**"I only wished t**[...] **way I spoke to y**[...] **I was unforgivably** [...] **Sir Isaac said in a low voice when they drew close enough to converse.**

"Thank you," she replied softly. "I appreciate the trouble you have gone to in order to convey your apology."

"Trouble?"

"Asking me to dance when I am sure there are many others in this room whose company you would find more agreeable. I was not—I was not all that I should have been at our last meeting, either," she added hesitantly, hoping he would grasp her meaning.

The demands of the dance separated them for a few moments. As she moved with as much grace as she could muster, Louisa found herself feeling impatient. Why was it that a man and a woman could not have a straightforward conversation in company, without the need for the ruse of dancing?

## Author Note

When embarking upon my first historical romance novel, I could think of no better setting than the wild and rugged Cumbrian coastline. It is a corner of England that, even nowadays, feels quiet, unspoiled and remote. The perfect place for a scandalized spinster to escape to and the perfect place for a brooding baronet to hide.

Lowhaven is based upon Whitehaven, a port town that grew exponentially during the Georgian period, with its busy quays receiving imports of tobacco, rum and sugar and exporting coal from the nearby mines. For me, settings become like characters themselves, and as a northerner, I was excited by the idea of exploring Regency life in a place that is not readily associated with the era in the same way as, for example, Brighton or Bath. Today Whitehaven is a lovely town to visit, with many of its fine Georgian buildings still extant, and its once-bustling harbor transformed into a peaceful marina, filled with boats. I hope to return soon—in the interests of research, of course.

Britain in the late 1810s was an unsettled place, emerging from war, grappling with extreme weather events and failed harvests, and similarly the hero and heroine of this story have been through a lot. At its heart, though, this is a story about seizing second chances and about finding happiness during one long and (occasionally) hot summer. It was uplifting to write, and I hope you find it as uplifting to read.

# SADIE KING

—

## Spinster with a Scandalous Past

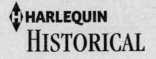

HARLEQUIN
HISTORICAL

# HARLEQUIN®
## HISTORICAL™

Recycling programs
for this product may
not exist in your area.

ISBN-13: 978-1-335-59598-0

Spinster with a Scandalous Past

Harlequin Enterprises ULC
22 Adelaide St. West, 41st Floor
Toronto, Ontario M5H 4E3, Canada
www.Harlequin.com

**Printed in U.S.A.**

**Sadie King** was born in Nottingham and raised in Lancashire. After graduating with a degree in history from Lancaster University, she moved to West Lothian, Scotland, where she now lives with her husband and children. When she's not writing, Sadie loves long country walks, romantic ruins, Thai food and traveling with her family. She also writes historical fiction and contemporary mysteries as Sarah L King.

### Books by Sadie King

### Harlequin Historical

*Spinster with a Scandalous Past*
is Sadie King's debut for Harlequin Historical.

Look out for more books by Sadie King
coming soon!

Visit the Author Profile page
at Harlequin.com.

For my family

# Chapter One

*June 1818*

As the carriage rattled along the road towards Low-haven, Louisa Conrad wondered what on earth she had been thinking. The sound of braying horses rang in her ears, and if she closed her eyes she could still feel herself tumbling down, could still feel her body thud against the coach's solid wood as it landed on its side and took her with it.

In her lap, her hands tremored. She clasped them together and pressed her lips into a tight smile, forcing calm where there was none to be found. Her gaze moved between the two brothers sitting before her, but only one of them returned her smile. The other did not even look at her, apparently preferring the country views offered through the small carriage window.

Briefly she furrowed her brow at him, before giving her full attention to his sibling as he struck up a conversation once again.

'I'm sure that you will find Juniper Street to your liking,' Mr Liddell said.

'I'm sure I shall, sir,' she replied crisply. 'And I believe that after the journey we've had I will appreciate it all the more.'

'Indeed, indeed. A wholesome meal and a good night's repose cures most ills, I find.' His eyes shone, almost teasing. 'You have both had quite an adventure.'

Beside her, Nan shifted, gripping the cushioned seat so hard that her knuckles turned white. Louisa couldn't decide what was distressing her maid more. The terror of the stagecoach accident, or everything that had happened since.

'I'm not sure I would describe it quite like that,' Louisa answered him. 'Those poor horses were dreadfully frightened after the coach turned over. I'm quite sure that the coachman was beside himself with concern for their welfare.'

'Of course—well, until the next time he's whipping them relentlessly so that he might travel at a dangerous speed,' Mr Liddell countered, a smile playing on his lips.

Louisa gave him a small nod, suppressing her own smile but finding that she could not, in earnest, disagree. Nan, meanwhile, chose that moment to clear her throat, no doubt to remind Louisa of the impropriety of their situation. They would have words later, that was for certain. Strong words about getting into the carriage of some unknown gentlemen, about reckless decisions and their consequences, about the manifold horrors which might have occurred.

Louisa had already prepared her defences. What else could they have done when they were stranded in the middle of nowhere, miles from the nearest inn? Were they not fortunate that the gentlemen happened upon them just moments after the coach had overturned?

Her hands trembled again, reminding her that she was not certain of her own argument. After all, Nan's undoubted reservations would be more than justified. Shaken and disorientated, the coach stricken and their luggage scattered on the ground, she could hardly claim to have been thinking clearly. No, instead she had allowed them to be swept along, embracing the notion of rescue without reservation. In those few moments she had been utterly unguarded. And Louisa, more than most, ought to remember the dangers inherent in letting down one's guard.

'Forgive me, Miss Conrad, I am making light of a difficult day, but you might have been seriously injured. I would urge you to consult a doctor once you are settled at your aunt's house. I can ask our physician to pay a visit to you, if you wish?'

'That's very kind of you, sir,' she replied, 'but I'm sure there's no need. We are, as you see, unharmed.'

She forced a smile, ignoring the ache in her ribs which served to remind her that she was not being entirely truthful.

'My brother is right.'

Louisa blinked, startled by the low timbre of the voice which had interjected. The other brother looked at her now, fixing his deep blue eyes upon her so intently that she almost wished he'd return to looking out of the window. Sir Isaac, Mr Liddell had called him during their fraught introductions earlier. Sir Isaac Liddell of Hayton Hall. As she stared back at him now, Louisa realised that this was the first time Sir Isaac had spoken to her in the several hours they'd been travelling together.

'My brother is right,' he repeated. 'We will send our physician.'

Louisa nodded her assent, sensing it was not worth her while to disagree. This appeared to satisfy him, as he said nothing more, but continued to look at her for a little longer than would be deemed polite. Louisa dropped her gaze, and after a moment she sensed him resume his interest in the scenery outside.

'What did you say your aunt's name was, Miss Conrad?' Mr Liddell asked, apparently keen to break the awkward silence which had descended in the carriage.

'I'm not sure that I did, but it is Miss Clarissa Howarth.'

'Miss Clarissa Howarth,' he repeated. 'I know that name. Is your aunt the rector's daughter from Hayton?'

Reluctantly Louisa nodded, feeling immediately guarded at this new line of questioning. 'That's correct, sir.'

Mr Liddell nudged his brother. 'Do you remember Reverend Howarth, Isaac?'

'Of course,' Sir Isaac muttered, not troubling himself to tear his gaze from the window.

From across the carriage Louisa found herself observing him, both offended by and grateful for his apparent lack of interest. With his striking blue gaze safely averted, she felt able to note his other features: near-black hair, a strong, angular jawline, and a sun-kissed complexion which hinted at time spent outdoors. He was dressed from head to toe in black, apart from the white shirt which she glimpsed beneath his coat, and it struck Louisa that he would not look out of place as a character in one of Mrs Radcliffe's gothic romances.

He was handsome, she concluded, but disagreeable. Not that either aspect of Sir Isaac Liddell mattered to her.

'It must be some time now since Reverend Howarth's passing?' Mr Liddell continued.

She nodded, returning her attention once more to the talkative brother. Unlike Sir Isaac, his features were fair, his hair the colour of sand and his eyes a pale blue-grey. In both looks and demeanour, it was hard to believe that they were related.

'Yes,' she replied, 'almost fifteen years.'

'And now your aunt lives on Juniper Street,' he said, in a way which seemed to be neither a statement nor a question.

'She does, yes.'

Now it was Louisa who turned to look out of the window, emulating Sir Isaac's aloof posture in the hope that it would signal an end to the conversation about her family history. Answering questions about Aunt Clarissa was all very well, but she was not keen to see where Mr Liddell's enquiries might lead. He'd already discovered where she'd come from, not long after they'd settled into the carriage.

'Berkshire…?' he'd pondered, before remarking upon how far she'd travelled and recounting a tale of some arduous journey south he'd previously undertaken.

She'd only half listened, and after a while he'd seemed to sense her weariness, smiling an apology and insisting that she needed to rest. Now, so close to her destination, she was determined that they would not revisit the subject. Louisa Conrad was a stranger here, and that was how it was going to remain.

Fortunately, it appeared she wouldn't have to deflect his attempts at conversation for much longer. Outside the carriage window, the wild Cumberland countryside had given way to a gentle townscape of smart grey and white buildings, and the streets were alive with coaches, carts and crowds, as people went about their business.

Her first glimpse of Lowhaven was a reassuring one, and she recalled the excitement she'd first felt when her parents had proposed this sojourn to her. A change of scenery, they'd called it. An opportunity to travel, just as she'd always wished.

She suspected there was more to their desire to send her away than mere broadened horizons, but she didn't care, and had loved the idea from the very first moment. Her eagerness had been dampened somewhat by the travails of the journey, but now, as it reached its welcome conclusion, it returned with renewed vigour. Even Nan looked happier, staring wide-eyed out of the window, her mouth agape at the town as it unravelled in front of her.

'Juniper Street is not far from the port,' Mr Liddell informed them. 'I do hope you won't find the noise and traffic too disturbing.'

Louisa thought about her family's estate, enveloped in rolling green fields and an almost unendurable silence. About the large country house, containing too few people and too many opportunities to ruminate on what might have been. Without doubt, she'd had her fill of living quietly in recent years.

'If it's near to the port then it is near to the sea, which will do very well for me,' she countered cheerfully. 'Besides, lively places can be very diverting.'

Mr Liddell let out a soft laugh. 'If diversion is what you seek, Miss Conrad, then I do believe you will find it in Lowhaven.'

The carriage drew to a halt on a dusty street, lined on either side by rather humble-looking stone townhouses, uniformly built, but with little embellishment. After a moment the coachman opened the door and Mr Liddell exited, offering Louisa his hand as she descended the steps, with Nan following closely behind her.

Louisa smoothed her palms over the crumpled, muddied skirt of her day dress as she took her first breath of Lowhaven's fresh sea air. *Yes,* she thought, *this will do very well indeed.*

'Our driver will fetch your luggage to the door for you, Miss Conrad,' Mr Liddell said.

Louisa turned to face him, realising then that Sir Isaac had not followed them out of the carriage. Instead he remained within, his sombre countenance visible through the little window to which he'd given so much of his attention throughout the journey. Briefly Louisa shook her head at his rudeness, before regarding Mr Liddell once more. There might have been two gentlemen in the carriage today, she thought, but really only one of them could be regarded as their rescuer.

'Mr Liddell, I must thank you most sincerely for coming to our aid today. Truly, you are a good Samaritan. I only hope we have not caused any significant delay to your own journey.'

The gentleman shook his head. 'None whatsoever. Our home is merely a few miles up the road. It was a pleasure to escort you, and to see you safely to your destination, and I will see to it that our physician calls upon you later. I hope that your stay in Lowhaven is agreeable. It is not comparable with the fashionable resorts of the south coast, but nonetheless it has its charms.'

'I'm obliged to you, sir. Will you not stay for some

tea? I'm sure my aunt would be glad to welcome you both,' she added, glancing warily once more towards the carriage.

'You're very kind, Miss Conrad, but I'm afraid we must take our leave,' he replied, tipping his hat briefly. 'Perhaps our paths will cross again, while you are here.'

Before Louisa could respond, Mr Liddell had climbed back into the carriage and closed the door behind him. Through the window he gave her one last broad smile, before his coachman cracked his whip once more and they were off.

For a moment Louisa just stood there, staring after that handsome carriage, surrounded by the luggage which Nan was frantically trying to put into order. After the ordeal of their journey, it seemed miraculous that they had finally arrived. In fact, it almost didn't seem real: the accident, the rescue, the kind gentleman, the rude gentleman—all of it.

Louisa let out a weary sigh. What a long and strange day it had been.

Then, behind her, a door opened and a voice she hadn't heard for years rang out in delight.

'Louisa! Oh, my dear Louisa! Is it really you?'

Louisa turned around and walked straight into the outstretched arms of her Aunt Clarissa, who embraced her quickly before stepping back to regard her niece. The woman looked older than Louisa remembered, her face heavily lined, her once blonde hair now silver and peering wildly from beneath a lace cap. Thinner, too, Louisa thought. She could compete with the minuscule Nan in terms of slenderness.

'You look well, my dear, all things considered,' her aunt said carefully, and Louisa couldn't help but suspect that she was referring to more than just the long journey. 'Your mother was right; you've grown into quite a beautiful young lady.'

Louisa laughed aloud, gesturing at her mud-spattered travelling clothes. 'I look far from beautiful right now, Aunt! And I don't believe I merit being described as "young" any more, either.'

Clarissa raised a curious eyebrow. 'Oh, nonsense— you're barely five-and-twenty; you're not allowed to deny your youth for a few years yet!' She placed a gentle hand on Louisa's arm and steered her towards the door. 'However, you do look as though you've become acquainted with our Cumberland countryside already. Come, let's get your luggage brought in, then we can have some tea and you can tell me all about it.'

'Tell you all about what, Aunt?'

'Your journey, of course—I'd say it's quite a story, judging by the state of your dress.' Clarissa smiled, a look of amusement sparkling in her keen blue eyes. 'But above all you must tell me—how on earth did you come to be accompanied here by Samuel Liddell of Hayton Hall?'

# Chapter Two

Samuel Liddell patted his older brother on the back as they walked through the grand wooden door of Hayton Hall. 'I'd say that was a very successful trip,' he declared. 'A number of business matters put to bed, and we rescued a fair maiden in distress on the way home.'

Isaac grunted as he loosened his cravat and threw off his coat, wearied both by the long journey and his brother's endlessly cheerful disposition.

It had been only a short stay in Penrith, and that had been quite long enough. With every passing hour Isaac had found himself yearning to return to the peace and tranquillity of Hayton Hall. The bustle of towns had never suited him and, after spending so long away from them, he now found that he disliked them all the more. He'd never felt so relieved when they'd finally left the coaching inn that morning and begun the final part of their journey home.

A journey which had taken far longer than it should have, thanks to a stagecoach accident on the road and Samuel's insistence that they deliver that young woman and her maid to her aunt in Lowhaven.

'Related to the old rector, Howarth, and coming all the way from an estate in Berkshire,' Samuel remarked, mulling over the details he'd managed to prise from their unexpected carriage guest. 'A gentleman's daughter, to be sure.'

'The very reckless daughter of a gentleman,' Isaac countered as he marched towards his library. 'Getting into a carriage with us—we could have been anyone.'

Samuel followed, his amused chuckle seeming to echo down the hall. 'Well, fortunately for her, we were perfect gentlemen. Or at least I was. You barely looked at her.'

Isaac grunted again as he collapsed into his favourite armchair. Samuel was wrong about that: he had looked at her. Had observed the deep brown of her eyes, her pink pursed lips, and the way her striking blonde curls peered from the edges of her damaged bonnet. He'd noted the mud on her dress, and the way she'd winced and put her hand against her ribs every time the carriage met a bump on the road. He'd caught her frowning at him, more than once, and sensed that his aloofness displeased her. Not that any of it mattered to him.

He slumped back in his chair and closed his eyes as Samuel rang for some tea. No, he thought. Fair maidens and their opinions of him were of no consequence.

'You'd better make sure that you do send the physician to attend to her,' Isaac said. 'Despite her protestations, I do believe that she was injured.'

'Ah, so you are taking an interest in her?' Samuel teased.

Isaac's eyes flew open and he sat up straight. 'I'm merely concerned for her welfare after being in such a bad accident. And might I remind you that it was you who invited the lady and her maid into our carriage?'

'And you'd have left them stranded on the road?' Samuel scoffed.

'Of course not,' Isaac snapped. 'I am many things, but I am not heartless.'

Isaac watched as his brother sat down in the armchair opposite him, sighing heavily as he resigned himself to a lecture. It had been like this ever since Samuel had returned from his European travels, apparently determined to atone for his lengthy absence by seeing to it that his grieving recluse of a brother got his life in order.

Sometimes he was glad of it, content to have his morose moods offset by a dose of his brother's buoyancy and relieved to have the large rooms of his ancestral home filled with lively chatter once more. At other times Samuel's good intentions grated on him—largely because he no longer felt he needed to be looked after. And because his brother had not been there when he really had needed his care...during those darkest days when he'd wallowed, unwashed and undressed, drinking himself into oblivion.

Samuel must have seen something in his brother's expression to dissuade him from pursuing the matter of Isaac's heart, as when he finally spoke it was to change the subject.

'I'm glad you decided to come with me to Penrith. I know you have much to attend to on the estate, but I do believe it's done you the world of good.'

Isaac grunted, the temptation to offer one of his usual cutting retorts thwarted by the earnest look on Samuel's face. 'I suppose it did end up being something of an adventure,' he confessed, surprised to find himself thinking about the lady with the brown eyes and fair curls once more.

'Ah—you see!' Samuel declared, clapping his hands together. 'Even Sir Isaac Liddell is not immune to a bit of chivalry.'

'I wouldn't go that far,' Isaac retorted. 'As you said yourself, I barely acknowledged the lady.'

And he hadn't—not really. Noticing a pretty face was one thing, but his days of being a knight in shining armour to a fair maiden were long past. He was alone now; that was the cruel hand fate had dealt him, and that was how it was going to remain.

After being plied with tea, copious amounts of cake, and a conversation which bordered on an interrogation, it was with some relief and a very full stomach that Louisa made her way to her bedroom later that afternoon.

Aunt Clarissa had been horrified by the stagecoach accident, expressing her consternation that Louisa's parents had not seen fit to escort her on the long journey north. Louisa had protested mildly, informing her aunt that her family were all presently in London, and doing her best to ignore her nagging suspicions about exactly why her parents had left her to fend for herself. Why they were so keen for her to spend the summer here. What they thought it might teach her.

Her aunt's mood had mercifully lightened when the conversation had turned to Louisa's rescuers—or at least, the one she had seen.

'Mr Samuel Liddell,' she said, beaming. 'He has been away for some time, travelling in Europe, and has only recently returned to Hayton Hall. The Liddells are a distinguished family in this part of the country. You will recall that your grandfather was the rector of Hayton? He knew the family very well.'

'Yes, Mr Liddell spoke of my grandfather during the journey,' Louisa had replied. 'He said that he remembered him.'

'Mr Samuel would have been quite young back then. Your grandfather knew his father better. He passed away suddenly, years ago, before Mr Samuel came of age. I recall his mother followed not long afterwards. Mr Samuel's older brother inherited the baronetcy.'

The mention of Mr Liddell's brother had caused Louisa's stomach to lurch quite unexpectedly. Doubtless it was the memory of his sombre disposition and curt indifference which had vexed her.

'Sir Isaac Liddell was also travelling with us this afternoon,' she'd said, feeling duty-bound to report to her guardian the exact details of her rescue.

Her aunt's eyes had widened in surprise. 'Really? I did not see him.'

'He remained in the carriage when we arrived,' she'd explained, trying to suppress a fresh wave of irritation at his rudeness.

'I see. Well, my dear, you have had a rare introduction. Sir Isaac is almost never seen in town. Indeed, it is said that he seldom leaves his estate.'

Louisa had nodded, utterly unsurprised by her aunt's revelation. The gentleman she'd encountered earlier today had been inattentive and unsociable, and clearly had not wished to be in her company, so it was little wonder to her that he did not relish being in anyone else's.

On the other hand, she'd reflected, as she had sipped her tea, there were many good reasons to shut oneself away from society, as she knew only too well.

She'd been about to enquire what Sir Isaac's might be when her aunt had changed the subject.

'I'd suggest you don't mention the stagecoach accident or your subsequent rescue to your mother when you write to her,' she'd advised. 'I'm not sure that she would approve.'

Louisa had furrowed her brow at this. 'I've done nothing I should be ashamed of, surely? Nan was with me—and besides, I'm not sure what else I could have done. Mr Liddell was very kind, and Sir Isaac has insisted that their physician will call upon Nan and me, as a precaution.'

'I mean no criticism, my dear,' her aunt had replied, chuckling at her niece's defensive tone. 'Sometimes in life we find ourselves in difficult situations, and the choices offered to us are less than ideal. In those situations we are forced to trust our instincts. You should be reassured that, as an unmarried woman, you can rely upon yours. That's important—especially if this is the path you're set upon.'

Those words rang in Louisa's ears as she walked into her room to find Nan, still unpacking. The room Clarissa had given her was small, but well-appointed, tucked away at the rear of the house and overlooking a charming little courtyard. Beyond it were more houses, walls and courtyards; wherever she looked, there seemed only stone to be found.

It occurred to Louisa then that it had been a long time since she had looked out of a window and seen anything other than fields. Her last London season had been six years ago, and she'd seen nothing of any town since. Another aspect of the path she had embarked upon.

'Your books are on the table, miss,' Nan said as she bustled about. 'I know you'll be looking for them before you trouble yourself with your dresses.'

Louisa thanked her maid, moving to run her fingers over her most prized possessions as she gazed out of the window. The afternoon was ebbing away towards evening, but the light was still good, the early June sunshine warm and bright and uninhibited by cloud.

She wondered how often the room's previous inhabitant had stood there and enjoyed the view over the town. For years Aunt Clarissa had shared her home with another spinster, Miss Slater, until the woman had quite unexpectedly married at the age of five and fifty. The now Mrs Knight had subsequently relocated to Carlisle, with her husband, leaving Aunt Clarissa alone.

Louisa knew that this was partly what had prompted her mother to send her to Lowhaven—although she was not so naïve that she did not recognise the other motivations her parents were likely to have for wishing to remove her from Berkshire entirely.

'Have you told your aunt about what happened this afternoon?' Nan asked. 'I hope she is not too vexed by it.'

Louisa gave her maid a brisk nod. 'I have, and I must say she was only concerned that we might have been injured. The rest of the tale didn't seem to perturb her in the slightest.'

Nan stared at her mistress, her mouth agape. 'But, miss, your reputation—'

'In these parts I have no reputation, Nan. I am known to no one, so there is no one to discuss whether or not I should have got into that carriage, or to condemn me as silly, naïve or without virtue. And if I have my way that is how it shall remain. I am here to visit my aunt and to enjoy a pleasant summer before returning to Berkshire, and that is all.'

'I'm sorry, miss. I only worry for you, given what happened with your captain—'

Louisa held up a hand in protest and looked her maid directly in the eye. 'Nan, you will not mention any of that while we are here; I forbid it. You do not know who might be listening. I will not have my life become the subject of tittle-tattle between servants.'

Nan nodded meekly. 'Yes, of course, miss.'

Louisa's stern expression dissolved into a fond smile. She couldn't help it; she'd known Nan since she was a girl. At a little more than ten years her senior, her maid was not old enough to be a motherly figure, but nonetheless the pair shared a close bond which had only deepened as Louisa's life had taken increasingly difficult turns. Nan knew all of it, she'd seen everything, and yet she still cared.

Louisa retreated from the window once more, sitting down upon the bed which was situated in the centre of the room. She patted the sheets at her side, indicating that Nan should rest for a moment and join her.

'This is such a beautiful bedroom,' Louisa remarked, surveying her surroundings once more. 'I'm glad my aunt saw fit to put me at the back of the house. I'm not sure how well I would sleep with all the noise from the street outside. It was Miss Slater's room; my aunt told me so at tea.'

Nan's eyes widened at that. 'Well, I daresay that staying in this room is a good omen, miss. If its last occupant managed to find herself a husband in this town, perhaps you will, too.'

Louisa bristled. The words were kindly meant, but they stung her nonetheless. She closed her eyes for a moment, allowing herself the luxury of small remembered glimpses: his chestnut hair, his green eyes, his deep blue frock coat. The delicate feeling of his fingers caressing her face. The way that he always seemed to smell like the ocean, even though he'd been on land for months. The way he'd kissed her at their last meeting. The fearful urgency of it—as though he had already seen that a rising tide was coming and that it would part them for good.

Her thoughts darkened then, wandering to everything that had come after...everything she'd had to face alone. Everything that made finding a husband in a new town utterly impossible.

From beneath her lashes, a tear slipped out. 'You know that is out of the question, Nan. There is no one for me now, and that is an end to it.'

Then, before Nan could say anything further, Louisa fled from the room.

# Chapter Three

Isaac whipped his horse, pushing the poor beast to gallop as fast as its legs could manage. The weather was as foul as his mood, having turned in these last few days from still and sunlit to blustery and beset with heavy grey cloud. It hadn't begun to rain yet, thank God. Like everyone else, he feared that if it did, it might never stop.

He might have little interaction with the world outside Hayton Hall these days, but he was not immune to its worries. They'd endured two of the worst summers he could remember, cold and endlessly wet, damaging crops and causing many a harvest to fail. What Cumberland and England prayed for was a long, hot summer.

He'd pray, too, if he could bring himself to speak to his maker any more.

Isaac growled, cracking his whip again as he sped towards the cliffs before turning to chart a rough path along their rugged edges. In front of him the land sloped down towards Lowhaven, its orderly buildings and busy port nestled into the bay. He wouldn't go as far as that; it was out of the question. It was difficult enough to slip away from Hayton unnoticed. He was almost guaranteed to be seen in town, to be remarked upon, and he despised being the subject of gossip.

Perhaps he ought to turn back now, before he got too close…

'You're a damnable coward, Isaac Liddell,' he muttered to himself.

Samuel would certainly agree. He'd more or less said it himself, a few nights ago at dinner. The evening had started well enough, with Samuel in high spirits after they'd gallantly rescued that lady from her overturned coach. His good cheer had eventually grown on Isaac, and after a pleasant meal and a few glasses of port he had found himself smiling, too. He'd relaxed, allowing himself to take comfort in his brother's company, to reflect that it was preferable to dining alone.

Samuel must have sensed that his guard was down, or perhaps he'd really been in his cups—either way, his words had not been gentle.

'You should go out more,' he'd said. 'Put on your best clothes. Go to a ball. Go to London! Find yourself a nice wife. Stop hiding yourself away, licking your wounds and hoping the world will forget that you exist.'

Isaac groaned at the memory of it, the pained sound mercifully carried away by the howling wind. The brothers had always been very different men, in both outlook and temperament, but these past couple of years seemed to have placed an unnavigable chasm between them. Samuel had travelled and Isaac had lost; one brother's horizons had expanded, whilst the other's world had shrunk.

Samuel would never understand that Isaac's life could not be repaired by embracing society or getting himself on to the dancing card of a beautiful lady.

'Watch out!'

He'd been so absorbed by his own thoughts that he hadn't seen the woman until the very last moment. In fact, his horse saw her first. The creature reared, letting out a high-pitched whinny as it drew to a sudden halt. Isaac clung hard to the reins; he was a good horseman, but not beyond being unseated by a startled beast.

'Hell and damnation!' he cried out, finally bringing his horse under control.

The woman stared up at him, wide-eyed and apparently frozen to the spot. Her terror was written all over her face, which had turned a ghastly shade of white. Despite the fright she'd given him, immediately he recognised the deep brown gaze, contrasting starkly with the fair curls which sprang at the edges of her bonnet.

The fair maiden they'd welcomed into their carriage on the way home from Penrith. The one travelling from Berkshire with her maid before falling victim to a careless driver and an overturned stagecoach. He watched as she furrowed her brow at him, giving him the same disapproving look he'd spied during that long journey to Lowhaven. Instead of stepping aside, the lady remained in his way, and inexplicably he felt the heat of irritation rise in his chest.

'What the blazes are you doing, walking into the path of my horse?' he snapped.

His accusing tone seemed to bring her to her senses. 'What am I doing?' she repeated. 'I am walking, sir. I might ask what you are doing, riding your horse in such a reckless manner, with no consideration for those whom you might encounter up here.'

Her question was a fair one; he had been riding with little care. With a sigh, he dismounted from his horse. 'I do not expect to see anyone up here. Not on a day like today, at least.' He drew closer to the woman. 'I am very sorry to have frightened you.'

'I wasn't frightened,' she answered him, taking a step back.

If he'd been in a better frame of mind he would have found her indignation amusing. Instead he found himself struck by the petite, pretty, but very stern figure standing in front of him, well turned out in a fetching pale blue dress and matching spencer, steadfastly holding her bonnet in place as the fierce wind threatened to carry it away.

A gentleman's daughter, Samuel had called her, and indeed there was no mistaking the air of gentility about her.

As he considered this, Isaac found himself regretting his coarse words. He gave her a small, belated bow. 'Forgive me,' he said. 'If I am not mistaken, I believe we have met before. My name is Isaac Liddell. We—that is my brother and I—escorted you to Lowhaven after that dreadful stagecoach accident. You may not recall… In fact…' He shook his head at himself, unable to comprehend his sudden lack of ability to speak coherently. 'That is to say, you may remember my brother better, as he made all the arrangements.'

The lady offered him a brisk nod. 'I remember you,' she said simply. 'Sir Isaac Liddell of Hayton Hall.'

He winced at the cool way with which she accorded him his proper title. 'Did our physician attend you? I asked my brother to arrange it.'

'He did, thank you.' For the first time, a small smile played upon her lips. 'I daresay Mr Liddell likes to arrange things.'

Isaac frowned. 'What makes you say that?'

She beheld him with a steely gaze he couldn't read.

'I was merely thinking about the day of the coach accident, and the way he took charge of the situation,' she replied.

Isaac tried not to feel the sting in her observation— tried not to consider the implication that, while Samuel had been something of a hero, he'd done nothing much at all. 'I suppose some people are good at fixing things,' he said. 'Or at least they like to believe that they are.'

'Indeed. But not everything can be fixed, can it?'

Such a knowing remark unsettled him, and he felt his breath catch in his throat. 'Fortunately, rescuing a fair maiden after a stagecoach accident and sending for a physician are skills well within Samuel's repertoire.' He kept his tone light, cheery, almost jovial. Everything he did not feel in that moment.

The woman frowned. 'Excuse me? A fair maiden?'

Isaac suppressed a groan, realising he'd said that aloud. Damn, it had been so long since he had spent time in company, and even longer since he'd spoken to a lady. It seemed that his sense of etiquette was something else he'd lost.

'Forgive me,' he said again. 'It was how my brother described you. He meant it kindly, but it was impolite of me to repeat it.'

'I see.' The woman raised her eyebrows at him, then pursed those pretty pink lips once more before adding, 'I'd wager you cannot even recall my name, sir.'

Such directness took him aback, and he felt an unusual heat rising from beneath his collar and creeping to his face. During their first fraught encounter on the road, some brief and extremely awkward introductions had been made. She had given her name then—of course she had—but he was damned if he could remember it. Ever since then, in his mind she had been the fair maiden. Samuel's name for her had well and truly stuck, and he hadn't needed another when conjuring the memory of her dark gaze or her disapproving glances. A memory, he realised now, that he'd conjured more than once.

'Indeed I do,' he replied, floundering as he grasped at the only name he knew. 'I do recall, Miss… Howarth.'

'Miss Howarth is my aunt,' she replied flatly, although something like amusement flickered across her face. 'My name is Miss Louisa Conrad,' she added, extending a hand towards him.

He accepted the gesture as the olive branch it was clearly intended to be, and took hold of her hand with as much grace as he could muster. Although they both wore gloves, he found himself struck by the feeling of her small, delicate fingers resting briefly in his.

'It's a pleasure to make your acquaintance again, Miss Conrad. Please accept my sincere apology. I meant no disrespect.'

Miss Conrad laughed. 'To be honest, I'm not sure which is worse—being referred to as a fair maiden, or having your name forgotten entirely.'

Isaac winced at her gentle teasing. 'Truly, I am sorry on both counts,' he replied. 'You have my solemn promise that I will never refer to you as a fair maiden ever again.'

'Do not fret, sir. I have been called worse, I'm sure,' she quipped.

'Really?' asked Isaac, disconcerted by the forthright remark. 'That I cannot believe. Although you will have been seen arriving in Lowhaven with my brother and me.

Such an event is certain to set tongues wagging around these parts.'

Isaac had made the observation in jest, but immediately he could see that he'd offended her all over again. The look on her face hardened, and those dark eyes blazed with something he couldn't quite name. Hotter than hurt, but cooler than anger.

He shook his head at himself, unable to believe his own impertinence. Truly, what had become of him?

'I'm sorry, Miss Conrad, I didn't mean—'

'Oh, I'm quite sure you did,' she replied, her tone scathing. She gave a brief, insincere curtsey. 'I think I'd best take my leave of you now, sir. I wouldn't wish my unchaperoned presence here to provide any further fodder for the gossips. Good day.'

She spun round, determinedly marching away from him and back towards Lowhaven. Isaac stared after her for a few moments, dumbstruck at his own stupidity. What on earth had possessed him to talk so loosely to a woman he barely knew?

He sighed, and found himself wondering what Samuel would say if he'd borne witness to all that had just occurred. It was just as well he'd no intention of marrying again. After two years of solitude, it was clear that all his charm had simply withered away.

As she walked back to her aunt's house, Louisa felt that she ought to question her sanity. Aunt Clarissa had expressed reservations about her taking long walks alone, making vague insinuations about the possible dangers to a young woman, and saying how she really ought to accompany her but she feared she could not walk so far. It turned out that her aunt had been right—although perhaps not in the way she would have imagined.

It had only been days since Louisa had arrived in Cumberland. Already she'd got into the carriage of two unknown gentlemen, and now she'd argued with one of them for good measure. She shook her head, berating herself as she hurried in the direction of Juniper Street. Why had she spoken to him in that way, and with such a careless tongue? It was bad enough that her actions on the day of the coach accident had shown her to be a foolish and improper young woman, but to then suggest that there might be some further stain on her character, that people might see fit to besmirch her reputation— that was unforgivable.

It was also true, she reminded herself. She knew well enough what Berkshire society said about her. She had, without doubt, been called far worse than a fair maiden.

'A fair maiden, indeed,' she muttered as she marched along.

She tried not to imagine how the brothers must have made fun of her—how they must have laughed as they talked of the silly southern lady they'd rescued on their journey home. Certainly, Sir Isaac had all but told her what he thought of her, hadn't he? That she was the sort of woman about whom people chattered, and therefore, by implication, the sort of woman whose behaviour was unbecoming of a gentleman's daughter. That had been the point of his impertinent remark, hadn't it?

'Such a rude, disagreeable gentleman,' she said aloud to herself.

He had been rude—there could be no question about that. A man of honour would have kept such thoughts to himself, even if provoked by her own ill-advised commentary. A man of honour would not have cursed in her presence, either, or tried to suggest that she was to blame for his bad horsemanship.

She reflected once more upon the sight of him, his wild hair and thunderous expression as he'd stared down at her from his horse. A man of honour would have concealed such anger, not indulged it.

No, she thought. There was something altogether very disagreeable about Sir Isaac Liddell. Tomorrow she would walk a different route and hope that their paths did not cross again. He was a man whose company ought to be avoided.

# Chapter Four

Louisa's return to her aunt's house put a swift end to all thoughts of her unpleasant encounter. She was greeted in the hall by an agitated Nan, who was mumbling about how long she'd been away and where she'd got to, and how she had been beginning to worry. Like Aunt Clarissa, her maid did not approve of the long promenades she'd so quickly established as a habit.

Louisa tried not to show her irritation; she knew that they both had her best interests at heart. She couldn't possibly explain to them how free she felt, able to wander the countryside unburdened by the worry of who might see her and what they might say. She couldn't expect them to understand what these past years had been like for her, confined to her family's estate, unwilling to venture beyond their own land. It had been her choice, she knew that; she'd been her own gaoler. But here she was unknown; Cumberland was indifferent to her, and it was liberating.

She smiled as Nan took her spencer from her and gave her skirts a swift brush with her hand. 'I haven't been away all that long, Nan—and besides, what is the hurry? I have nothing I need to attend to.'

'You do today, miss. Your aunt has visitors in the parlour and you've some mud on the hem of this dress. Do you wish to change first?'

Louisa frowned. 'No, the dress will do. Who are the visitors, Nan?' she asked, curious now. She glanced at the long-case clock in the hall, realising it was past noon. Her long walk had indeed encroached upon calling hours.

'A Mrs Pearson and her daughter. I gather they are fairly new in town and only recently acquainted with your aunt.'

'I see,' she replied. 'Well, then, Nan, I think I'd best be introduced, hadn't I?'

Nan led her mistress to the parlour, where she opened the door for her before briefly bobbing a curtsey and taking her leave. Tentatively, Louisa walked into the room, feeling suddenly self-conscious as her aunt's two guests stared at her from across the table where they were enjoying cake and tea. She was not used to company…not used to making polite conversation. Briefly, the thought of her earlier walk returned to her. She'd already failed in one social encounter today. She hoped she wouldn't give a bad account of herself in another.

'Ah! There you are, my dear,' said Clarissa from her chair. 'Come, sit down and have some tea. I'd like you to meet Mrs Mary Pearson and her daughter, Miss Charlotte Pearson.' She turned back to her guests. 'This is my niece, Miss Louisa Conrad.'

Louisa gave them both a polite nod before taking a seat beside her aunt. 'It's nice to meet you both,' she said, pausing briefly to accept a cup of tea from her aunt's young maid, Cass, who had entered the parlour to wait upon her. 'I apologise for not being here sooner.'

'Oh, not at all, Miss Conrad,' said Mrs Pearson. 'Your aunt was just telling us how much the Lowhaven air is agreeing with you on your daily walks.'

'It is indeed,' Louisa replied. 'The surrounding country is beautiful, and walking by the sea suits me very well.'

'I am glad to hear it. Regrettably, my health doesn't permit me to venture far, but Charlotte likes to promenade—don't you?' Mrs Pearson addressed her daughter, who gave an assenting nod. 'Perhaps you might accompany one another.'

'Ah, that would be wonderful,' Clarissa declared. 'It is better if young ladies walk out together, I think. It is the proper way of things.'

'Yes, indeed,' Mrs Pearson agreed. 'The right and proper way.'

Charlotte gave Louisa a brief look of amusement which said that she had heard such a sentiment expressed at least a hundred times before. Louisa returned it, before allowing herself to make a discreet study of her new acquaintance. Her smooth, freckled face pronounced her youth, and Louisa suspected she could not be much older than twenty. She had the most striking red curls and bright blue eyes, which sat in direct contrast to her mother's ashen complexion, sunken features and greying brown hair. If Mrs Pearson had not already declared herself to be in poor health, Louisa should have easily supposed it.

'Have you ventured far on your walks, Miss Conrad?' Charlotte asked her, clearly determined to make some conversation.

'Just the environs of the town,' Louisa replied. 'Although I did wander a little along the coast today. The cliffs are magnificent.'

Charlotte nodded. 'That is indeed a pleasant walk. There is another I might show you, too, which takes you inland towards a village called Hayton.'

Louisa smiled, glancing at her aunt. 'My grandfather used to be the rector at Hayton. I have heard much about the place, although I confess I have not yet had the opportunity to visit.'

'Ah!' Charlotte exclaimed, clasping her hands together. 'Then we must go! It is very charming, and so quiet. Not at all like Lowhaven. I can show you the church and the rectory, and if time allows we can walk towards Hayton Hall. It is not far from the village, and it is the most spectacular-looking house. Indeed, I think it is the best in all of Cumberland.'

Clarissa smiled at the two young ladies. 'This sounds like a wonderful outing,' she said. 'If I was a younger woman, I might join you. I seldom visit Hayton these days, for all that it is only a few miles along the road. And Charlotte is right; Hayton Hall is very old, you know, and very fine.' Clarissa paused, stirring her tea. 'Although I believe these days it is best viewed from a distance.'

'Oh, Charlotte knows not to venture too close to the house—don't you, Charlotte?' her mother interjected.

Louisa sipped the tea thoughtfully. 'Of course. That is only polite, surely? The family must be afforded their privacy when in residence.'

Clarissa shifted a little in her chair. 'I think it would be fair to say that Hayton Hall has been closed to the outside world for some time.' She patted Louisa's hand. 'It is a sad story, I'm afraid, my dear. Two years ago

Sir Isaac suffered the loss of both his wife and his only child. Since then he has seldom been seen by anyone.'

Louisa felt her heart beat a little faster. 'That is terribly sad,' she said.

Aunt Clarissa nodded her agreement, giving Louisa a conspiratorial look. Neither of them was careless enough to mention that Louisa had met the reclusive baronet and risk revealing the circumstances in which this rare encounter had occurred. And Louisa, for her part, had no intention of telling anyone the sorry tale of their second meeting.

She dropped her gaze, staring into her empty cup and trying not to think of those deep blue eyes staring down at her from the horse. Trying not to think about how she'd failed to spot the sadness lurking behind the near-permanent scowl. A sadness which she, of all people, ought to have seen.

'I hear he has been seen a little more of late,' Mrs Pearson interjected. 'Since his brother returned to Hayton. Hopefully he can bring Sir Isaac some comfort.'

Clarissa gave her friend a grim smile. 'I think we ought to pray for it,' she replied. 'For that is what the poor man deserves—our prayers and our pity.'

Louisa retired to her room early that evening, not long after giving up on the dinner which she had pushed around her plate. She'd brushed off her aunt's professions of concern with an insistence that she was merely tired after an eventful day, explaining away her lack of appetite with the excuse that she'd eaten too heartily at tea that afternoon.

After changing into her bedclothes and dismissing Nan, she'd climbed between the sheets, intent upon reading her book for as long as the remaining daylight and the glow of a single candle would allow.

Hoping she would be able to take her mind somewhere else for a little while, Louisa picked up Mariana Starke's *Letters from Italy*. She might never venture beyond the confines of England, but she could indulge her desire to travel by seeing the continent through another's eyes until she fell asleep.

But, try as she might to fill her head with Mrs Starke's descriptions of vineyards, volcanoes and ancient towns buried by lava, her thoughts kept wandering back to the cliffs above Lowhaven. To the intensity of Sir Isaac's stare, the gentle touch of his gloved hand. To the way his dark hair had been made wild by the wind. To the unpleasant way their brief exchange had ended, and to the cross words she regretted now that she knew the nature of what pained him.

Words she ought to have regretted anyway, she thought as she slammed her book shut. Sir Isaac had been rude, but it shouldn't have been beyond her to meet his rudeness with some grace. Instead she'd been angry—and why? Because he'd spoken the truth, that was why.

She was reckless and improper. She made herself vulnerable to gossip and she bore the taint of scandal. Her reputation might not be known in Cumberland, but it followed her all the same, etching itself on every word she spoke, every decision she made. She was not free of it. She would never be free of it. She was fooling herself if she thought she could be at liberty here, or anywhere. She might as well lock herself away on her family's estate again—this time for good.

Louisa closed her eyes, pressing her lips together tight

as a single tear slipped down her cheek. It seemed she and Sir Isaac had more in common than she could have supposed. They had both loved and lost, and had chosen to shut themselves away, to hide their pain from the world. She wondered if solitude had been a salve for him or if, like her, he had found it only allowed the wounds to fester. She wondered if she would ever see him again, and if she'd find the courage to apologise to him, to acknowledge his suffering without betraying her own.

A knock at the door caused her to sit bolt upright, her eyes wide open now as the unexpected intrusion brushed all thoughts of Sir Isaac Liddell away. After a moment Aunt Clarissa peered round the door.

'I'm sorry to disturb you, dear,' she said, somewhat tentatively.

Louisa gave her a small smile. 'You're not, Aunt. I wasn't yet asleep. Is everything all right? Are you quite well?'

'Oh, yes, nothing is amiss,' Clarissa replied, coming into the room and closing the door behind her. 'It was just that I had meant to tell you at dinner that we have an engagement with the Pearsons on Friday evening.'

'I see. I'm sure that will be lovely. At their home?'

'No, not at their home.' Clarissa paused, seeming to hesitate. 'At the Assembly Rooms. There is to be a ball, it seems. I pay little heed to these events usually, but Mrs Pearson has asked if we will both come.'

Louisa gave a slow shake of her head. 'I'm not sure, Aunt. I...'

Clarissa gave her a pained look. 'I am sorry, my dear, but I have already accepted. Mrs Pearson asked me earlier today, just as she was leaving. In truth, I think she wishes you to attend as a companion for Miss Pearson.

I have not known Mrs Pearson for very long…to have refused her invitation would surely have seemed ungracious, wouldn't it?'

Louisa sighed. 'Indeed, I suppose it would. I regret that I will be rather poor company for Miss Pearson, though, after so long away from society.'

Clarissa reached over and patted her hand. 'You are a charming young lady, and I won't hear anything different said by anyone. Your only flaw is that you are too hard on yourself, my dear. The past is the past. This is a fresh start for you, Louisa. If you want my opinion, a new town, some new friends and a busy social calendar is exactly what you need.'

Louisa gave her aunt a knowing look. 'A friend like Charlotte Pearson, perhaps?'

Clarissa chuckled. 'I cannot deny that I have thought that Miss Pearson would make a suitable companion for you this summer. I simply want you to enjoy your time here, Louisa.'

Louisa shuffled under her sheets, suddenly discomfited. 'That is kind of you, Aunt. You are close to my mother, and I know she has told you much of what occurred several years ago. You have my deepest gratitude for welcoming me into your home in spite of it.'

Her aunt frowned. 'My dear, you speak as though you murdered someone! What happened to you is a tragedy, and if your Berkshire society chose to shun you for it then that reflects poorly on them, not you.'

'But I did not conduct myself as a young lady should…'

'You conducted yourself as many a young woman has and as many young women will continue to do whilst ever there are young men in the world to turn their heads. Your family approved of him, yes? And you were to marry, yes?'

Louisa nodded. 'We had an understanding.'

'Well, then, you were a victim of dreadful circumstance, Louisa, and that is all there is to be said.' Clarissa gave her a tender smile. 'Your mother has told me how these past years have been for you, and I pray that being here in Lowhaven will put an end to all of that. Starting with this ball at the Assembly Rooms on Friday.'

Aunt Clarissa bade her a swift goodnight, leaving Louisa to blow out her candle and settle down beneath her sheets. Oddly, she felt more peaceful now, her aunt's soothing words having replaced the more distressing thoughts she'd entertained earlier. Aunt Clarissa knew about her past and loved her despite it. Perhaps one day she could manage to love herself again, too.

She fell asleep quickly, dreaming not of windswept cliffs and heated conversations, nor of lost sea captains and promises unfulfilled. No, instead thoughts of candlelit rooms, country dances and beautiful gowns spread through her sleeping hours, and when she woke in the morning she wondered if her aunt might be right. Perhaps this truly was a new beginning, after all.

## Chapter Five

Isaac gulped down the last of his brandy, wincing as it burned the back of his throat. He seldom took strong drink in the afternoon these days, but today he'd decided to allow himself a single glass. Around him the library was gloomy, the grey day outside providing little by way of either light or solace. With a heavy sigh he hauled himself out of his armchair and set about lighting a candle by which to read. If he could concentrate on a book. If he could concentrate on anything at all.

Beyond the library Hayton Hall was silent, except for the occasional footsteps of a servant going about his duties. Samuel had been out for most of the day, having given no indication as to when he was likely to return. And, although he was loath to admit it, Isaac found himself craving his brother's company, his merry demeanour and even his gentle teasing. Increasingly, it struck him just how much he hated being alone. Just how much he resented the life he'd been condemned to. It was not the sort of life he wanted at all.

Unfortunately for him, it was the only kind of life he was ever going to have. He'd made a vow once, to love and to cherish until death. He'd spoken those words in a church on a fine summer's day, never considering that death would come so soon. Never even contemplating that the years of loving and cherishing would be so painfully brief. Making such a vow again was completely out of the question. His heart had been shattered by his loss, and although it had now mended enough that he felt able to live again, he was not sure he was capable of loving again.

Not the way he'd loved Rosalind. Not how a woman deserved to be loved.

He missed Rosalind as he would miss his own skin. That was how losing her felt—as though someone had flayed the flesh from his bones and he'd been left to walk around raw and bleeding ever since. And the child, too. How he missed his long-awaited, much-beloved son.

In the months after their deaths, with enough darkness and enough drink, he had pretended that they were by his side, his liquor-addled mind conjuring a vision of his wife sitting just across from him, their little boy perched on her lap. He had heard her laughter, seen her brown curls shaking as she teased him about some trivial matter or other.

He'd always been so serious, but she'd been able to counter that with a kind of inherent, light-hearted joy that had made his soul burn for her. He'd loved marriage, loved the companionship of having a wife. He'd loved waking up beside her each day and embracing her before bed each night. Others might be cynical about getting wed, doing it for money or connections, but he had entered into it for neither reason.

He'd married for love.

By God, he had loved her.

'And now look at you…can't even talk properly to a woman, you damn fool,' he muttered to himself.

The incident on the cliffs had been preying on his mind ever since he'd returned home on his horse. He'd left the poor, weary animal with his groom and marched inside, reeling at how Miss Conrad had slighted him, how she'd walked away as though he was the most offensive creature on earth. A few clumsy words—that was all he'd uttered. He wasn't used to conversation any more, or to women, and for some unfathomable reason he had tried to compensate with a loose tongue and ill-judged humour.

She might have been more forgiving.

She might have tried to understand him.

She might have stayed and talked for a little longer.

Inside Hayton Hall he'd poured himself a brandy, just as he'd done today, and inside that glass his indignation had dissolved into regret. He had been rude, he knew that, and a young lady of impeccable character like Miss Louisa Conrad had been quite right to walk away in the face of such insult.

Miss Louisa Conrad… He had rehearsed that name over and over in his mind, so that he might never forget it. He'd promised never to call her a fair maiden again, and yet that was exactly what she was—all dark gaze and honey-coloured curls. Now, a day later, he knew he owed the fair maiden an apology.

This would be no easy task to accomplish. A note simply would not do, but neither could he just turn up on her doorstep. Going to Lowhaven and exposing himself to comment was inconceivable at the best of times, and seeking out a lovely young lady like Miss Conrad was all but guaranteed to send the town's gossips into a frenzy. Perhaps he could ride that same route again and hope to see her. But then he'd be leaving it all too much to chance, and...

'You're a damnable coward, Liddell,' he said, closing his eyes and dragging his fingers down his face.

'Brother, are you quite well?'

Across from him stood Samuel, a look of concern etched upon his face. He'd been so preoccupied with his quandary over the matter of Miss Conrad that he had not even heard his brother return. He looked up now, wondering how long Samuel had been standing there. How much of Isaac's self-critical monologue he'd heard.

'I'm fine,' he replied, forcing a smile. 'Just a little tired, that's all.'

'I see.' Samuel sat down opposite him, and Isaac watched as his brother's gaze shifted warily to the empty glass on the table. 'How many of those have you had?' he asked.

'Only one,' Isaac snapped. 'Why?'

'I'm just making sure you're not falling back into your old ways, brother.'

Isaac flinched at the memory of how he'd lived during those long months he'd spent lost to his grief. Festering in the darkness in his library, surrounded by empty glasses laced with the residue of day-old drink and crumpled newspapers, half-perused and then abandoned. He had tried futilely to numb the pain with so much brandy that it was a minor miracle that he hadn't been struck down with barrel fever.

He was aware that Samuel knew it all—that he'd interviewed the servants almost immediately upon his return to Hayton Hall, ensuring that he had sufficient insight into exactly how his older brother had been faring during his long absence.

'Such bad habits are far behind me,' Isaac replied, glaring at him. 'That was the case even before you dragged yourself home from your continental adventures. I am quite capable of looking after myself these days, Samuel.'

To his surprise, his brother held up his hands in a gesture of surrender. 'I know that. Believe me, I'm not trying to be a nursemaid to you. But I am trying to encourage you to do more, to go out a bit more—for your own good.'

'I do go out,' Isaac countered, sitting back in his chair, arms folded. 'I accompanied you to Penrith at your request, didn't I? And I am out most days on my horse. I went riding just yesterday, if you recall,' he added, his mind wandering immediately to the cliffs, to those dark eyes staring boldly up at him as he spat out his fury.

'I do recall that you went riding alone,' Samuel agreed. 'I recall too that you came back in the most foul temper. A mood which, dare I say, has persisted ever since. A black mood even by your standards, Isaac.'

Isaac curled his lip. 'As I said, I'm just a little tired.'

Samuel, however, was clearly not going to let the matter drop. Instead he sat forward, his elbows pressed against the arms of his chair. 'I regret that I was not here for you, you know. I regret that I did not return home as soon as the news about Rosalind and the baby reached me. I can offer no excuses.'

He drew a deep breath, and instinctively Isaac found himself dreading whatever was coming next.

'But I am here now,' he continued, 'and I think it is time that a few things changed at Hayton Hall.'

Isaac frowned. 'Such as?'

'You are Sir Isaac Liddell, Baronet. It's time you started to act like it again.'

'I do act like it,' Isaac protested. 'I care for my estate and always have. Even when I was at my lowest ebb I did not neglect my duties.'

'That is not all that your position in life involves, and you know it,' Samuel countered. He pointed at the window. 'It involves going out there, visiting your tenants and going into town. It involves being a part of society. You might not spend all day in your robe any more, drinking yourself to death, but you must surely see that you are still living a half-life.'

At this, Isaac groaned. Samuel was right—of course he was. In his widowhood he'd become sullen and reclusive. To such an extent that sometimes he wondered whether he knew how to hold a proper conversation any more. His encounter with Miss Conrad yesterday had shown him just how low he'd sunk. Hot-tempered and impertinent, he had undoubtedly caused great offence.

Rosalind wouldn't have looked at him twice if he'd behaved in such a manner with her. Not that he wanted any woman to look at him the way she had—of course not. But a small, suppressed part of him did desire to see the old Isaac return, to see the man his wife had loved stare back at him in the mirror once more.

'All right,' he said at length. 'I place myself wholly at your disposal, brother. What would you have me do?'

Samuel smiled. 'Quite simply, Isaac, I want you to start venturing into society once again. I want you to show your face in the village, and in Lowhaven, and I want you to go to the events that those in our society would expect you to attend.'

'You really want me to offer myself up as fodder for the gossips?' Isaac scoffed, shaking his head.

'People will simply take it as an indication that you have come out of mourning at last,' Samuel replied flatly. 'They will be glad of it, I am sure. You must stop believing that the world is somehow against you, because truly it is not. We will start by attending a ball at the Assembly Rooms in Lowhaven this Friday.'

'But that is only a few days from now, Samuel.' Isaac stared at him, aghast.

Samuel nodded. 'You must start somewhere, Isaac. Let this be your new beginning.'

'All right,' Isaac conceded with another groan.

'Good,' Samuel replied, rising from his seat. 'Because I am rather looking forward to this ball. A pleasant evening among friends and perhaps a dance or two with some of the young ladies will suit me very well.'

Isaac gave him a wry smile. 'Indeed, brother. I expect you'll find yourself on scores of ladies' dance cards before the night is over.'

'As might you,' Samuel answered him as he made his way to the library door. 'Even you are not immune to the charms of a pretty face.'

Isaac made no attempt to reply, but instead sat back in his chair, exhausted at the mere prospect of what the next few days would hold. Putting on his best clothes and going out in company for the evening was one thing, but dancing with a woman was quite another. Although, he reminded himself, there was one young lady with whom he did wish to speak, and if she happened to be there requesting a dance with her might be his only means of offering an apology.

His stomach churned at the thought of such an interaction, at the possibility of her rebuke. At the small chance of her acceptance and the pleasant prospect of being the recipient of that dark gaze once again.

Samuel was right, it seemed. He was not immune to a pretty woman's charms. Not in the least.

# Chapter Six

The sun was still bestowing its pink-orange glow upon Lowhaven when the Pearsons' carriage drew to a halt outside the Assembly Rooms that Friday evening. The Pearsons had arrived to collect Louisa and her aunt a little early, which had thrown the household into brief disarray as Nan hurried to finish dressing her mistress while Aunt Clarissa cajoled them from downstairs.

'It seems that the Pearsons keep to their own time,' she'd said as Louisa had finally emerged, 'and we must keep to it, too, since they are good enough to take us in their carriage.'

Louisa had met the remark with silence. She was not oblivious to her aunt's humble circumstances—no carriage and only two servants in her household—but acknowledging the ageing woman's situation so directly made her uncomfortable. Perhaps, she realised, it was because this was the future that she imagined for herself: independent, but only so far as a small income might allow.

The journey in the carriage had been brief and lively, with the two older women complimenting the younger women's gowns and speculating as to how full both their dance cards might be.

Louisa had felt herself grow anxious at the latter remarks. While she was enjoying having an occasion to wear the pretty rose-pink silk gown that Nan had selected for her, she was nonetheless adamant that dancing was out of the question. Her aunt had asked her to come as Miss Pearson's companion, and she would fulfil her duty, but that was all.

She'd felt relieved when Mr Pearson, a stout man with greying red hair, had changed the subject to ask if she'd found Lowhaven agreeable so far. An easy question, she'd thought, at least for the most part. As long as she did not include clifftop arguments with disagreeable baronets when determining her answer.

The scene which greeted Louisa as she stepped out of the carriage was one of crowds and chaos, as it seemed most of Lowhaven had descended upon the fine white building to enjoy an evening of music and conversation. As she was jostled up the steps and towards the entrance she found herself taking hold of Charlotte's arm, more for her own reassurance than anything else, but Charlotte accepted the gesture warmly.

'We shall be fine if we stay together, I think,' the younger woman whispered to her. 'I promise I shall not leave your side, Louisa.'

Louisa blinked, momentarily taken aback by Charlotte's familiarity in using her first name before deciding to embrace it. By her own admission Aunt Clarissa had identified Charlotte as a suitable companion for her; perhaps during the course of the summer they could become firm friends, too. It had been so long since Louisa had enjoyed a friendship.

She smiled. 'Thank you, Charlotte,' she said.

The two young women made their way inside, trailing behind their older companions as they wove their way through the congregating masses towards the ballroom, from which they could already hear the cheerful sound of violins playing.

Halfway along the corridor Louisa heard Mr Pearson announce his intention to visit the card room and to leave the ladies to their own devices. She smiled, thinking of her own father, who would do much the same thing when out for the evening. Her face grew serious once more as she remembered how long it had been since she had enjoyed such times in the company of her parents.

'Do not worry,' Charlotte said to her, misinterpreting her countenance. 'We shall do quite well without Papa.'

The four ladies settled themselves in a spot at the edge of the ballroom, with Aunt Clarissa and Mrs Pearson fortunate enough to find two seats upon which to make themselves comfortable. Louisa and Charlotte, meanwhile, stood close together, sipping from the small cups of punch they'd each been offered by a passing waiter. The drink was strong, and Louisa resolved to take only a little of it. She would act as an unmarried woman in her position ought to act: with good deal of sense and restraint. She would be a charming and responsible companion to Charlotte, and would give Lowhaven society no reason to gossip on her account.

'Do you know many people here?' Louisa asked Charlotte.

Charlotte shook her head in reply. 'Not so many, no,' she replied. 'I'm afraid we may be standing here like wallflowers for some time.'

Louisa smiled reassuringly. In truth, she did not mind.

It was rather pleasant to stand to one side and watch others as they danced in the warm glow of the candlelight. Her days of hovering beside her mother, trying not to fidget as she waited for some young gentleman to request an introduction and thereafter a dance, were long past. She knew, however, that Charlotte would be experiencing such nervous anticipation right now, and that her hopes for the evening were altogether different from those of a woman settled upon spinsterhood.

'I am sure you will be dancing before too long,' Louisa whispered encouragingly.

At length, Louisa was correct. When one dance ended and before the next began Charlotte was approached by a young man of her acquaintance and swiftly whisked away to dance a lively cotillion. Conscious she was now alone, Louisa stepped back towards her aunt and Mrs Pearson, intent upon looking at ease in their company while standing quietly with her thoughts.

She had managed well so far, she believed, cultivating an air of serenity whilst drawing no attention to herself. Perhaps venturing into society as a stranger was not so bad, after all.

'I'm afraid you may see little of my daughter for the rest of the evening,' Mrs Pearson observed as she approached. 'I usually find that once she secures one dancing partner, she shortly thereafter secures a dozen.'

'I am glad of it,' Louisa replied. 'Although Miss Pearson seemed to suggest that she did not know many of the people here.'

'She knows plenty who are of consequence,' Mrs Pearson answered, giving her a sharp look.

Louisa glanced apologetically at her aunt, fearing she

had unwittingly overstepped the mark. 'Of course,' she replied with a conciliatory nod.

But neither Mrs Pearson nor Aunt Clarissa were paying any further heed to her faux pas, their attention instead captured by something beyond her. Something which had made her aunt's mouth fall open in disbelief.

'Well, I never…' Aunt Clarissa began.

Louisa spun round, watching as the crowd seemed to part like the Red Sea. Standing in the chasm they'd left were two gentlemen—both of them known to her, and both causing her to take a sharp breath, albeit for very different reasons.

The fair-haired gentleman was smiling broadly, his open, friendly expression taking her back to those hours she'd spent in his fine carriage, reeling from the ordeal of the overturned stagecoach. But it was the other gentleman standing by his side who had really captured her attention—and, indeed, the attention of everyone else in the room. The dark, wild-tempered man from the cliffs…the one who'd inflamed her with his insolence and preyed on her thoughts ever since.

She heard herself gasp as he turned and caught her gaze. Then she felt the earlier calm she'd relished simply ebb away.

Isaac ought to have been mortified by the scene his presence had created—by the gawping expressions and unsubtle whispers which welcomed him to his first social outing in more than two years. Indeed, it was exactly this reaction he had dreaded. He had been so reluctant to attend tonight that Samuel had had to all but drag him out of Hayton Hall and into his carriage.

Yet now, standing there, he could think of nothing

but one lady's face, wide-eyed and uncommonly beautiful, just as she had been the last time he'd seen her. He could think of nothing but speaking with her again, of finding some discreet way to deliver the apology which was due to her. The sight of her staring at him with that same aghast look in her eyes that he'd seen when he'd almost trampled her with his horse was enough to make him feel ashamed all over again. How wretched he had been. How uncouth.

'Well, brother, it seems we've caused quite a stir,' Samuel observed, an amused smile playing on his lips.

'Exactly why I did not want to come here,' Isaac replied, although his protest sounded hollow.

Samuel helped himself to a couple of glasses of punch from the tray of a passing waiter, handing one of them to his brother. Isaac took a long sip, savouring its sweetness and the way it warmed his throat, as every pair of eyes in the room seemed to remain intently upon him. At least the drink was strong, he thought. He would need plenty of it if he was going to survive the long evening ahead of him.

'Ah, I see Miss Conrad is here,' Samuel observed, with a polite nod in her direction.

'Miss Conrad?' Isaac asked, feigning ignorance.

'The fair maiden,' Samuel whispered. 'The one whose aid we came to on our way home from Penrith. Surely you cannot have forgotten her, brother?' He nudged Isaac firmly in the ribs, making him wince. 'Come, let us say hello. I am curious to know how she is enjoying her stay in Lowhaven.'

Dutifully, Isaac followed his brother. He hoped he looked sufficiently detached, and that no one would detect his heart hammering in his chest as he walked across the room towards her. As he drew closer, he noted that the two older ladies sitting down behind her had got to their feet. One of them looked familiar, although he could not recall why. He noted, too, how Miss Conrad's eyes seemed to widen even further, her posture so stiff and brittle that she looked as though she might break.

His stomach lurched at the realisation that it was his approach which had provoked such a response.

'Miss Conrad!' Samuel exclaimed, giving her an impeccable bow. 'It is very good to see you again.'

'Mr Liddell.' Miss Conrad met Samuel's enthusiasm with a brisk nod. 'And Sir Isaac, of course,' she added, although she barely lifted her dark eyes to acknowledge him.

Isaac watched as Miss Conrad gestured awkwardly towards her companions and hurriedly undertook the necessary introductions. Isaac bowed politely at the two older ladies, realising that the one with the familiar face was Miss Howarth, the old rector's daughter. The other lady, Mrs Pearson, he did not know, and nor did he warm to her as she stood there, her sharp gaze flitting between them all like a crow choosing its supper.

With the formality of introductions now complete, he found himself watching Miss Conrad once more, his gaze lingering upon her while Samuel gave an account of their meeting Miss Conrad to Mrs Pearson, who had enquired as to how they were acquainted.

He noted that his brother's tale was less than truthful, omitting all mention of taking the young lady and her maid into their carriage. Apparently protecting Miss Conrad's reputation meant more to Samuel than providing evidence of his own gallantry. Guilt surged through him as he compared his brother's gentlemanly behaviour with his own clumsy, brutish tongue that day on the cliffs.

'I daresay that must have been frightening, Miss Conrad,' Mrs Pearson observed. 'Coachmen these days can be so reckless. I am surprised that neither you nor your aunt mentioned it before. It is quite a story,' she added.

Isaac found himself raising an eyebrow at the cutting nature of the remark. It was as though the woman sensed there was a shared secret she was not being made privy to.

'Ah—yes, well, fortunately the coach was able to continue on its way and no harm was done,' Miss Howarth interjected smoothly. 'And my niece is very grateful to you both for stopping to retrieve the fallen luggage,' she added, giving both gentlemen a smile which told them that she appreciated their discretion.

Miss Conrad, however, appeared not to be listening, her eyes cast down, her thoughts elsewhere. Isaac wished he could read them…wished to know what had her so preoccupied. Wished to know if she could stand this latest meeting, or if she wanted to turn and walk away all over again.

Around them the music ceased, and the bustle of men and women changing dancing partners began. Before he could think about what he was doing, Isaac reached out and offered her his hand.

'Would you like to dance, Miss Conrad?' he asked her, and finally she lifted her gaze and those deep brown eyes met his once more.

## Chapter Seven

Louisa felt the heat rise in her cheeks as Sir Isaac led her towards the centre of the ballroom. It seemed to her as though every pair of eyes was upon them—as though every person there had the same whispered questions on their lips. Who was this woman? And why had Sir Isaac chosen her for his first dance?

In truth, she desired to know the answer to the latter question herself. After their awful last meeting she had assumed he'd want no further association with her. He'd had to endure his brother's approach and the subsequent conversation—that had been a matter of politeness. But asking her to dance? There had been no requirement for him to do that.

She wished he hadn't asked her. She wished she hadn't felt obliged to accept. It had drawn attention to her, and that was the very last thing she wanted.

They lined up opposite each other and Louisa said a quick prayer, hoping she could remember the steps. She looked up at Sir Isaac, realising she must appear as anxious as she felt when he offered her a small, reassuring smile.

The candlelight seemed to illuminate his face, and her attention was drawn to the gentle creases around his eyes and the smattering of silver in his near-black hair. It struck her that he was older than she'd thought—but then she hadn't thought very much of him at their first or second meeting…at least, not much to his credit. Now, she couldn't seem to take her eyes off him. His countenance—indeed his entire appearance—was very different from that which she had witnessed on the cliffs. Tonight, he looked every inch an elegant gentleman, in his dark tailcoat and contrasting breeches, whilst his windswept hair had been tamed, and apparently so had his rough manners.

Realising she was staring at him, she lowered her gaze, instructing herself to be calm as the music began and they took their first steps towards one another. It was only one dance. It would be over soon enough.

'I fear I have made you uncomfortable, Miss Conrad,' Sir Isaac said in a low voice when they drew close enough to converse. 'I only wish to apologise to you for the way I spoke to you at our last meeting. I was unforgivably rude.'

'Thank you,' she replied softly. 'I appreciate the trouble you have gone to in order to convey your apology.'

'Trouble?'

'Asking me to dance when I am sure there are many others in this room whose company you would find more agreeable. I was not… I was not all that I should have been at our last meeting, either,' she added hesitantly, hoping he would grasp her meaning.

The demands of the dance separated them for a few moments. As she moved with as much grace as she could muster, Louisa found herself feeling impatient.

Why was it that a man and a woman could not have a straightforward conversation in company without any need for the ruse of dancing?

By the time they met again Louisa could barely keep command of her words as they burst forth. 'I was ungracious towards you,' she blurted. 'Truly, I am ashamed of it.'

Sir Isaac caught her gaze, offering her his hand again as the dance required. She accepted it delicately and together they turned, exchanging small smiles which seemed to express a mutual understanding that words could not.

'Then it seems we are both ashamed, Miss Conrad,' Sir Isaac said at last. 'Come, let us start afresh.'

Louisa gave a nod of agreement. Although she very much doubted that any acquaintance between them would be sustained, it eased her conscience to know that there was no animosity between them.

They spent the remainder of the dance largely in silence, punctuated only by Sir Isaac's polite enquiries into the length of her stay in Lowhaven and whether she was enjoying her summer sojourn. She allowed herself to relax, enjoying the dance and the company of a man who, she could not fail to observe, had both charm and handsome looks in abundance.

For this indulgence she chastised herself; her days of admiring a gentleman's appearance were as far behind her as she'd believed her dancing days to be. Occasionally, though, when the steps brought them close together or compelled them to go hand in hand, she felt a long-forgotten warmth spread through her limbs. And when she caught Sir Isaac looking at her, letting his deep blue eyes linger over her face, she remembered why dancing could be preferable to conversation.

Trouble. That was what she'd called it. *Trouble.*

Isaac sat back in the carriage, resting his head against the hard wooden side as he waited for Samuel to join him for their journey back to Hayton Hall. The hour was late and, given the evening's exertions, he knew he ought to be exhausted. But rest could not have been further from his mind. Instead, he found his thoughts revisiting certain memories, again and again.

Her dark eyes staring up at him. The soft feeling of her gloved hand. The arresting sensation of her nearness to him each time the dance commanded them to draw close. The touching sincerity of her apology. It had all caught him unaware and left him so overwrought that he'd managed only the barest amount of conversation. Truly, she must think him the most charmless man she'd ever met.

Trouble? Indeed, he was troubled.

'Well, brother, I do believe that tonight was a success.'

Samuel climbed into the carriage, sitting down opposite him with a satisfied sigh. His eyes were heavy and a little glazed, and Isaac noted the smell of strong liquor emanating from him. His encounter with Miss Conrad had left him feeling distracted for the rest of the night, and he had neither paid attention to his younger sibling's merrymaking nor indulged in the strong punch himself. Now, he found himself wishing he was in his cups, too. Some gentle inebriation might help to distance him from uncomfortable thoughts about a beautiful woman.

'It was not as bad as I feared,' Isaac conceded.

'You see! I was right that you should come,' Samuel declared, with a self-satisfied tap of his knee.

'Indeed... Although I am very weary now,' Isaac replied, suddenly desirous of a quiet journey home.

His brother, however, was not to be dissuaded from his chatter. 'I cannot see how! You barely danced, except with Miss Conrad. That was a surprise, I have to say... you whisking her away like that. I wondered what had come over you.'

'Nothing,' Isaac grunted. 'I merely thought it polite.'

'You were under no obligation. Mind you, she is remarkably handsome. I had thought to ask her myself, but...'

'But what?'

'She's very reserved. Dare I say a little cold, even? I recall thinking as much when we first met her. The way she sat in our carriage, stony-faced and hardly troubling herself to make conversation.'

Isaac felt his fists curl with irritation and he pressed them into the seat. 'She didn't know us, Samuel. She was forced by circumstances to accept our assistance. I think she can be forgiven for being a little wary.'

Samuel let out a wry chuckle. 'You've changed your tune. What was it you called her after we'd left her with her aunt? Reckless?'

'Damn you,' Isaac growled.

Samuel's face grew serious. 'You're quite taken with her, aren't you? I saw the way you were looking at her, you know. I'll bet most of the people in the ballroom did—including her. I've not seen you look at a woman like that since...'

'Don't say her name!' Isaac snapped. 'Don't you dare!' He sighed heavily, composing himself. 'I was not looking at Miss Conrad is any particular way. I was only…'

'Only what?' his brother challenged him, sitting upright now.

'Only—only seeking to apologise to her,' he admitted finally, rubbing his forehead with his hands.

'Apologise?' Samuel frowned. 'What could you possibly need to apologise for?'

'I saw Miss Conrad again—after the day of the stagecoach accident.' Isaac made his admission quietly. 'I was riding up on the cliffs near Lowhaven. Miss Conrad was out for a walk. I nearly trampled the poor woman with my horse. I was in a foul temper and I spoke to her in a way that I had no business to. Asking her to dance with me was the only way I could offer an apology discreetly.'

Samuel raised his eyebrows. 'I see. And when was this?'

Isaac shrugged. 'Less than a week ago. Does it matter?'

'I suppose not.' Samuel slumped back, closing his eyes. 'And that's all there is to it, is there? You've made amends to her and have no intention of seeing her again?'

'Indeed,' Isaac replied. 'Miss Conrad is visiting her aunt for the summer. I doubt that our paths will cross again.'

The only answer Isaac received from his brother was the sound of his loud snores punctuating the air as their carriage rumbled slowly along the road back to Hayton Hall.

Just as well, Isaac thought, settling into his seat. The last thing he wanted was for Samuel to hear how forlorn he sounded, or to realise just how unsettled the evening, the dancing, and above all Miss Louisa Conrad had left him.

\* \* \*

By the time the Pearsons' carriage delivered Louisa and her aunt back to Juniper Street, Louisa could barely keep her eyes open. The short journey home had been quiet, with the older members of the party all dozing and the younger two exchanging only brief whispers about the evening's events.

Charlotte evidently relished her near-constant dancing. Her cheeks were flushed, her face alight with a smile which no amount of weariness could remove. For Charlotte Pearson it had been a very successful night indeed.

Louisa, on the other hand, felt more conflicted about her first foray into Lowhaven society. She hadn't wished to dance at all, and had it not been for Sir Isaac Liddell's invitation she would have succeeded in that regard. Yet, try as she might, she could not bring herself to regret it.

Dancing with Sir Isaac had thrilled and discomfited her in equal measure. She had been pleased to make amends with him, but it was more than that—if she was honest with herself, she had enjoyed his attentions. She'd relished his proximity, and the sensation which had run through her each time he'd taken hold of her hand. She knew she shouldn't feel that way—the dance would have meant little to him, and he'd only asked her so that he could apologise. But still, she decided, there could be nothing wrong with her keeping the memory of it for herself and bringing it out on those occasions when she needed something to make her smile.

'Goodnight, Aunt,' she said, almost as soon as they walked through Clarissa's door, determining to go straight upstairs and to bed.

'Could you perhaps come into the parlour for a moment, my dear?' Clarissa asked her.

Louisa nodded, wordlessly following her aunt into the small room and closing the door. She felt her heart begin to beat faster as she wondered what was amiss. Aunt Clarissa's face was drawn and grey with tiredness; whatever it was must be serious if it could not keep until morning.

'I wanted to speak to you about Mrs Pearson, Louisa.'

'Oh?'

Aunt Clarissa shook her head, clearly troubled. 'Unfortunately I think Mrs Pearson was vexed not to have known that you'd met Sir Isaac and his brother before.'

'I rather think it's none of her business who I am acquainted with, Aunt,' Louisa replied.

'Indeed, but after we'd discussed Sir Isaac at tea…' Clarissa paused, then waved a dismissive hand. 'Oh, never mind about that. I wanted to speak to you about your remark…when you suggested that Miss Pearson did not know many people at the ball.'

'I was merely repeating what Charlotte had told me herself,' Louisa protested mildly.

In truth, her thoughts had been so preoccupied with Sir Isaac that she had quite forgotten the incident altogether.

'I'm sure you were, and I know you spoke in innocence. But I thought I ought to explain to you why I believe Mrs Pearson behaved the way she did.' Clarissa sighed, sitting down on one of the parlour chairs. 'The Pearsons only came to Lowhaven a few months ago. Mrs Pearson is a gentleman's daughter, from Northumberland, but Mr John Pearson's family have made their fortune in trade. From what I have heard, he has squandered it, and the family now find themselves in reduced circumstances. Since coming to town, I believe they've struggled to make good connections. That's what Miss Pearson will have been alluding to when she told you that she had not had all that many introductions.'

Louisa frowned. 'Charlotte seemed to manage well enough this evening. She had sufficient acquaintances to keep her dancing for most of the night.'

'Ah, yes, but I doubt that even one of those young men she danced with will be considered suitable by Mrs Pearson,' Clarissa countered, giving her niece a knowing smile. 'Even though I'm sure she knows well enough that the leading families in the area will want little to do with a hapless tradesman's daughter— especially since I doubt there is even a substantial dowry to tempt them.'

'It cannot be so bad, surely? They manage to keep a carriage and horses of their own.'

'They keep up appearances, my dear, but I believe it is bad enough. Mrs Pearson will want her daughter to marry soon, I think, and as well as possible.'

'I see,' replied Louisa, biting her lip. 'I am sorry, Aunt. I did not mean to offend Mrs Pearson.'

Clarissa got up from her chair, gently patting her niece on the arm. 'I wouldn't worry. I daresay you more than made up for it by securing her an introduction to Sir Isaac and his brother.'

The mention of Sir Isaac made Louisa's face grow warm. 'Oh, yes,' she replied.

Clarissa shook her head. 'I couldn't quite believe my eyes when they walked in together. And then for Sir Isaac to ask you to dance! You did well, my dear. Very well.'

'I'm quite sure Sir Isaac only asked me out of politeness, Aunt.'

At this, Clarissa laughed. 'I might be an old spinster, Louisa, but I know enough about the world to know that a gentleman never asks a lady to dance just to be polite. He did not dance with anyone else all night, you know. And from the way he looked at you, I was quite certain that he'd ask you to take a turn with him a second time.'

Now Louisa felt sure her cheeks must be glowing scarlet. 'Well, I am glad he did not, for I am convinced I could not have borne it,' she replied hotly. 'And now I am tired and must go to bed. Goodnight, Aunt.'

Before Clarissa could say anything further, Louisa opened the door and marched out of the room.

# Chapter Eight

'You've done well today, brother.'

Samuel's patronising tone made Isaac flinch, although he knew the remark was well-intended. The day was fine and bright and the two brothers rode side by side, paying visits to the farms and cottages situated across the not inconsiderable swathe of Liddell land.

'I was never so melancholic that I ceased to have any regard for my tenants,' Isaac countered, glancing briefly over his shoulder at his steward, who rode a little further behind. 'Although I will concede that I always had the very best help.'

'I do believe your visits today were appreciated, nonetheless. It means a lot for you to be seen.'

Isaac nodded. 'Indeed. I regret that I have been so absent these past two years. In plentiful times it may have been forgivable, but…'

'You are not responsible for bad harvests, Isaac,' Samuel interjected. 'Only the damnable weather can be blamed for that.'

'No, I know that,' Isaac replied quietly. 'But, as you say, it's important that I'm seen, and while my tenants suffered I was very much invisible.'

Samuel offered his brother a sympathetic smile, and together they rode on in silence. They had one more visit to pay on the edge of the village, before returning to Hayton Hall for luncheon. The mere thought of food made Isaac's stomach growl; they had been out for hours, and he'd barely had time to eat even a small breakfast before meeting his steward at nine o'clock.

Despite his hunger, he had to admit that the busy morning had buoyed his spirits. He'd enjoyed seeing the families, many of whom had lived and worked on his family's land for generations. And, he had to admit, he'd liked having Samuel accompany him as much as he'd appreciated the support of his steward. Samuel's light-hearted, relaxed manner and ability to regale an audience with tales of his European travels had put Isaac at his ease and made him feel less under scrutiny.

Yes, he thought. The morning had been a success.

He'd even managed not to think so much about Miss Conrad.

Isaac sighed, inwardly cursing himself for allowing his thoughts to roam back to that evening once again. Truly, it was ridiculous to think so much about a woman he'd met only a handful of times and danced with once. It was nonsensical to wake in the morning and realise he'd been dreaming about her, twirling in that captivating pink dress she'd worn. It was alarming to realise that the quiet moments of his day were dominated by her—her smile, her large brown eyes, her perfectly curled fair hair.

He supposed this was to be expected—that after so long on his own even the brief company of a woman like Miss Louisa Conrad could prove overpowering. He found the way that she haunted his thoughts unsettling, but at the same time he was forced to admit that he did not want it to stop.

'Almost there,' Samuel called out to him.

Good, he thought. He needed distraction, and there-after a hearty meal.

'Is it not the most charming little village, Louisa?'

Charlotte took hold of her companion's arm as they made their way along the dusty track which served as the main thoroughfare through Hayton. This was their first outing together since the ball and, as promised, Charlotte had determined that they would walk to Hay-ton, so that she could show Louisa around the village her family had once called their home.

Louisa found herself easily agreeing with her new friend's opinion—Hayton was indeed as picturesque as it was miniature, with a cluster of low stone cottages forming its centre, framed by trees and hedgerows in full leaf. At its furthest edge was the ancient church where, Charlotte had reliably informed her, the old rec-tory could be found.

As the two ladies made their way in this direction, Louisa considered what life in Hayton must have been like for her mother and her aunt. Quiet, certainly, with only a handful of neighbours and their parents for com-pany—somewhat different from the life her aunt led now, in a bustling port town.

Rather idly, she wondered which she preferred, and wondered, too, if the isolation of small village life had been the reason she'd never married. For whilst Aunt Clarissa's siblings had sought opportunities in the larger towns or, in her own mother's case, been removed to London by benevolent relatives, Clarissa had remained faithfully at the rectory, at her parents' side. She wondered how much that had been of her own choosing, or whether it had simply been the only option left.

'It is very lovely,' Louisa agreed at last.

'When I marry, I should count myself very fortunate if I was able to live in a place like this,' Charlotte gushed. 'Life in a small country cottage would suit me very well indeed.'

'Perhaps you ought to marry a rector, then. A man with a rural parish to tend to. That should assure you of the quiet life you seek,' Louisa said, a note of gentle teasing in her voice.

Charlotte wrinkled her nose. 'I doubt that would do for Mama.'

'What? Your mother would not approve of a match with a man of the cloth? To a gentleman with a steady income? I do believe most mothers would seek exactly such marriages for their daughters,' Louisa replied.

'Alas, my mother is not "most mothers",' Charlotte countered quietly. 'She is most particular on the subject of whom I might marry.'

Louisa gave her friend's arm a sympathetic squeeze, but made no further remark. She reflected briefly on Aunt Clarissa's words about Mrs Pearson, and the high aspirations she believed she had for her daughter. High indeed, Louisa thought, if she would not give her over to marriage with a clergyman.

'Well, here we are, Louisa,' Charlotte said as they arrived at the gates to the church. 'Here is where your grandfather used to minister to his congregation, and over there is the rectory.'

Louisa stood still at length, admiring the old stone church, its spire reaching far above the humble dwellings of the village. She looked, too, at the rectory, finding it to be a pleasing white house of considerable size. She found herself thinking again about the years both her mother and her aunt had spent here, and how little she knew of it.

'It's strange to see it,' Louisa observed, speaking some of her thoughts aloud. 'I cannot claim to have really known my grandparents. They sent my mother to London to stay with relatives not long before she came of age. I knew her family in the south far better.'

'But you are here now, with your aunt,' Charlotte replied. 'You must know her well enough to want to come all this way to visit?'

'I had not seen Aunt Clarissa since I was a girl, but it is true that we have written often.'

'And after all these years you wished to see her and spend the summer here?' Charlotte asked.

Louisa gave a hesitant smile. 'Yes.'

'I wish you would not leave so soon…' Charlotte groaned. 'I fear I will have only just got to know you and you will be going back to Berkshire. Perhaps you will find a reason to stay?' she added, her expression brightening once more. 'Perhaps you will find a husband here.'

'Oh, no, I shall never marry,' Louisa replied, the instinctive response rolling from her tongue before she could think about it.

'Never?' Charlotte exclaimed. 'But how can you say so?'

Louisa sighed, taking Charlotte's arm again as they turned away from the church and began their return journey through the village. Quietly she cursed herself for being so careless with her words. Such a forthright statement demanded some form of explanation.

'I was engaged once, to a captain in the navy. He died at sea during the war…before we were able to wed. I swore then that I would not marry.' She tried her best to sound matter-of-fact, not to betray her emotions. Not to betray all that she had left out.

'Oh, Louisa, that is very sad. I am sorry for you. But you are still young. I do not think your captain would wish for you to remain alone. Surely if he loved you as you loved him, he would not?'

Louisa offered her friend a small smile, wishing she could explain, but knowing she could not. If Charlotte knew the whole story she would understand. But if Charlotte knew the whole story she would not want to be associated with her at all.

'I'm sure he would not. But it is my wish, and I am very much settled upon it.'

'Mama says the life of a spinster is one that no woman should desire. I have to bite my tongue to stop myself from pointing out that one acquaintance she's made in Lowhaven is just such an unmarried woman, and that she seems to do perfectly well by herself.'

Louisa laughed at this. 'Indeed, my aunt is an example to us all.'

'I suppose that while you are here you might learn something from her about managing alone?'

'Yes, I suppose I might,' Louisa replied, wondering, not for the first time, if such motivation had informed her parents' enthusiasm for sending her here. Wondering, too, if they'd hoped seeing her aunt's life for herself might put her off spinsterhood entirely.

'Mama hopes I will learn from you,' Charlotte continued. 'She says you will be a welcome influence upon me…that you are a gentleman's daughter of good repute and great sensibility.'

But Louisa was no longer listening—which was just as well as she might have reddened at Mrs Pearson's overly generous characterisation of her. Instead, she was staring straight ahead, her eyes wide, at the two approaching men on horseback—both of whom she recognised, and one of whom she had not wished to see so soon.

She had barely managed to collect herself following that evening at the ball, never mind recover from that ill-tempered conversation with her aunt on the subject of her dancing. Truly, she was not sure she could face him again. And yet, she realised as he continued his approach, it seemed she must.

Isaac had known it was her from the moment he saw her in the distance, standing in front of the old church. He hadn't been able to see her clearly, or to recognise her pretty features with any precision, but he'd known. He'd known instinctively from the way his heart beat faster and his empty stomach seemed to tie itself in knots.

For a moment he'd thought about turning his horse around and galloping in the other direction, to put some distance between himself and Miss Louisa Conrad and how she flustered him. However, he'd known that would only cause more problems than it would solve—notably in the form of questions from his brother, who still rode at his side. Besides, he was beginning to suspect that mere miles would not be enough to stem the tide which threatened to overwhelm him when he so much as dared to think about her.

'Ah, look—there is Miss Conrad,' Samuel called. 'And who is that with her? A friend? I wonder what she is doing in Hayton. We should stop to say hello.'

'Huh…' Isaac grunted, trying his best to look uninterested.

He wished he could be uninterested. But as he drew closer and saw her looking up at him, those dark, inquisitive eyes staring into his, he realised his folly. This lady—who'd clambered into his carriage, who'd berated him on the clifftops, who'd danced with him—interested him. Now fate had put her in his path once more, and Isaac found himself feeling unfathomably anxious about speaking to her, about giving a good account of himself.

He swallowed hard. His mouth was as dry as a desert, and his mind seemed barren like one, too.

He dismounted his horse, trying to find the right words.

*Damn you, Liddell,* he said to himself. *What is the matter with you?*

# Chapter Nine

'Good day, Miss Conrad. What a pleasant surprise to see you in Hayton.'

Samuel spoke first—of course he did—finding exactly the words which Isaac lacked. Isaac forced a smile and a courteous nod at the two young women, ignoring the prickle of resentment he felt at his brother's friendly, easy manner. Rosalind had always been better in social situations, too, but she'd been his helpmeet. He'd felt gratitude and admiration for her grace and charm. The superior qualities of a younger brother, by contrast, could only ever be irritating.

Samuel dismounted his horse and Isaac watched as Miss Conrad dropped her gaze and gave them both a polite curtsey.

'Sir Isaac, Mr Liddell…may I introduce my friend, Miss Charlotte Pearson?' she said, raising her eyes to meet his once more.

Realising he was staring, Isaac turned quickly to regard her companion, whose acquaintance Samuel was already making, going to great pains to stress his delight. She was a striking young lady, her fair complexion contrasting with the bright red curls which peered wildly from the edges of her bonnet. She seemed younger than Miss Conrad, and both her appearance and manner betrayed a giddiness over which she didn't seem to have mastered complete control.

He wondered then how old Miss Conrad was. Younger than him, certainly—he was nine-and-thirty, and she looked ten years his junior, at least. Yet there was something in those dark eyes of hers, something about the seriousness of her countenance, which suggested a maturity beyond her years. He ruminated on this observation for a moment, before a nudge from his brother forced him to return his mind to the conversation.

'We would be delighted to accompany you back through the village. It would be our pleasure—wouldn't it, Isaac?' Samuel was saying.

'Yes. Indeed—yes,' Isaac replied hastily, realising he'd missed much of the discussion.

He watched with a mix of delight and anxiety as Samuel and Miss Pearson led the way, leaving him in the company of Miss Conrad. Giving her another nod, he took hold of his horse and together they began to walk, slowly and silently at first, as though each one did not know what to say to the other.

'You have enjoyed your walk to Hayton, I hope?' Isaac began, settling upon what he believed would be an easy topic.

There were so many things he wished to say to her, so many things he wished to know—too much to convey and to discover in a short promenade through the tiny village. He would have to content himself with more mundane subjects.

'Yes, thank you,' she replied. 'As you know, my family used to live in the village. Miss Pearson offered to accompany me while I explored the area. She has been very kind.'

'Miss Pearson is related to the Mrs Pearson you were with at the Assembly Rooms?' Isaac asked.

She nodded. 'Yes, they are mother and daughter. They live in Lowhaven. Mrs Pearson is acquainted with my aunt.'

Isaac furrowed his brow a little. 'I do not think I know any Pearsons from Lowhaven.'

'They are fairly new in town, much like myself,' she replied. 'Although they reside now in Lowhaven, whereas I am only visiting.'

'For the summer,' Isaac said, the temporary nature of their acquaintance striking him again.

Miss Conrad smiled. 'Yes, as I think I told you when we danced. I am here only for the summer.'

He nodded briskly, hoping she wouldn't be able to detect the heat that had risen within him when she had made reference to their dancing. God, how his mind had lingered upon the memory of that night. She spoke of it so matter-of-factly; he knew he never could.

'And you enjoyed the ball?' he asked her, wilfully ignoring the way his instincts were crying out at him to avoid the subject altogether.

'Yes, very much. I confess that I was somewhat out of practice when it came to dancing. I hope I did not miss too many of the steps.'

'You were perfect, from what I could see,' he answered her, a little too forthrightly. Reining in his feelings, he added, 'Although I am no expert, since I am more than a little out of practice myself. In truth, I hadn't danced in a long time until I danced with you.'

She smiled again. 'Then I hope I was a worthy partner.'

Damn, he thought. Worthy? She had no idea.

They were approaching the end of the village, and ahead he could see Miss Pearson and his brother had stopped to wait for them. He felt his heart begin to beat faster; they were almost out of time together and all he'd managed was a conversation about trivialities.

'I don't see a lot of people,' he blurted out. 'Other than my brother, of course. What I mean to say is I don't venture much into society. But I do like to walk, and to ride. I often ride out to the cliffs where we met that time. If—if I was ever to see you there again, I should be very glad to continue our conversation.'

He glanced at her, wondering if she had understood his meaning—nay, hoping she had. She turned to meet his gaze, and for a moment he believed he might lose himself in the depths of those eyes.

'Thank you, Sir Isaac,' she replied demurely. 'On the next fine afternoon, after calling hours, I believe I will walk that way again, too.'

What had come over her? What had she done?

Those same two questions circled around Louisa's mind all the way back to Lowhaven. She barely absorbed a word of anything Charlotte said to her, peppering their very one-sided conversation with 'yes' and 'indeed' in the right places as her friend gushed excitedly about her encounter with Mr Liddell.

She could think of nothing else but Sir Isaac's words to her. The way he'd complimented her dancing, the way he'd made sure she knew the significance of it for him—his first dance in a long time. The way he'd asked to see her again, to meet with her…alone. That *was* what he'd meant, wasn't it? She hadn't imagined that, had she? She hadn't misinterpreted his meaning? No, she wasn't so naïve as to have misunderstood him. But she had been foolish enough to answer in the affirmative.

She had said she would meet him, even though she knew she should not.

She'd been reckless—again.

In truth, she'd felt so flustered throughout their conversation she'd hardly known what to say to him. One look into those bright blue eyes had been enough to render her mind utterly incapable of conjuring any suitable conversation. Thank goodness he had taken the lead, in the end. Their encounter, though polite, had been thick with undertones—layer upon layer of words and thoughts unexpressed. She'd felt it, and she sensed he had, too. She hadn't felt this way in the company of a man since…

No. She would not think of him now. It would not do any good.

'Are you all right, Louisa?' Charlotte asked her, apparently finally running out of things to say about the charming Mr Liddell.

'Yes, I am well…just a little tired,' she replied, offering her friend a small smile of reassurance and hoping it would be sufficient.

'You haven't said much about your promenade with Sir Isaac,' Charlotte remarked. 'I observed you dancing with him at the ball, you know. And Mama told me that you were already acquainted with both Sir Isaac and Mr Liddell.'

'Yes, I met them both on my journey to Lowhaven, and, yes, I did dance with Sir Isaac,' she said. 'Both seem to be very agreeable gentlemen,' she added.

'Agreeable—and handsome,' Charlotte said with a giggle.

'Charlotte!'

'Oh, Louisa, surely even a committed spinster like you can see all that both gentlemen have to recommend them. Good looks and a good deal of wealth, I should say. Especially Sir Isaac, given his rank.'

Louisa flinched, not enjoying the brazen tone Charlotte had adopted. 'These are not the only qualities a woman ought to consider in making a marriage, Charlotte,' she tried to advise her.

'Tell that to my mother,' Charlotte retorted. 'For her, they are the only qualities worth noting. Anyway, you have not yet told me—what did you and Sir Isaac discuss?'

'Nothing of any import,' Louisa replied with a small shrug. 'He asked if I had enjoyed seeing Hayton, and we spoke a little about the ball.'

Charlotte's eyes widened. 'About dancing together?'

'Not really,' Louisa lied, wanting to put an end to this conversation.

'Oh. Well, still… It is fortunate that we saw them here today. Mama has been disappointed that I missed out on an introduction at the ball. Mr Liddell said it was quite by chance that they were riding through the village today, as they had been visiting Sir Isaac's tenants.'

'I see,' Louisa replied, realising with a pang of guilt that she had neglected to enquire as to the reason for their visit to the village. In fact, she hadn't asked Sir Isaac any questions at all.

She wondered then what he must think of her. Reserved—aloof, even? Or merely dull and uninterested? On the other hand, he'd made it plain he wanted to see her again, so she couldn't have done so badly. She bit her lip, resolving to be a better conversationalist next time they met. After all, there would be a next time. In a moment of madness she'd agreed to it. She could hardly go back on her word.

Isaac couldn't recall when he'd last been this hungry. As he tucked in to his plate of bread and cold meat, washing it down with a small glass of wine, he smiled, reflecting upon how well he felt. It had been good to spend the morning outside, to be with his brother and to ride in the warm summer air. It had been good, too, to see his tenants. It had been another step along the road out of mourning, and another way in which he had signalled to the world that he was ready to re-join society. And he was—truly, he was.

But none of that was the reason he felt so exhilarated.

He'd behaved boldly with Miss Conrad—had been far bolder than he'd thought himself capable of being. It was hard to comprehend what had come over him, but ever since that day on the cliffs that woman had been on his mind. Today's encounter had been a coincidence, but even as they'd walked together he'd felt keenly that he did not want to leave the next time they saw each other to chance. He wanted to talk to her, to get to know her. He wanted to see her alone.

God, he had all but asked her to come alone.

And she'd all but said that she would.

'Well, that was quite an unexpected pleasure,' Samuel said between mouthfuls of food.

Isaac had been so absorbed in his thoughts that he'd almost forgotten his younger brother was sitting opposite. 'What was?'

'Seeing Miss Conrad today. And meeting her friend, the lovely Miss Pearson. A charming girl…very lively.'

Isaac nodded. 'Indeed, she gave that impression. I'm not sure she ever stopped smiling.'

Samuel buttered another slice of bread. 'I found her very agreeable.'

'She seemed very…young,' Isaac remarked, searching for the right words to describe the lady who had clearly caught his brother's attention.

'Not so much younger than me, I don't think,' Samuel retorted. 'Twenty, perhaps? I doubt I have more than ten years on her. Remember, I am much younger than you,' he added, with a grin.

'Huh…' Isaac grunted, occupying himself with his food once more. 'We know nothing of the girl's family other than that they are new to Lowhaven. Miss Conrad told me so.'

'Ah, yes. And how *was* the stoic Miss Conrad?'

'Well, I believe. I wish you would not mock her simply because she seems to be immune to your charms,' Isaac bit back, his tone sounding harsher than he'd intended.

'I don't think you're immune to hers, though,' Samuel replied, giving him a pointed look.

'Nonsense.'

Samuel sighed. 'There is no shame in it, Isaac. Rosalind would want you to be happy.'

Isaac felt the heat of anger flash through him. 'Don't you dare to presume what Rosalind would or would not have wanted!' he snapped.

His ire was directed at Samuel, but Isaac knew that in truth the only person he was frustrated with was himself. He was no naïve youth, ignorant of his growing infatuation with Miss Conrad. But neither was he deaf to that inner voice which niggled at him, suggesting that his preoccupation with her amounted to a betrayal of his dead wife, that it was utterly contrary to his commitment to remaining alone.

A mere two years had passed since Rosalind's death; how could he possibly contemplate moving on? How could he even think of allowing himself to love again when he knew only too well the pain it had brought him? That was if he was even capable of love, he reminded himself. Surely his heart bore too many scars for that.

'All right, all right,' Samuel said, holding his hands up. 'All I'm trying to say is if you like Miss Conrad then you should pursue her. Just be cautious. The last thing you need is some disappointment with a woman to send you back into hiding with a bottle of brandy.'

'Then you have nothing to fear. Because I have no intentions towards Miss Conrad, or any other woman of my acquaintance.'

Damn, how that lie stung his lips. He gave his brother a hard stare, hoping he would not manage to see through the façade. In truth, he barely understood his own intentions. Barely knew what he wanted. All he did know was that he was tired of grief and tired of being alone. He wanted companionship and conversation and joy. He wanted to sit beside a beautiful woman and make her smile, even if it was only for the summer.

He could only hope he would find some of those things next time he rode out to the cliffs.

## Chapter Ten

In the days after her visit to Hayton it did nothing but rain. Louisa was forced to remain indoors, sitting often with her aunt in the parlour while she read or passed the time with light conversation.

Louisa had sensed some tension between Clarissa and herself, ever since the night of the ball. She knew it was her doing, that the way she'd spoken to her aunt about Sir Isaac had made the older woman wary. She regretted that this was the case, but she did not know how to remedy it. To bring up the subject would be uncomfortable, and might lead her aunt to begin the discussion about the master of Hayton Hall anew—which was the last thing she wanted. But to avoid it, as she had done thus far, allowed it to fester between them, making the memory of her cross words no doubt a source of mortification for them both.

Oh, how she wished she hadn't spoken out of turn.

How she wished she'd said nothing about Sir Isaac at all. Especially not a lie—and it was a lie. She knew she'd have enjoyed a second dance with him very much indeed.

Nan was driving her to distraction, too, fussing around

her as she tried to read a book or write a long-overdue letter to her mother, to whom she hadn't written since she'd sent word of her safe arrival several weeks ago. She knew her maid had found the adjustment to a smaller household difficult, and that having to assist with kitchen or cleaning tasks did not suit her as well as keeping solely to the duties of a lady's maid. Nonetheless, she found Nan's frequent intrusions irritating; she didn't need anything brought to her and she didn't desire company. If anything, she wanted to be left alone: to think, to reflect and—dare she admit it?—to daydream a little. It had been a long time since she'd allowed herself a luxury such as that.

On the first fine day in almost a week Louisa ventured outdoors as soon as the calling hours were over. She'd done her best to make it appear like an impromptu walk, deflecting her aunt's suggestion that she send a note to Charlotte by insisting throughout the morning that she planned to stay at home, only to then change her mind at the last possible moment. Such deceit had left her feeling flustered, but she knew she couldn't take Charlotte with her, or indeed anyone else. Nan had made some vague overtures about accompanying her, but had been easily put off when Louisa had let it be known that she planned to walk up to the cliffs and take the sea air.

'I'll come if you wish, miss,' she'd said, gesturing at the sewing in her lap, 'but then this mending will need to wait until later.'

'Oh, no, Nan,' Louisa had replied hastily. 'I don't want to keep you from your work. Besides, I will only be gone a short while.'

A short while—indeed, it would have to be.

As Lowhaven's busy streets increasingly gave way

to countryside, Louisa reflected upon the risk she was taking. Meeting a man, unchaperoned, was not something any young woman should do. She tried not to think about what Aunt Clarissa would say if she knew, how she would lecture her and insist she ought to know better.

She tried not to think about the rumour and gossip she would be subjected to if she was seen. Instead, she tried to calm her nerves, to retain some perspective. After all, she had already met Sir Isaac on the cliffs once, and she had been alone then, too. To a casual observer this might simply appear to be a chance encounter between two acquaintances. Besides, she reminded herself, he might not even come. He might be busy, or he might have reflected upon his own recklessness in suggesting it and thought better of it.

Louisa began the slow ascent along the rough track leading to the cliffs, her boots sliding on the muddy ground which had been saturated by days of rainfall. It wasn't too late for her to turn back, she considered. To return to her aunt's house and forget all about Sir Isaac Liddell and his unusual suggestion. Perhaps that would be wise. And yet, despite her reservations, she kept going, spurred on by an instinct, a sort of curiosity she could not quite name. God knew, wisdom had never been her strong suit...

Isaac arrived on the clifftops a little before four o'clock. For the first time in a while he was alone, which in itself was a luxury he permitted himself to enjoy after all the socialising he'd done recently.

He'd had to put on a convincing show for Samuel in order to escape without arousing his brother's suspicions. Freshly shaven and smartly dressed, he'd joined Samuel for a late luncheon. Halfway through his third piece of cold meat and his second cup of tea, he'd casually announced that he planned to take some air later, now that the weather had improved.

'Then I will gladly accompany you, brother,' Samuel had predictably replied.

Isaac had put on his best and most cheerful smile. 'In fact, if you don't mind, I would prefer to ride alone today. It is nothing untoward, I promise you. I merely feel the need for a little quiet contemplation. I've spent a lot of time in company of late.'

Samuel had seemed unconvinced, but not prepared to challenge his brother further on the matter.

As ever, the early afternoon had brought no callers to the door of Hayton Hall, and after several hours at his desk, attending to estate matters, Isaac had ridden out to that spot on the cliffs where he and Miss Conrad had first met. Now, as he sat on a rock and stared out at the vast blue sea, he contemplated what a fool he was. He had no idea if she would come today or not. She'd said she intended to walk here on the next fine day, but that had doubtless been a flustered response to his impertinence. It was entirely possible that she'd returned to her aunt after meeting him that morning in Hayton and thought better of it. Indeed, he would hardly blame her if she had.

'You should never have asked her, Liddell,' he muttered, giving the ground a swift kick with his left boot.

'Do you often talk to yourself?'

Isaac sprang to his feet, turning around as she approached him. The sight of her took his breath away, from the perfect blonde curls tamed into place by her bonnet to the casual spatter of mud along the bottom of her violet day dress.

He removed his hat, running a swift hand over his black hair. Thank God there was no strong wind to tousle it today. He wished to give her no occasion to remember the wild, dishevelled creature he'd been at their last clifftop meeting.

'Miss Conrad,' he mumbled, greeting her with an awkward bow.

She returned the gesture with a polite nod, before raising her eyebrows expectantly at him. 'Well?' she asked.

He frowned briefly, before her meaning dawned upon him. 'Oh!' he replied, laughing. 'Yes, I'm afraid I am guilty of giving myself a quiet lecture or two when the occasion demands it.'

'And does sitting by oneself on the cliffs require such a thing?' Her question seemed serious, but her eyes, he could see, were smiling.

He felt a flush of colour rise in his cheeks. 'Only if you're the sort of man who recklessly suggests that a woman meet him upon those cliffs alone,' he confessed. 'Forgive me, Miss Conrad. I am very glad you came, but truly I do not know what came over me when we met in Hayton. I know just as well as you do that we should not meet alone.'

She gave another small nod, her expression unreadable. 'I won't tell if you won't,' she replied.

He gave her a small smile. 'There is no one for me to tell—except my brother, perhaps. But I've always found confiding in Samuel to be unwise.'

'Oh?'

Isaac let out a wry chuckle. 'Samuel is younger than me by almost ten years. I find telling him anything usually leads to either teasing or a lecture—although recently it's been more of the latter than anything else. He has become very insistent that I should make more of an effort to go into society. I have not found it easy to be in company since my wife's death.'

Isaac paused, realising he was saying far too much already.

'Forgive me, Miss Conrad,' he continued after a moment. 'I do not know why I am telling you all this. Would you like to walk? Or perhaps to sit awhile on the rocks?'

'We could walk a little,' she replied. 'Although I promised my aunt that I would not be out for too long.' She glanced at his horse, standing obediently at his side. 'Will he be all right to walk with us?'

Isaac had almost forgotten the poor creature was there. 'What? Oh, him! Yes, it was not a long ride from Hayton. He will not be tired yet.'

He gathered the reins tightly in his hand, and with all the courage he could muster he offered Miss Conrad his free arm. His breath caught in his throat as he watched her hesitate, her dark eyes seeming to search his for something—he didn't know what. Then, before he could retract the gesture and apologise once more, she reached out and took it. Her nearness warmed him like the sun could never hope to, and it alarmed him to acknowledge how quickly his thoughts turned to letting the damned horse go and enveloping her in his embrace.

Louisa's heart hammered in her chest as they took a gentle stroll along the coast. She'd barely known what to do or to say since she'd arrived here. The way he looked at her, the way he spoke to her with such openness and familiarity—she could not fathom it.

Why her? What had she ever done apart from be defensive or reserved or muted in his presence? Now, as she walked with her hand clutching his arm, she tried to focus on her surroundings—the squawking of the gulls, the sound of the waves crashing against the rocks far below. Anything but the heat of his arm against hers... anything but the proximity of him.

Those thoughts, she knew, led to other thoughts—brazen, forbidden thoughts. Not the thoughts of a spinster. No, she told herself, this would not do. She was allowing this tide to carry her along, but she had been here before, and she knew what it would cost her. She had to remember the vow she had made to herself. She had to remember what was at stake if she didn't.

'Why—why did you ask me to meet you, Sir Isaac?' she asked, rushing out the words before she could change her mind.

He turned to look at her, studying her face, and she realised he was trying to understand what had prompted her question. She pressed her lips together, trying to swallow down her turmoil. Then he looked away again, staring far into the horizon as he spoke.

'I am drawn to you, Miss Conrad, in a way that I have not been drawn to another human being for a long time. I mentioned my wife before... You must know I lost her, and my son—it is an oft-repeated tale around these parts.'

'Yes,' she interjected. 'My aunt told me not long after that last time we met here on the cliffs. I was sorry to hear of it. Losing those you love brings much suffering.' She felt the truth in those words with a tightening in her chest.

He drew a deep breath. 'Since their deaths I have

struggled. I have kept away from society, tried to protect myself by remaining alone. But that is a fool's errand which brings only misery. Then I met you, and I feel as though I'd like to get to know you.'

He turned his gaze to meet hers once again, and there was no mistaking the warmth in his eyes.

'I know you are not in Lowhaven for long, and I do not ask nor expect you to have the same interest in me. But, nonetheless, if you would consent to spending some time in my company, I believe I would enjoy that.'

'You seek my friendship?' Louisa asked him, desiring clarity.

He nodded. 'If you will give it.'

She smiled then. 'Readily I will give it, sir. You do yourself a disservice if you think I have no interest in you.'

'Even after the last time we met up here?'

She laughed. 'Well, perhaps not after that…but I will admit you redeemed yourself a little when we danced together at the ball.'

'Only a little?' he teased.

'All right, perhaps slightly more than a little,' she replied, still smiling.

He looked at her again, that azure gaze of his growing more serious now. 'You must call me Isaac. If we are to be friends, it is only right.'

She hesitated for a moment, remembering how easily she'd slipped into more familiar terms with Charlotte after only a brief acquaintance. But this felt different—more significant somehow. She wasn't sure she could countenance it—not yet.

'I shall call you Sir Isaac, for that is the name you properly deserve. But I will not object if you'd prefer to call me Louisa, and perhaps, in time, Isaac will do just as well on its own.'

'I will hope for it, Louisa,' he replied, and it didn't escape her notice how broad his smile had grown. 'Even the mere promise of it will do very well for me.'

Louisa drew a deep breath, averting her eyes to concentrate once more upon the seascape. She'd agreed to be his friend, and indeed she sensed that a good friend was something he needed as much as she did. Nevertheless, she knew she had to draw firm lines in their acquaintance—and if that meant maintaining some formality in addressing him, then so be it.

A friendship was all well and good, but any deepening of affection between them could not be permitted. It was clear that Sir Isaac had suffered a great deal, and although he did not know it, so had she. Nothing good could come of becoming too attached, for either of them. Anything beyond friendship was, quite simply, out of the question.

## Chapter Eleven

On the day of their next clifftop meeting Isaac found himself gripped by a potent mix of good humour and crippling self-reproach—and he was not sure which feeling disconcerted him the most. He was not renowned for having a cheerful disposition—even before Rosalind's death a solemn countenance had always come easier to him than a smile—and although he'd been a contented spouse, he'd been ill at ease showing it.

He'd often considered it was the force of habit…that his position in life—eldest son, then landowner and baronet—and all the years of bearing so much responsibility had etched a profound seriousness upon his soul. The loss of Rosalind and his child had also meant the loss of his reasons to smile, and so he hadn't.

Not until this summer.

Not until he'd met Louisa.

Acknowledging how much he enjoyed the lady's company, however, came with a considerable amount of guilt. That inner voice which berated him for betraying Rosalind's memory seemed to grow louder, as though it sensed he was contemplating his own readiness to move on. And he was, wasn't he? He'd emerged from the worst of his grief some time ago, and slowly he'd begun to accept just how much he hated being alone.

That acceptance had now bred other feelings—feelings which he had never expected to experience again. The enjoyment of a lovely woman's company. The pleasure of her hand holding his arm. Bit by bit his resolve had weakened, his desire for companionship increasingly defeating his commitment to solitude.

But it was only companionship, he reminded himself. It was only friendship. Surely fostering a friendly acquaintance with a lady during the course of a summer was not such a terrible transgression? In any case, he doubted that Louisa would have any interest in anything more than friendship with an older, morose man such as him. She was young and beautiful, charming and refined. She was hardly likely to consider disagreeable and damaged Sir Isaac Liddell a catch.

Such murky thoughts continued to preoccupy him at breakfast, combining with his growing anticipation of his later clifftop meeting to make him feel quite sick. As he forced down several slices of toast in the company of his brother he made a concerted effort to appear nonchalant about his plans for the day ahead. Fortunately, Samuel made life easy for him in this regard, informing him that he would be detained all day in Lowhaven on matters of business, and that he would not return before dinnertime.

'I am sorry, brother,' Samuel said regretfully. 'It cannot be helped. I hope you will go out riding without me. I can see all the fresh air you've enjoyed recently has done you the world of good.'

Isaac nodded. 'Indeed, I do not mind some time by myself. In fact, I think I might take a long walk today.'

Samuel looked up from his newspaper. 'Oh?' he said. 'Anywhere in particular?'

Isaac shrugged. 'No,' he replied, pushing his empty plate away. 'I am happy to see where the wind carries me.'

Of course the strong sea breeze took him to the coast, and the afternoon sun was shining down from its high position in the sky by the time he reached their meeting place. To his surprise, Louisa was already there, and inwardly he chastised himself for not leaving earlier. Clearly walking to the cliffs had taken him much longer than he'd anticipated.

As he approached, he offered her a warm smile, feeling his mood lift once more as she smiled back at him. He could not help but notice how lovely she looked in a cream and cornflower-blue dress, its vertical stripes seeming to lengthen her petite frame and make her appear taller as she stood to greet him. He'd seen her wear blue more than once now, and thought the colour suited her very well—a thought he would keep to himself, he decided. He'd asked for a friendship, not a courtship, after all.

'I am sorry to have kept you waiting, Louisa,' he said as he reached her, tipping his hat in greeting.

'I have not been here long,' she answered him, glancing back towards the sea. 'Indeed, I have enjoyed watching the waves. It is nice to have a little peace and quiet now and then.' She turned back to him, frowning as she peered over his shoulder. 'You have not brought your horse today?'

'No, I felt like walking to meet you. Besides, he is a

grumpy creature—like his master. It is better not having him here, forced to follow us around.'

Louisa laughed at that. 'I do not think you are so very grumpy,' she countered.

He grinned appreciatively at this compliment of sorts, then offered her his arm, which she accepted without hesitation. Together they began to walk, sauntering slowly along the clifftops, neither of them apparently in any hurry to go anywhere in particular.

He stole a glance at her, spying her contented expression beneath her bonnet. She seemed more relaxed today…more at ease in his company. He wished then that he could be so calm. In truth, the closeness of her, the feeling of her hand resting in the crook of his arm—all of it had ruffled him again, made him think about things which mere friends were not meant to consider.

'So…peace and quiet,' he said, determined on some meaningful conversation. 'You do not have much of that in Lowhaven, I expect?'

She shook her head. 'Such is life in a busy port town, I believe. It is all very new to me. I am far more accustomed to living in the country.'

'And what is the country like in Berkshire?'

'Tranquil.' She smiled fondly. 'And very green. Although there I am without the pleasure of seeing the sea every day.' She gestured towards the vast expanse of water stretching to the horizon. 'I will miss this when I leave Cumberland. The coastal air here has agreed with me very well.'

He nodded, accepting the compliment on behalf of his county. 'Do you enjoy walking at home, too? Or riding, perhaps?'

'Oh, yes—both. Although walking is by far my favourite outdoor pursuit. Indeed, it's a habit I have continued here, much to my aunt's displeasure. She does not think it is right for a young woman to be out so much on her own.'

'Ah, well, of course your aunt's concern is entirely justified,' he replied, giving her a mischievous grin. 'The unchaperoned lady is vulnerable to approaches from all sorts of ruffians and scoundrels.'

She laughed as she looked up at him, giving his arm a squeeze. 'Indeed,' she said. 'As I know only too well.' Her smile faded, and those brown eyes seemed to darken as her face grew serious once more. 'Aunt Clarissa means well, but I do wish she would not make such a fuss. I have been of age for some years now, and I am very accustomed to taking care of myself.'

'You are?' Her declaration surprised him. 'Forgive me, Louisa,' he said, frowning, 'but I assumed you lived with your parents.'

She nodded. 'Yes, I do. Our home is a lovely country estate, and when my parents and brother are in town—which they frequently are—I do very well staying there by myself.'

'You do not go into town with them?'

He watched as she seemed to hesitate, as though his simple question was giving her pause for thought. 'No,' she said after a moment. 'Not usually.'

How odd, he thought. In his experience, unmarried young women were seldom permitted any respite from the watchful gaze of a parent or guardian. Seldom permitted even the semblance of a reprieve from society or from the task of securing a husband.

'And your mother? She is quite content with this arrangement?'

The question slipped out before he could properly consider it, and the moment he uttered the words, he could see that he had overstepped the mark. Immediately Louisa looked away from him, staring straight ahead, her pretty features hardening against what she doubtless perceived to be criticism.

Inwardly, he chastised himself. After avoiding society for so long, what right did he have to question her apparent preference for doing the same?

'Forgive me,' he began. 'I…' His voice faltered, and he found himself at a loss as to how to explain himself.

She glanced at him then. 'There is no need to apologise, Sir Isaac,' she said stiffly. 'My mother is as content as I am. While in residence alone I am properly cared for by my maid, and I send regular reports to my parents, who are always anxious to be reassured of my good health. So, you see, there is nothing for you to concern yourself with on my account.'

Her rebuke, though politely delivered, stung him. What a prying, interfering man he must have seemed to her. How insulting he must have appeared towards her family. He'd been so gripped by his curiosity, by his desire to get to know her, that he'd managed to offend her all over again.

His earlier buoyant mood all but evaporated, and in its place the mist of malaise began to settle once more.

'I see,' he replied, his expression grim. 'I am glad the arrangement suits you. I can only hope that your time in Cumberland will bring you similar joy.'

Louisa could see that she had upset him, but in truth she was at a loss as to how to repair the damage. The fault was undoubtedly hers—there had been no need to mention her self-sufficiency, or her unconventional familial arrangements, and yet for some reason she had. She'd been momentarily unguarded and had said too much about herself. She'd given Sir Isaac cause to wonder about her unusual manner of living. Indeed, was there a gentleman alive who would not have wondered at it?

Her father had only reluctantly accepted her wishes, and that was because he understood the reasons for the choice she'd made. To an outsider it must seem baffling, but she could hardly explain herself. She could hardly admit to her past, which had given her little option but to embrace a solitary existence.

She needed to make amends to her new friend—she knew that. However, she also needed to put a stop to any further discussion about her life in Berkshire. On that subject, she needed to be the closed book she'd promised herself she would be. Her past was hundreds of miles away, and for this summer, at least, that was where she was determined it would remain.

'Tell me about some of your favourite places here,' she said, resolving to change the subject. 'Where do you like to ride, or to walk?'

She was relieved to see his face light up at her question. 'Anywhere quiet. I avoid the town whenever possible—not that there is anything wrong with Lowhaven, of course, but such a busy place inevitably presents the possibility of being seen by an acquaintance and forced by duty to converse.' He paused, glancing at her. 'You must think me very dull, Louisa. Or very disagreeable. Or both.'

She shook her head. 'Not at all. I think you are none of those things. The point in being out riding or walking by oneself is to be alone, not to seek out company. I would avoid the town too, in your position.' She offered him an encouraging smile. 'Please, tell me about a place you like to go.'

'There is a village a little way down the coast called St Bees. Before you reach the village there is a headland which reaches out west. It is a stunning spot, and home to all kinds of sea birds. There is a legend that an Irish princess called St Bega was shipwrecked there in the ninth century, after fleeing from being forced to marry a Viking prince. She became an anchoress, devoting herself to a life of piety and solitude. The village is named after her, and the priory there is dedicated to her.'

'How fascinating,' Louisa replied. 'Does the legend say what became of her?'

'She lived in St Bees for some time, but fearing the pirates who were raiding along the coast she eventually went east, perhaps into Northumberland.' He grinned at her. 'She appears to have caught your imagination, just as she catches mine.'

Louisa felt her cheeks begin to colour, although she wasn't sure why. 'It's quite a story,' she replied, turning to look ahead and steadfastly avoiding his gaze. 'I wonder if it is true.'

'I often ponder the same question,' he replied, not seeming to notice her unfathomable discomfort. 'I must confess, over the past couple of years I have often found myself sitting on that headland, staring out across the sea towards Ireland and reflecting on her perilous escape and her decision, once safe, to remain alone. I've had solitude forced upon me by the unhappiest of circumstances, but she chose it.'

'As you said, it was a matter of religious devotion,'

Louisa countered. 'There are many good reasons why people choose to remain alone.'

She bit her lip, realising that once again she'd said more than she ought to. She felt the weight of his gaze on her as he considered her assertion, but still she avoided looking at him. Indeed, she did not dare, lest he read something in her expression which she did not want him to see.

'I wonder if you speak from experience,' he ventured, apparently not quite daring to ask the question.

Perhaps it was the fine day, or the sea air, or the note of earnest concern in Sir Isaac's voice, but something in that moment caused Louisa's resolve to soften. She looked up at him, her heart lurching at the sincerity of his intense blue gaze, just as it had when she'd first learned of all that he'd lost. When she'd first understood just how much they had in common.

'I lost someone once,' she began, the words falling from her lips before she could truly contemplate them. 'Someone I loved very much. He died in the war.'

She paused, trying to ignore her racing heart, trying to remind herself that she'd said nothing more to Sir Isaac than she'd confided in Charlotte. Yet as she stared up at him, watching the frown gather between his eyes as their shared understanding dawned upon him, she knew that this would be nothing like talking to Charlotte. Nothing at all.

## Chapter Twelve

'His name was Richard. He was a captain in the navy.'

Instinctively Louisa drew closer to Isaac, glad of the comforting feeling of his arm holding hers. It had been a long time since she'd talked properly about Richard, and longer still since she'd said his name. She'd begun this story now, for reasons which seemed quite beyond her understanding, and she was committed to telling it. Or at least part of it.

The parts she would tell were painful enough. The parts she would omit were wholly unutterable.

'We met at a ball, at the home of some friends of my family, who live near Reading. Richard was a relation of theirs, and had come to stay with them in the country while recovering from an injury he'd sustained when his ship was badly damaged in a storm. I was young…only nineteen; Richard was a little older at six-and-twenty. Suffice to say we danced and we talked, and were quite taken with one another. Over the following few months I saw a lot of him; our affection grew, and before long we were engaged to marry. By this time Richard's injury had healed and he'd received word that he was to return to sea. He'd applied for a new ship, his old one having been declared unfit for service, and had been appointed to another command. I'm not sure why, but it all seemed to happen very quickly, and we agreed we would marry once he returned.'

Louisa paused, swallowing hard. Even after all this time, telling this story seemed to affect her physically. Her mouth was dry…a dull ache was spreading through her chest.

'However, it was not to be. A couple of months after he took command, Richard's ship was sunk in the English Channel by the French. None of the crew survived.'

Beside her, she heard Isaac draw a deep breath, and she found herself looking out towards the sea, a strange sort of weariness settling over her like mist. She'd parted with as much of the story as she was willing to, and even that had been a trial. She prayed he would accept the sorry tale, just as Charlotte had done. She prayed he would not ask too many questions of her.

'I am very sorry for your loss, Louisa,' he said, his voice grave and sincere. 'And I thank you for telling me. I am sorry if my remarks about your living arrangements in Berkshire caused you any distress. I understand perfectly now why you remain alone.'

She offered him a tight smile. 'It's not a story I tell very often,' she replied. 'At home, it's a story everyone knows, and here… Well, it's been nice that almost no one knows.'

'I can understand that,' Isaac replied. 'After Rosalind and our son died I wearied quickly of all the condolences, all the pity. I just wanted to escape. I couldn't do that, so I retreated instead.'

'It is surprisingly easy to hide on a country estate,' Louisa mused, half to herself.

She felt the pain of guilt grip her as she thought about all the reasons she'd been hiding. About all the things a man like Sir Isaac could never know.

'It seems we have more in common than I'd realised,' he observed. 'I am sorry that you have had your life marred by sadness at such a young age, and before you were even wed. I have always been grateful that at least Rosalind and I did have some years together.'

She nodded. 'Our time together was so very short. Sometimes it feels as though I dreamt him—as though he was never in my life at all.'

'I often think that about my son, since he was here so briefly,' Isaac replied, his voice almost a whisper. He shuddered, as though brushing off unwelcome thoughts. 'It's been two years since they died, you know, and sometimes I wonder if I will ever fully recover from my grief.'

'I don't believe you ever do,' she replied. 'I think you simply learn to live with it…that it becomes a part of who you are.'

'Indeed. As long as you do not let it consume your whole self,' he said pointedly. 'Grief cannot be allowed to govern your life, to dictate to you over every decision you make.'

Louisa bristled, feeling his insinuation sharply. In the wake of losing Richard her grief had been utterly consuming, but even then it had not exercised full control over her choices. She pressed her lips together, thankful that Sir Isaac did not know anything of the other circumstances she'd grappled with during those long, dark months.

Sir Isaac seemed to notice her discomfort, because

after a moment he smiled wryly at her and added, 'I realise that I have no business saying that. I've spent much of the last two years allowing my grief to do exactly that. But it a lesson which I think I am beginning to learn.'

Louisa found she could only answer him with a tight smile. The growing wind whipped at her face and she drew closer to him once more, as though the mere feel of him could ground her, could stop her from thinking too much. Her summer in Lowhaven was meant to be a reprieve, and this walk with Sir Isaac was meant to be an enjoyable interlude with a new friend. Thoughts of the past, of her reasons for being here and her choices, had no place here.

Clutching his arm ever tighter, she drew a deep breath, burying those thoughts in the back of her mind as she so often did.

For a brief moment she felt the muscles beneath her fingers tense, before he brought his other hand to rest over hers. It was a tender, reassuring gesture, and one which, despite her instincts, she allowed herself to appreciate. He had responded to her sorry tale with kindness and sincerity, and had related to her grief with something far deeper than mere sympathy. It was hard to believe that this gentleman, who spoke to her so gently and honestly, was the same sullen and disagreeable man she'd first met.

Sir Isaac was right; they did have much in common. She'd recognised that herself, when she'd first learned of all that he'd lost. But she also knew that their shared knowledge of grief, of pain and of self-imposed solitude was only the half of it. The other half—the unspeakable half—was something Sir Isaac could never know. The other half of her story, she reminded herself, was something which no gentleman in his position could countenance.

Isaac replayed her sorrowful story over and over, picking through its details and feeling his heart lurch at the knowledge of her pain. He understood it now. The serious countenance, the aloofness, the reserve. The stoicism, as Samuel had correctly called it.

At the time, Isaac had objected to his brother's remarks about Louisa's character, and yet he'd been right, hadn't he? She was all of those things, and for good reason. For the same reason, it transpired, he had for being solemn and reclusive. Indeed, they had both locked themselves away, both sought refuge from the prying eyes of the world in secluded country houses. They'd both nursed their grief alone.

He could never have imagined on that first day they'd met, when she'd stumbled into his carriage, that they'd have quite so much in common.

Isaac made himself comfortable in his library, sending for some tea to quench his growing thirst after walking home from the cliffs. As he sat back in his favourite armchair, he found himself wondering how Louisa felt about being alone now…if she was as weary of it as he was. He wondered what had brought her to Lowhaven—if it was more than a simple desire to visit her aunt. After all, since she'd been in town she'd evidently not hidden herself away, attending balls and befriending the likes of the Pearsons. Befriending him.

She hadn't hesitated to accept his offer of friendship, had she?

*You do yourself a disservice*, she'd said, *if you think I have no interest in you.*

How those words had warmed him since.

'Friendship is one thing, Liddell,' he muttered to himself. 'But anything else is out of the question.'

And it was—it had to be. During these past months he'd come far—much further than he could have imagined possible during those early dark days he'd spent shrouded in his grief. He was loath to admit it, but Samuel's insistence that he re-enter society had been good for him.

If he hadn't been in that carriage returning from Penrith that day he would not have met Louisa. If he hadn't attended the ball in Lowhaven he would not have danced with her. If he hadn't been visiting his tenants he would never have had the chance to boldly suggest that they begin to meet. He would not have begun a friendship with her. But no matter how lovely she was, or how much they had in common, he knew it could never be more than that. He'd learned to live with the past now—it no longer dictated to him. But it was still there, nonetheless.

It still weighed heavily upon his heart.

It still surrounded him in every room, every inch of Hayton Hall.

Louisa had said that Richard's presence in her life had been so fleeting that it felt like a dream. For Isaac, it was the opposite. Rosalind was still everywhere in his home—from the rooms she'd tastefully had modernised, with fresh paint and plasterwork, to the clothes and other personal effects which remained tucked within the ancient cupboards and drawers passed down to him by his ancestors.

He'd clung on to her possessions, unable to look at them, but equally unable to let them go.

Well, he reasoned, perhaps it was time to do either one or the other.

Isaac hauled himself out of his seat and walked over to the large walnut chest sitting solidly in the shadows. He pulled open the middle drawer, noticing immediately the musty smell which rose up, as though stale, years-old air had finally managed to escape the confines of that dark, disused space. It caught him off guard, and he felt the past begin to claw at him.

He paused then, before placing a tender hand upon the pretty blue shawl and lifting it carefully. As though it might break. As though the memories it contained might disintegrate as soon as the cloth met the cool library air. He unfolded it, grateful that after all this time it no longer smelled of her. The whiff of neglect which tainted it now was bad enough, but for it to have held on to even the merest hint of her perfume would have been unbearable.

The last time she'd worn this she'd been heavy with child, sitting in the library and poring over one of her favourite novels by Mrs Radcliffe. *The Italian*, probably, but now he thought about it he realised he couldn't recall.

He clutched the shawl against his chest, feeling the fragility of the soft silk beneath his fingers. He was still fragile, too, he realised. His heart, though mended, was scarred for ever. There was no point allowing his thoughts to linger upon just how much he and Louisa seemed to understand each other, or the way his heart skipped a beat as she took his arm, or the way he would lose himself in her deep brown gaze. He'd found solace in her friendship, but he should not imagine that there could ever be anything more between them than that.

He remained rooted to the spot as the door creaked open and a maid delivered his tea, still holding on to that shawl and, with it, all the reasons he knew he could never allow himself to love again even if he wanted to.

The problem was, he reflected as he poured himself some tea, increasingly he suspected that to love and to be loved was exactly what he wanted.

# Chapter Thirteen

Louisa sat beside her aunt in the Pearsons' splendid parlour, trying her best to sit still and look interested in the conversation. Outside the sun shone brightly, and from within this dark room, dominated by a deep blue Chinese wallpaper and an over-indulgence in mahogany furnishings, Louisa felt its pull, as though the fine day itself demanded she get up and leave this place at once.

But of course she could not. She had been informed that morning by her aunt that they would be visiting the Pearsons' home for tea, and it had been made very clear to her that she was expected to attend.

'It will be nice for you to see their home. It's a rather fine house on the edge of town. It is a bit of a walk, but I am sure we can manage it together. Unless you have another commitment?' Aunt Clarissa had asked, her eyebrows raised in surprise at her niece's apparent reluctance.

'No, not at all, Aunt,' Louisa had replied, swiftly recovering herself. 'I had just hoped to walk more of the coast this afternoon.'

'I'm sure if the opportunity presents itself Miss Pearson will walk with you,' her aunt had responded. 'Walking with another young lady is preferable, Louisa. You walk too often by yourself. You must have gone out alone not less than four times this past week!'

Four times, indeed, and each time to meet Isaac at the cliffs. Neither of them had hesitated to take advantage of the dry, sunny days, to fill them with conversation and good company. For the past two days, however, she'd been prevented from seeing him. Yesterday, her aunt had asked her to accompany her into town to visit the linen drapers, and today it was what was turning into a lengthy social call.

She tried not to begrudge it, reminding herself that Aunt Clarissa generally made little imposition upon her time. Nonetheless, she found herself repeatedly gazing out of the window, her mind wandering to the cliffs, to the image of Sir Isaac sitting upon a rock, waiting for her. She hoped he would not wait too long. She wished she'd been able to send word, to let him know she would not come today.

She wished, above all, that she could have gone to see him.

He had been so humorous at their last meeting—so light of spirit. Sharing silly anecdotes with her about his childhood and his family. He'd told her some of his memories of her grandfather, the stern but kind village rector, who had enjoyed the respect and affection of his parishioners. His tales had breathed life into her family history, and for the first time since coming here she'd felt the strength of her connection to Hayton. It had dawned on her that this quiet little corner of Cumberland was a part of her story, too.

How they'd laughed at his recollections of his boyhood scrapes! How they had smiled. She had enjoyed seeing that more relaxed, more cheerful side of Isaac— enjoyed, too, the reprieve from the more difficult subjects they'd previously discussed. To her relief, Isaac had asked her nothing more about Richard, and nor had he spoken of Rosalind. It was as though he'd sensed a need to lift the mood between them. To relish the present, rather than dwell on the past.

Not that she regretted sharing something of her past with Isaac. Indeed, telling him about Richard had brought her a sort of solace she hadn't expected. She supposed that was because she'd shared part of her story with someone who understood loss, who'd known grief. She supposed it was because they were friends.

She did not allow herself to contemplate that Isaac was the only friend she had who could cause her stomach to perform somersaults at the merest touch or the briefest glance. There was, after all, no point in considering that.

'Are you quite well, Miss Conrad?' Mrs Pearson asked, interrupting her thoughts.

'Oh, yes, thank you,' she replied, offering her hostess a polite smile.

Mrs Pearson narrowed her eyes slightly, glancing at the window which had held Louisa's attention before returning her focus to her guest. 'Charlotte tells me she has not heard from you since your visit to Hayton. She wondered if you'd been ill.'

Louisa glanced at Charlotte, noting how she sipped her tea and steadfastly avoided her gaze. 'No, not ill,' she began. 'I…'

'You've been quite preoccupied with writing to your friends and family in Berkshire—haven't you, my dear?'

Aunt Clarissa interjected. 'And the weather has been so dreadful of late I don't think any of us will have ventured much outside of our homes.'

'Quite so,' Mrs Pearson agreed, still looking at Louisa. 'I have felt the damp air in every bone in my body. I believe I must ask my physician to strengthen my tincture. Still, the sun has shone a good deal during the past week. Hopefully it will last, and you two young ladies can take the benefit of it together.'

Charlotte gave an enthusiastic nod. 'We could walk to Hayton again, if you like,' she said, addressing Louisa. 'Last time we did not make it as far as Hayton Hall, and it would be a real pity if you did not see it. I suppose if we are fortunate we may even see Sir Isaac and Mr Liddell out riding again.'

Aunt Clarissa looked up, her teacup poised at her lips. 'Again?

'Oh, don't you know? Sir Isaac and Mr Liddell accompanied them back through the village,' Mrs Pearson explained. 'Charlotte tells me that she talked at length with Mr Liddell, but could not get a word in edgeways with Sir Isaac as Miss Conrad had him entirely under her spell.'

Aunt Clarissa looked squarely as Louisa, her eyebrows elevated in curiosity and surprise. 'Oh?'

'We really only saw them very briefly, as they were visiting Sir Isaac's tenants,' Louisa explained, as evenly as she could manage.

'We talked for as long as it takes to walk very slowly from one end of the village to the other,' Charlotte added with a giggle. 'I found Mr Liddell very agreeable. He was very charming and witty.'

'Younger sons often are,' Mrs Pearson replied, putting her teacup down. 'When the eldest son has the property and the title, wit and charm are the only currency their brothers have to trade.'

'We should go and see Hayton Hall tomorrow,' Charlotte suggested. 'Let's go while the weather remains fine. What do you say, Louisa?'

Louisa sipped her tea, buying herself a moment's thought. She felt the eyes of the room upon her, all three ladies waiting expectantly for her response. What could she say? She didn't have any plans for tomorrow. Only hopes. Only possibilities. She'd had to let those slip by her today, and she would have to do so again. To do anything other than that would appear odd, at best, and rude at worst. She could not risk causing offence.

'Of course,' she replied finally. 'That would be wonderful.'

She hadn't come. Again. As Isaac rode home, furiously whipping his horse, all the possible reasons for her absence whirred around his frenzied mind. Was she unwell? Had he offended her? Had some other commitments detained her for these past two days?

She had not mentioned anything at their last meeting. Indeed, she had smiled and nodded when he'd asked her if it was likely she'd be walking on the cliffs the next day. Nothing had seemed to be amiss when they'd parted. Their conversation had been agreeable. He'd regaled her with some family tales, which she'd seemed to appreciate, before indulging with her in a lengthy discussion about books they'd enjoyed.

She liked to read; he'd learned that. Travel diaries, especially. She yearned to visit the continent, she'd admitted rather bashfully, as though such a sense of adventure was to be berated rather than commended.

He'd held back from telling her that he'd never left England…that his younger brother was superior to him in first-hand knowledge of other countries and cultures. Instead, he'd told her about his love for *Waverley*, and the other novels by the same anonymous author, how he found himself swept to other times and places whenever he lost himself in their pages.

'I know that they are very famous,' she'd said. 'But I confess I have not read any of them.'

He'd thought about all the hours he'd spent in his library, devouring those stories, trying to distract himself from his grief.

'If you like, I can lend you my copy of *Waverley*,' he'd offered, to which she'd assented.

He still had to consider how he would get the book to her, as its three volumes were too large to fit in his pocket. Just as well, he thought. He'd have felt even more of a fool if he'd brought them with him.

Why hadn't she come?

Isaac whipped his poor horse again, riding hard as Hayton Hall came into view. All other possibilities exhausted, he allowed himself now to contemplate the worst. She was ill, or there had been some sort of accident. God, how he wanted to know! How he wanted to help if he could. But how could he? He could hardly turn up at her aunt's house unannounced.

Yet that was all he wanted to do, and it was all he could think of—going to her, summoning his physician to attend her. Anything. Anything that might help.

He shuddered, remembering how he'd sat beside a bed and watched the life of the woman he adored ebb away. He could still see the sickly pallor of her skin, still feel the cold clamminess of her face. Those memories, he knew, would haunt him for ever.

He could not bear to feel such helpless agony again.

He arrived back at his home, all but flinging the reins of his exhausted animal at his groom. He marched inside, the sound of his footsteps thudding on the wooden floor as he made his way down the corridor towards his library. Once inside, he shut the door firmly behind him, leaning his head against it for a moment, trying to gather his thoughts.

He breathed in deeply, perturbed to realise that today he found no comfort in the familiar smell of the old wooden shelves and leather-bound books. His library had for so long been his sanctuary, his place of retreat. Now he realised he no longer wished to be in hiding. He no longer wanted to be alone.

'What the devil is the matter with you, Liddell?' he muttered to himself.

His foolish desire for companionship had really started to get under his skin, conspiring with the worst of his fears and his memories to drive him quite mad. He was a widower almost in his middle years, not some hot-headed youth, and yet here he was, entertaining impulsive ideas about running to the bedside of a woman with whom he'd promenaded a handful of times.

He had to acknowledge that her friendship had come to mean a lot to him even in such a short space of time, that he enjoyed being with her and talking to her. That her company enlivened him in a way he'd believed he would never experience again. He felt as though she understood him. Yet friendship was all there was between them, he reminded himself. It was all there could ever be. Anything else would be a betrayal of Rosalind and a risk to his fragile heart.

He pulled himself up straight. Louisa was his friend, he told himself. Of course he had to know if she was all right. There was nothing more to it than that.

'Isaac?' Samuel's voice sounded muffled through the thick oak door. 'Is something amiss?'

Isaac sighed. The last thing he needed at this moment was an inquisition from his brother.

'I'm well, thank you,' he called back, stepping away from the door and walking over to his desk.

'May I come in?'

'Of course.'

Samuel entered, a deep frown etched on his face as he glanced around him, apparently—and not too subtly—surveying the room. Looking for clues, Isaac thought wryly.

'You came home in an awful hurry. I thought perhaps something might have happened,' his brother said tentatively.

Isaac picked up a handful of papers from his pile of correspondence. 'I was out riding and recalled I had a pressing matter to attend to,' he replied, waving the papers nonchalantly in his hand.

Samuel narrowed his eyes. 'A pressing matter?' he repeated.

'Yes,' Isaac laughed. 'You do not run the estate, Samuel. You do not see the volume of work I have to contend with, even with my steward's assistance.'

'And is that what you have been doing on so many afternoons recently? Attending to pressing estate business?' Samuel asked, clearly unconvinced.

'No, I have been riding, or walking—as you know.'

Isaac tried to maintain an even tone, but he could feel his patience beginning to wane. He did not have time for this.

'For hours on end?'

'I have been enjoying the scenery Cumberland has to offer, and it is a vast county. So, yes, for hours on end, brother.'

'I see,' Samuel answered, in a way which told Isaac that he didn't see at all. 'Well, if there is anything I can do to assist with this pressing matter, you know I am at your service.'

Isaac gave a tight smile, feigning interest in his paperwork once more. 'Thank you, brother. I will bear that in mind.'

Samuel gave a brief nod and took his leave. The moment the door shut behind him Isaac sat down at his desk and got to work. His explanation to Samuel had not entirely been a lie—he did have a pressing matter to attend to. And while his brother had been interrogating him he'd settled upon the only way he could conceive of to address it.

He wrote furiously, committing his words to paper before he could lose his nerve. Before he could think too much about what he said or how he said it. As soon as he had signed his name he folded the letter and enveloped it within another blank sheet, then rang for his butler.

Moments later, the man arrived.

'Yes, sir?'

'Smithson, I need this delivered to Miss Louisa Conrad in Lowhaven,' Isaac instructed, handing over the letter.

Smithson looked at the paper in his hand, upon which Isaac had hurriedly written Louisa's name and address. 'Right now, sir?'

'Yes. Please see to it that this reaches Miss Conrad

as soon as possible. I am anxious to know that the lady is in good health, Smithson,' Isaac added, 'so any information you manage to discover in this regard would be appreciated.'

The butler nodded. 'Very good, sir,' he replied, turning to leave.

'Oh, and Smithson?'

'Yes, sir?'

'Please ensure that this remains confidential. Particularly, that no word of this letter should reach my brother's ears.'

'Of course, sir.'

Isaac sat back in his chair as Smithson left the room, rubbing his face with his hands. The mix of weariness and agitation he felt following the day's exertions was potent, and he knew his judgement was not as sharp as it ought to have been. Writing to her and having her sought out in this manner was impulsive, and if discovered it would provoke comment and speculation.

But damn it all if he cared about that! All he cared about was knowing—knowing what had happened yesterday, knowing what had happened today, and knowing that she was all right. He would endure any amount of trouble for that.

## Chapter Fourteen

Louisa knew her aunt had questions for her; she could almost see the words forming upon her lips the moment they left the Pearsons' home in the late afternoon. Their walk home was a quiet one, with little in the way of conversation to divert Louisa from observing the way Clarissa looked at her, with brief but unsubtle glances, as though she was trying to get the measure of her niece and decide upon the best line of enquiry.

Louisa did her best to ignore it, feigning interest in the town's busy streets as they passed along one and then the next. As they approached Juniper Street she noted, as she always did, how the sounds of the port grew louder. She could hear the clatter and shouts of the dockworkers as they loaded and unloaded cargo at its numerous quays.

She recalled how she'd remarked upon its ceaseless din to Isaac, who'd laughed wryly at the observation. It was one of the busiest ports in England, he had told her, with all manner of goods passing through it, from cocoa and sugar being brought in, to coal and lime being shipped out. She'd quite marvelled at the prospect of it, feeling suddenly worlds away from her home in quiet, rural Berkshire. It had been a liberating thought.

Now she found herself considering how frequently her thoughts turned to Isaac and how, in her mind, she called him only that: Isaac.

'Louisa, is there something between yourself and Sir Isaac Liddell?'

Aunt Clarissa put the question to her almost as soon as the door closed behind them. The young maid, Cass, who'd been busying herself with collecting their shawls, gave them both a quick curtsey, sensing the need to take her leave. The awkward moment offered Louisa a brief opportunity to steel herself. She had not expected her aunt to be quite so direct.

'I barely know the gentleman, Aunt,' she replied, as nonchalantly as she could manage.

Clarissa frowned. 'That is no answer, Louisa. Marriages have been made on the barest of acquaintances, and other associations between men and women on far less than that.'

'Aunt!' Louisa protested, feeling the heat rise in her cheeks.

'Do not give me your blushes, my dear. We are both women of the world. Your mother may have tiptoed around these matters with you, but I will not. What Mrs Pearson said today about you and Sir Isaac—she made it sound unseemly. I cannot bear for you to be subjected to such comments again. Not after all that you have endured.'

Louisa sighed, glancing down the corridor, mindful of who might be listening. 'Perhaps we should talk in the parlour, Aunt,' she suggested.

Clarissa nodded in agreement and they moved into

the little room, with Louisa closing the door behind them. Together they sat down, and Louisa took a moment to collect herself. She did not wish to lie to her aunt, but she couldn't bring herself to be entirely truthful, either. She did not wish to contemplate her aunt's response if she knew about her secret clifftop meetings with Isaac. She did not want to consider the consequences of her reckless actions.

Above all, she did not want to consider whether there was, in fact, something more than friendship forming between herself and Sir Isaac Liddell. Something she knew she could not countenance, no matter how their heartfelt conversations and the tender feeling of her hand holding his arm had made her feel.

'There is nothing unseemly or otherwise between myself and Sir Isaac,' she said in the end. 'I will admit that when I have seen him I have enjoyed his company and conversation. He is very agreeable. But that is all. Charlotte is merely being fanciful if she imagines anything else.'

Clarissa gave a tight smile. '"Fanciful" is certainly a word I would apply to young Miss Pearson,' she replied. 'She ought to mind what she says. It's one thing to speak like that to her mother, but what if she recounts her stories in such a way to others?'

'We cannot control how others behave,' Louisa said simply. 'We can only be responsible for our own actions.'

The truth in this last statement made her stomach churn.

Clarissa exhaled deeply, reaching over and patting her niece on the hand. 'I'm sorry, my dear. I feel as though I have interrogated you. I was just so taken aback by Mrs Pearson's remarks.'

Louisa nodded. 'I will admit what she said managed to set me on edge. I fear I have not endeared myself to her of late. She made her displeasure with me plain enough when she alluded to me being remiss in keeping up my friendship with Charlotte.'

'Yes, I noted that. But you are going out with Miss Pearson tomorrow, which I am sure will placate them both.'

Relieved that their conversation had lightened, Louisa rose from the table. 'I think I will freshen up before dinner, Aunt, and perhaps read for a little while. I do find the bedroom you gave me so very peaceful.'

Clarissa gave her niece an appreciative smile. 'It is nice to hear you remark upon it,' she replied. 'Miss Slater used to say the same thing. Or rather, Mrs Knight, as she is now.'

Louisa nodded. 'Do you ever hear from Mrs Knight?' she asked gently.

'She writes to me occasionally, tells me of life in Carlisle. Her Mr Knight keeps her very busy.'

Clarissa was still smiling, but Louisa could not fail to notice the sadness that had crept into her eyes.

'Her marriage seemed to happen very quickly,' her aunt went on. 'But then at our age there is little time left to lose. I suppose she is a reminder that it is never too late.'

'Very true, Aunt.'

Clarissa got to her feet. 'It is true, Louisa, and certainly true in your case. I know you have determined upon spinsterhood, and I understand your reasons why. Nonetheless, I would caution you to think hard about your decision. Remaining alone is far from your only option. The way the likes of Sir Isaac Liddell regard you should be sufficient to remind you of that.'

'Aunt, you surely know that it is my only option,' Louisa replied. 'No gentleman could risk an association with me if he knew all about me. A gentleman like Sir Isaac would imperil his good name overnight. I could not countenance doing such harm to anyone.'

Clarissa sighed. 'As I've said to you before, my dear, you are too hard on yourself. You know that I have never condemned you for what happened, and neither have your parents. There will undoubtedly be gentlemen who would take the same view as I do. Perhaps Sir Isaac might be one of them,' she added meaningfully.

'Perhaps,' Louisa replied, unconvinced. 'Alas, it is a moot point, since there is nothing between Sir Isaac and me,' she reiterated quickly, trying to ignore how hard her heart was beating.

Clarissa gave her knowing look. 'Perhaps not on your part, but you cannot speak for him. He was obviously captivated by you at the ball, and I don't doubt that in essence what Charlotte told her mother about your encounter with him in Hayton was true. I can well imagine that he did not leave your side.'

'We enjoyed only a brief and very polite conversation,' Louisa countered, feeling her cheeks begin to burn as thoughts of their long walks and intense conversations returned to her once again.

'Oh, my dear! It is not so much what is said, but what is left unsaid, believe me.'

'You sound as though you speak from experience, Aunt.'

'I had a life before spinsterhood.' Clarissa's lined face

crumpled and she sat back down upon her chair. 'I was engaged once, you know. Goodness, we were young… and so much in love. His name was Frederick.'

Louisa took her seat again beside her aunt. 'What happened?'

'Frederick was a curate, but he had not yet managed to secure a living. Of course he needed an income, so that we could marry and begin our lives together. After our betrothal he joined the army as a chaplain and boarded a ship bound for the Caribbean. I heard nothing from him for several months. I remember being so worried… Then one day a letter came—not from him, but from his captain. In it, he told me that there had been some sort of epidemic and poor Frederick had perished, not many weeks after they had arrived.'

Louisa felt her eyes prick with tears and she tried furiously to blink them away. She felt every detail of her aunt's story keenly. Indeed, its resonance with her own could hardly be more acute.

'Oh, Aunt Clarissa…' was all she managed to say.

Clarissa gave her a watery smile. 'It was a long time ago. You see, my dear, we are really quite similar. Like you, I loved and lost, and I chose never to marry after that. It was a choice I was able to make as Frederick had left me a small inheritance in his will. Nothing extravagant, but it has helped to give me my independence.'

'And you have been happy all these years?' It was a searching question, but Louisa couldn't help but ask it.

'I have done well enough by myself,' her aunt replied. 'Although it is far from easy, being a woman in my position. You see for yourself how modestly I live, and keeping myself even in this manner has become more difficult since Mrs Knight's departure and the loss of her… Well, her contribution to the household. I find my-self a little more reliant on the help of my family than I'm accustomed to—a fact which makes me uneasy.'

Louisa frowned. 'Your family? Do you mean my mother and father?'

Clarissa nodded, then quickly patted her niece reas-suringly on the hand. 'But please do not consider that has anything to do with why you are here this summer. You know I would always gladly have you here with me, whatever the circumstances.'

Louisa gave her a meek smile. 'Do you ever wish you had married?' she asked quietly.

Clarissa sighed. 'In truth, I never met anyone after Frederick who could hold a candle to him, so the de-cision to remain unmarried was relatively easy in that regard. I can't say what I would have done had I found myself falling in love again,' she added, looking point-edly at her niece.

'I do not think I could bear to fall in love again. Not since losing…' Louisa bit her lip, unable to finish her sentence. Unable to say Richard's name. Unable, per-haps, to face contemplating just how close to falling in love again she might be.

'But one day you might, my dear, and if you do please heed my advice—follow your heart. Life is too short to hold yourself to solemn oaths made in the throes of grief.'

Louisa drew a swift breath, poised to argue. Ready to repeat that in her case it was about more than honouring her fiancé's memory. That it would be futile to fall in love again, for surely she could not marry. No gentle-man would want her for a wife if he knew the truth.

Then she looked at her aunt's face, racked with the

pain of baring her soul, and she realised that she had not the heart to say any of it.

'Thank you, Aunt,' she answered instead, with a small and unconvincing smile.

All evening Aunt Clarissa's words preyed on Louisa's mind. After dinner she went straight up to her room, where she tried and failed to concentrate on the book perched on her lap. She'd known nothing of her aunt's story, nothing of the loss she'd experienced—a loss which bore such similarity to her own. In grief they were kindred spirits, a fact which made her aunt's words of caution about choosing to remain alone all the more discomfiting.

Louisa knew that for her marriage remained absolutely out of the question. Yet, despite this, the prospect of spinsterhood seemed more daunting than ever.

'A penny for them,' Nan said that night, apparently tiring of her mistress's prolonged silence as she unpinned her long blonde hair in readiness for bed.

'I learned something about my aunt today,' Louisa replied, giving in to the overwhelming need to confide in someone. Nan, she knew, could always be trusted with her secrets.

'Oh?'

'It turns out we have a lot in common. Like me, she lost the man she was meant to marry. He was an army chaplain, and he died in the Caribbean.'

'Your poor aunt,' Nan remarked. 'I wonder why your mother never told you.'

'I suspect she didn't regard it as her story to tell.'

Nan nodded at that. 'That's true, miss. She is very discreet. I suppose that explains why your aunt has never married…why she stayed up here with your grandparents rather than go off to London like your mother did.'

'Indeed.'

Louisa gazed absently into the mirror in front of her, considering her aunt's insistence that her choice had been straightforward because she had never met anyone else. It occurred to Louisa now that her aunt's decision to remain in rural Cumberland, to embrace quiet village life, had all but ensured that she could not fall in love again. This part of the world hardly teemed with eligible men the way London society did during the season.

Although, Louisa reminded herself, they weren't entirely absent.

She shook her head slightly, trying to brush off all thoughts of a certain gentleman standing before her on the clifftops, his thick black hair tousled by the wind and his deep blue eyes staring intently into hers. She spent too much time thinking about him, and it did her no good. She could not allow herself to form an attachment, to indulge in thoughts about anything more than a summer-long acquaintance. She could not allow her heart to rule over her head. She had done so once, long ago, and she knew what it had cost her. She would bear the scars of her choices for the rest of her days.

'Oh, miss, I almost forgot,' Nan said, reaching into the pocket of her apron. 'A note arrived for you today.'

Louisa turned round. 'A note?'

'Yes.' Nan passed a small folded paper to her. 'It was the strangest thing. The man who delivered it would not say on whose behalf he was calling. He would only say that I was to ensure this note reached you, and he enquired after your health.'

Louisa looked down, running her finger over the

letters of her name. She did not recognise the pristine handwriting, but she knew instinctively who it must be from. She felt her heart begin to beat a little faster, and she hoped that in the candlelight Nan could not see the colour creeping into her cheeks.

'And what did you say?' she asked.

'I told him you were well, but that I would not say more without knowing who was asking.'

Louisa nodded, turning back and placing the note upon her dressing table. 'All right. Thank you, Nan.'

In the mirror she could see her maid frown. 'Aren't you going to read it, miss?'

'I will…in a little while.'

She could see immediately that Nan was not satisfied. She watched as her maid parted her lips, ready to speak, before she pressed them together once again. Clearly, out of respect for her mistress, she had decided that she ought to hold her tongue.

She finished brushing and arranging Louisa's hair quickly and in silence, perhaps not quite trusting herself not to say anything more on the subject.

Louisa thanked her quietly, then picked up the note, clutching it in her palm as she climbed into bed. Once Nan had left, she unfolded it, her heart hammering hard in her chest as she found herself anticipating its possible content.

This was ridiculous, she told herself. It was just a note. And yet as she held the paper in her hands and absorbed the words she felt a strange warmth spread from her stomach all the way down to her toes.

*My dearest Louisa,*
*Please forgive me for writing to you in this way,*

*but I find I am unable to prevent myself from being an utter fool.*

*I am sure there was a very good reason why I did not see you today, or yesterday, and of course you owe me no explanation for it. Indeed, you owe me nothing, since you have been so generous with your time already.*

*However, I cannot seem to rid myself of the feeling that something is amiss, that you are unwell or some other dreadful fate has befallen you.*

*I hope whoever accepted this note at your aunt's home will have been able to give my butler the assurance of your continued good health, which will help to ease my mind.*

*But, dearest Louisa, I must tell you that my mind is never so much at ease as it is when I am in your company. I hope we will be able to meet again soon.*

*Yours,*

*Isaac*

Louisa read the note three or four times before sitting back and holding it against her chest. She closed her eyes for a moment and took a few deep breaths, trying to calm her racing thoughts.

Isaac's concern for her was as clear as it was endearing, although she hated to think that her absence had caused him such distress. But the manner in which he wrote told her more than that. His words hinted at a growing fondness for her, a tenderness which she knew she increasingly felt, too.

She had missed his company today. She knew she would have preferred an afternoon spent in the fresh air talking to Isaac over the confines of a stuffy parlour and polite conversation. Nonetheless, the strength of the feelings his note had provoked surprised her. Alarmed her, even. It was bad enough that she spent far more time thinking about him than she should. That she found her thoughts lingering on the sight of his deep blue eyes or the low sound of his laughter. That meeting him on the clifftops had been the best part of an otherwise pleasant but unremarkable week.

To be so overcome by a simple note was too much. It had been a long time since the words of a gentleman had affected her in such a way. It would not do at all. Not when she still bore the scars of the past. Not when she still bore the unmistakable taint of scandal. Not when there could never be any hope of anything more than friendship between them, no matter what her unruly heart might yearn for.

Louisa climbed out of bed and sat down at the writing desk, determined to respond. Indeed, time was of the essence. She was due to visit Hayton again the following day, with Charlotte, during which she felt certain she could contrive a way to call at Hayton Hall and deliver her reply herself.

She would assure him that all was well, but she could not allow him to form an attachment to her. It was quite obvious that their meetings had already sown the seeds of affection between them. She could not, in all good conscience, allow them to grow.

It would only end in heartbreak for them both.

## Chapter Fifteen

After sending Smithson out with his instructions to deliver the note yesterday, Isaac had felt himself begin to sink. For the rest of that day he'd sat in his library, staring blankly at the volumes of books on his shelves, a black mood threatening to envelop him. He'd attempted to remedy it with a large brandy, but had managed no more than a sip before setting the glass aside, realising that he did not really want it.

Gone were the days when he'd wished to drown his feelings in the bottom of the decanter. Gone were the days of surrendering himself so completely to his melancholy. And so, with a resigned sigh and a few 'damnations' muttered under his breath, he'd rung for some tea and forced himself to confront what ailed him.

Louisa. Or, more precisely, Louisa's absence.

His anxiety had gnawed at him as he'd thought about the way he'd reached out to her, his mind reeling with the same handful of questions. Had Smithson been able to find her? Was she well? Had she read his note? And if she had, how had it been received?

This latter question had troubled him greatly. He

knew his words had been unguarded, and that he'd written in earnest about how her friendship had made him feel, what the time he'd spent in her company had meant to him. On reflection, his words had been too plain, perhaps, for either of them to countenance.

God, the wait for news had been unbearable.

Finally, just before dinner, Smithson had returned. By then Samuel had joined Isaac in the library, to peruse the newspapers and enjoy a small glass of port. Isaac had noted how his brother lowered the paper, peering curiously over it as Smithson approached his master. Isaac had got up from his chair then, steering the man towards his desk and away, he hoped, from Samuel's keen ears.

His butler, who was as discreet as he was loyal, had delivered his message in hushed, cryptic tones, but to Isaac his meaning was clear enough.

'I did as you asked, sir, and can confirm that all is well.'

It had taken a good deal of effort for Isaac to suppress his smile. 'Thank you, Smithson,' he'd replied, in the most businesslike voice he could muster. 'That will be all.'

'What was all that about?' Samuel had asked, almost as soon as the butler had left the room.

'Oh, just a household matter,' Isaac had lied. 'Nothing to concern yourself with.'

Knowing that she was in good health had buoyed Isaac's spirits, although he still worried about her reaction to the words his note had contained. He'd expressed himself hastily, and although not a word of it was untrue he feared she might be discouraged by his actions. He'd asked Louisa for her friendship, and yet he feared he was starting to behave as if he wanted far more than that.

Perhaps, he considered, he did want more than that. He knew he shouldn't, that there were scores of reasons why allowing himself to love again was a bad idea— not least the memory of his dead wife and the risk to his barely mended heart. Not least the risk of his love being rejected…a risk which was very real, given that he was neither young nor particularly agreeable.

Even Samuel, who had seemed to perceive the depth of Isaac's interest in Louisa before he did, had urged him to be cautious. And yet in sending that note he had been anything but cautious.

Damn, what had got into him?

Today that heavy feeling had returned, weighing him down in his chair as he sat in the library on a warm, sunny summer's day. He fidgeted uncomfortably, un- buttoning his collar in a vain attempt to combat the growing heat in the usually cool room, before shaking his head disapprovingly at himself.

His appearance today left much to be desired. After several hours of restless contemplation his shirt was badly crumpled, and his cravat hung loosely about his neck. He'd spent much of the morning staring wist- fully out of the window, his mind returning repeatedly to the windswept cliffs. He'd briefly considered riding out there, just in case, but ultimately decided against it. She hadn't come to meet him yesterday for reasons which remained unknown to him, and in his note he had not asked to meet her there today.

He'd decided it was best to be patient…to await her reply. God, how he prayed that she would reply.

A knock at the door interrupted his spiralling thoughts.

'Come in,' he replied, rather impatiently. It was probably Samuel, he reasoned, coming to check on him, to ask why he wasn't going out riding, or to insist that Isaac accompany him to some place or other. Truly, there was never any end to Samuel's machinations.

To his surprise, however, it was Smithson. The man looked flushed and a little out of breath, as though he'd run down to the library in a great hurry.

'Forgive me for disturbing you, sir,' the butler panted. 'But I thought you'd want to know that there was a lady at the door just now. She was here to deliver a note.'

Louisa turned away from the front door of Hayton Hall and hurried back down its wide drive. At the gate stood Charlotte, waiting for her, and even from this distance she could see that she was put out: arms folded, lips pouting.

Louisa let out a sigh. Managing Charlotte had been trickier than she'd expected, and she'd almost tied herself in knots trying to explain to her companion why she needed to call here and deliver a note.

'It's a silly thing, really,' she'd said, as casually as she could manage. 'When we met in Hayton, Sir Isaac and I talked a little of the books we like to read. I told him of my love for travel literature and he said he knew of a book I must read, but he could not remember the title. He wrote to me later, to give me the details. Since we are here today, I thought I might drop off a little note to thank him for his kindness.'

Charlotte's eyes had widened. 'You're exchanging letters with Sir Isaac?'

'No.' Louisa had been emphatic. 'It is one note. To thank him. It is only polite.'

'If my mother found out I was writing to a gentleman she'd say I was being improper, even if it was only to converse about books,' Charlotte had retorted.

'Well, your mother is not my mother, and she doesn't need to know anything of this,' Louisa had replied, a little more sharply than she'd intended. 'If you wouldn't mind waiting for me at the gate? I will only be a moment.'

Charlotte had acquiesced, although Louisa wasn't sure she was convinced by her explanation. She'd felt her heart thudding rapidly in her chest as she'd made her way towards the house, and briefly she'd considered Charlotte's insinuation about the propriety of her behaviour. If Charlotte disapproved of her writing to a gentleman, Louisa did not wish to imagine what she would say if she knew she'd been meeting him, alone and in secret.

She'd pushed the thought from her mind, turning her attention instead to the large, grand house before her. It was very old, certainly—much older than she'd expected. It had many lattice windows, and a roofscape rising at several points, giving it a castle-like quality. She'd wondered about its history, and for a moment had yearned to ask Isaac to tell her about it. Then she'd remembered the note in her hand and what she must do.

It was the right course of action. For both their sakes.

At the front entrance she'd knocked hurriedly, before she could change her mind. When the door had been swiftly answered by a grey-haired butler with a kindly face, she'd pressed her note into his hands and mumbled something barely coherent about being grateful if he would ensure that it reached Sir Isaac.

The man had nodded, his mouth agape, as though caught completely by surprise. He'd recovered himself quickly, and had started to say something about fetching his master, but Louisa had all but fled from the door then. It was one thing to deliver this note—quite another to watch Isaac's face as he read it in front of her.

She was certain she could not bear it.

'All that trouble over a book,' Charlotte huffed now, as Louisa finally reached her at the gate. 'You should have let me accompany you. I might have been able to see Mr Liddell if he's at home.'

'A good book is worth any amount of trouble,' Louisa replied, deciding that humour was the best remedy for her friend's growing bad mood. 'And I did not ask if either Sir Isaac or his brother are at home, as I would not wish to disturb them.'

Charlotte sighed as they linked arms and began to walk. 'I do hope I see Mr Liddell again soon. Perhaps there will be another ball at the Assembly Rooms, and...'

'Miss Conrad! Miss Pearson!'

Both ladies spun round to see Samuel Liddell, running down the path towards them. Louisa watched as Charlotte's pout quickly dissolved into the broadest smile.

'It seems you're going to get your wish, Charlotte,' she observed, feeling her heart sink at the prospect of her swift retreat being thwarted.

'I saw you both from the window,' Mr Liddell puffed when he finally caught up with them. 'Did you call at the house? It looked as though you were coming back down the path.'

'Louisa called,' Charlotte answered, before Louisa could speak. 'She had a note for Sir Isaac—something to do with a book.'

Mr Liddell frowned. 'A book?'

Louisa nodded. 'Yes, a travel book,' she explained, trying her best to sound nonchalant. 'I shall not bore you both with the details.'

Her breath caught in her throat as behind Mr Liddell she saw Isaac emerge from the front door of the house. He marched briskly down the path, his eyes intent upon her even from this distance. As he drew closer she noticed he looked more dishevelled than the last time they'd met. His dark hair was untamed, and he wore neither a coat nor a waistcoat over his white shirt, which looked loose and crumpled next to the smooth lines of his pantaloons and Hessian boots.

She swallowed hard, wondering if he'd already read her note. Surely he was not going to speak to her about it now, in front of his brother and her friend, was he?

'Ah! Here he comes now, Miss Conrad,' Mr Liddell said, after briefly turning to follow her gaze. 'I'm sure he will be at your service regarding this book of yours.'

Louisa inclined her head, hoping she looked more serene than she felt. By the time Isaac reached them her heart was pounding so hard that she believed it would burst out of her chest. She stared up at him, locking eyes with that cool azure gaze of his. He looked strained, she realised. His face was pale and drawn, as though something was weighing heavily upon him.

Her stomach lurched as she considered that she might be the cause of his unrest.

'Miss Conrad brought a note for you, Isaac, concerning a book,' his brother informed him.

Isaac nodded in acknowledgement, although his eyes never once shifted from Louisa. 'Yes, I have received it, thank you.' He gave her a tight smile. 'Perhaps we might all step into my library for a few moments? I believe the book you seek is in there.'

Louisa's eyes widened at the suggestion. 'I'm not sure, sir,' she began, feeling increasingly flustered. 'Miss Pearson and I must—'

'Louisa?' Charlotte interrupted her, frowning. 'I thought Sir Isaac had already given you the details of the book and you'd merely written to express your gratitude?'

'She did,' Isaac replied quickly, not missing a beat. 'But there is another book we discussed too, if I recall. The one by the anonymous author. I had promised to lend it to her.'

'Splendid,' said Mr Liddell, clasping his hands together. 'Might I suggest that since you've come all this way we give you both a tour of Hayton Hall? It would be our pleasure.'

Louisa's heart descended into the pit of her stomach. 'No, really…' she tried again.

'That would be wonderful!' Charlotte spoke over her, all but squealing with delight and taking hold of Mr Liddell's arm as soon as he offered it. 'Come, Louisa, let's make haste.'

Louisa continued to stand there, dumbstruck, a wave of horror washing over her as the futility of any further objection dawned upon her. She'd come here today to draw a firm line under an acquaintance which was in danger of becoming far more than it could or should be. Going into Isaac's home, seeing where he worked and ate and read all those wonderful books they'd discussed, was not at all what she had intended.

Beside her, she felt Isaac draw nearer. He did not offer his arm, but simply walked by her side as they sauntered towards the house. No words passed between them. Nothing about her absence at the cliffs, or his note, or her reply. Just silence. Difficult silence.

Ahead of them she heard Charlotte, already deep in conversation with Mr Liddell. She wished then that she could feel so light-hearted, that this was simply an enjoyable tour of a gentleman's ancestral home. That her friendship with Sir Isaac Liddell had not grown so fraught and so complicated.

But as she drew nearer to his fine country house once more, she realised that nothing between herself and the master of Hayton Hall would ever be straightforward. No amount of wishful thinking could change that.

## Chapter Sixteen

As they walked through the front door of Hayton Hall and towards his library Isaac wasn't sure what would drive him to madness first: his head or his heart.

His mind was still reeling at her unexpected presence here, and at the words in that damnable note she'd delivered—the one he'd read frantically before screwing it up and flinging it across the room, only narrowly missing poor Smithson's head.

His thoughts raced at the impulsive way he'd invited her into the library. He had meant to lend *Waverley* to her, that was true, but he could not deny that in that moment outside it had been a ruse to secure a few more moments of her company and an opportunity to speak to her. But how on earth was he going to speak in earnest with his brother and Miss Pearson present?

His heart, meanwhile, lurched from joy to despair, her company both lifting his mood and leaving him anxious that he might, in fact, never see her again. Certainly that was what her note suggested, wasn't it? That there would be no more clifftop walks, no more heartfelt conversations. That she would not, it seemed, permit a friendship between them any more.

In the library she seemed nervous, cutting herself adrift from him and pacing a little as she made a point of admiring the many shelves filled from floor to ceiling with his family's collection. He left his brother to attend to Miss Pearson, who lingered by the door with a bored expression on her face, and fetched the first volume of *Waverley* before taking it over to Louisa.

Her eyes seemed to widen as he approached, and her clear discomfort made his heart lurch. Had he really offended her so terribly by writing to her in the way he had? Was his admission that her company soothed him genuinely so distasteful to her?

'This is *Waverley*,' he said, loud enough for Samuel and Miss Pearson to hear. 'Well, the first volume, at least.'

Isaac held the book out to her, and Louisa's fingers brushed against his as she accepted it. Her unexpected touch jolted him, and his mind immediately returned to the clifftops…to the day she told him that she'd loved and lost, just as he had. To how he'd placed his hand over hers. To how deeply they'd seemed to understand one another. That day they'd drawn closer—a fact which he'd been grappling with ever since. Perhaps she had, too. Perhaps that was why his note had caused her to end their friendship so abruptly.

'Thank you,' she replied, offering him a tight smile but avoiding his gaze as she admired the fine leather cover.

'There are two more volumes,' he explained, 'if you will permit me to fetch them. They are not in their usual place, but I am sure they are here somewhere.'

A loud sigh punctuated their strained conversation. 'Forgive me, Sir Isaac, but I am feeling suddenly rather hot and thirsty after our walk,' Miss Pearson interjected, fanning her face with her hand. 'Could I trouble you for some tea?'

'It is rather too warm here in the library,' Samuel replied, before Isaac could utter a word. 'The small parlour is far more agreeable at this time of the day. Perhaps we might all retire there?'

Miss Pearson's face brightened at the suggestion. 'Oh, yes, let's! But do not trouble Sir Isaac and Louisa, Mr Liddell, if they are busy with their books. They can join us when they have finished fetching the rest of *Walpole*, or whatever it is.'

'*Waverley*,' Isaac muttered, raising his eyebrows at his brother.

Samuel, however, seemed helpless in the face of the young lady's machinations. 'Well…of course, Miss Pearson,' he began, looking uncharacteristically flustered. 'If you will be comfortable, then I'm sure we could…'

'Excellent!' Miss Pearson declared, seeming suddenly less fatigued as she took hold of Samuel's arm. 'I'm sure Sir Isaac and Louisa will do very well without us,' she added, casting the words carelessly over her shoulder as she all but dragged Samuel along with her and breezed out of the room.

The door slammed shut behind them and the library grew suddenly very silent. Isaac looked over at Louisa, offering her a smile and hoping it would convey his apology. He'd already noted her discomfort, and knew that being left alone with him would surely only make it worse.

'I will try to find the other two volumes as quickly as I can. Then we can join the others,' he said, returning his attention to his shelves.

'Thank you,' she said again, before adding, 'This is a lovely library, sir, and a lovely house. When was Hayton Hall built?'

'At the beginning of the seventeenth century, by the first baronet,' he replied, turning back to face her. 'My family has lived here ever since.'

'My goodness,' she replied, looking around once more. 'There is so much history here.'

Her expression of sheer wonder brought a smile to his face. 'I can show you the oldest book in the library, if you like.'

She nodded eagerly and, feeling that the ice between them had finally been breached, Isaac rolled up his sleeves and fetched the ladder, climbing up to retrieve the infamous volume without a moment's hesitation.

All the while he felt her hovering at the bottom of the ladder, her eyes upon him, following his swift movements up, then back down again. The observation intrigued him, and when his feet touched the ground once more he saw that she was blushing. *Blushing!* Whatever had he done to make her blush?

'The first book of *Don Quixote*,' he said, handing it to her. 'An early translation. It's about as old as the house.'

Louisa gasped, clutching it tenderly in her hands. 'I have never read it, have you?'

He shook his head. 'I must admit I have not. A book this old feels almost too precious to be read. You might like the story, though. I believe it's about an idealistic traveller,' he added, with a grin.

What on earth was wrong with him? She'd as much as told him that their friendship was over, and yet here he was, trying to tease her.

She smiled back, although he noticed that it didn't

reach her eyes. 'As much as I'd love to travel, I cannot admit to being idealistic,' she replied.

No, she wasn't—he knew that. Her life, like his, had brought her too much heartache for her to be quixotic.

Around them the library remained quiet. By now his brother and Miss Pearson would be enjoying their tea in the parlour on the other side of the house. For propriety's sake they had only a few more moments together. If he was going to speak honestly to her, then it was now or never.

'Have I offended you, Louisa?' he asked quietly, barely able to bring himself to do so.

She stepped back, just a little. 'No.'

'Your note said that we should not meet any more.'

'It is for the best,' she replied. 'We take a risk each time we meet alone.'

'Then we don't have to meet alone,' he answered. 'We can meet here, with my brother and Miss Pearson and even your aunt in attendance, if you wish. Invite the whole of Hayton, for all I care, if it means still spending time with you.'

She bit her lip, casting her eyes down, and he sensed that he was not winning the argument. 'But your note, Sir Isaac, the way you expressed yourself...'

'I was concerned when you didn't come to meet me. I had to know you were all right. And I felt that I must tell you what our time together has meant to me,' he said flatly. 'Please, Louisa, call me Isaac.'

Louisa looked back at him then. 'I had to go to the linen drapers with my aunt, and then to the Pearsons' house for tea,' she explained. 'That was why I didn't come. I am sorry to have worried you. I would not want you to fret on my account.'

Isaac smiled at her. 'I must admit I could not seem to help it,' he replied.

'Do you not think that is exactly why we must no longer meet?' she asked him.

'Why?' he challenged her. 'We are friends, are we not? Would you really wish for me not to care about you?' He sighed heavily, rubbing his forehead as the meaning of her objection suddenly dawned on him. 'You do not care for me,' he stated. 'I understand. I am too old for you, perhaps? Or too sombre. Indeed, I am well aware of my own shortcomings.'

'No.' He felt her hand upon his arm. 'You are neither of those things, Isaac. It is not that.'

His heart lifted at finally hearing her drop the damnable 'sir' from her address. Their eyes met, and before he could think about what he was doing he leaned towards her, his lips tentatively meeting hers.

He knew he shouldn't kiss her…that he ought to think of Rosalind…that he ought to remember the grief that love and loss had inflicted upon him. But, to his shame, those thoughts had flown from his mind, replaced by other, less familiar and more confusing ideas about the warm proximity of this woman, the orange sweetness of her lips.

His senses heightened as she drew closer, placing a gentle hand on his upper arm as she kissed him back. It was all the encouragement his foolish, impulsive heart needed. He wrapped an arm around her, pulling her close, then unfastened the ribbon of her bonnet and pushed it away. He ran his fingers through the loose curls of her hair, his lips trailing kisses from her mouth to her soft cheeks, her delicate jaw, and down her neck.

The taste of oranges combined with the scent of lavender as his senses were utterly overwhelmed by her. When their lips met again her tongue greeted his, and his mind began to entertain thoughts which he knew would be his undoing. *Their* undoing.

She pressed a hand against his chest, pushing him away. 'No, Isaac, we must stop.'

She was as breathless as he was—breathless and beautiful, her lips and cheeks made pink by his attentions. She stepped back from him, reaching down and picking up the bonnet which moments ago had been discarded on the floor.

He held up his hands, half defensive, half frustrated. 'I'm sorry,' he said. 'I should not have kissed you.'

He watched as she replaced her bonnet, noticed how her fingers shook as she tied the ribbon into an untidy bow. 'No, you should not,' she replied, her voice wavering. 'You must know I cannot—not after Richard...'

'Of course,' he replied grimly, his heart still racing, his mind still reeling from the taste of her lips, the feeling of her pressed against him.

What the hell had he been thinking? Had he gone completely out of his wits?

'Please, forgive me. I shall forget it ever happened, Louisa. You have my word.'

She nodded briskly. 'We should join your brother and Charlotte for tea. They will wonder what has become of us.'

'You go ahead,' he replied, giving her a thin smile. 'I will join you in a moment.'

He watched as she hurried from the room, then slumped down in his favourite armchair with a groan. He needed a few minutes to collect himself—and to chastise himself.

What a fool he was. There would be no more cliff-top walks, no more pleasant conversations now. Kissing her had sealed the fate of their friendship, and it was all his fault.

Worse still, he realised, was that for all he'd promised to forget their kiss, he believed that was the very last thing he was capable of doing.

'You're your own worst enemy, Liddell,' he muttered to himself.

It took Louisa a few minutes to locate Charlotte, following the trail of her giggles as they echoed around the ground floor of the house. In the end she found her in a cosy parlour, sitting far too close to Mr Liddell on a green velvet sofa and enjoying a cup of tea. Neither of them got to their feet when she walked in; they were far too deep in some whispered flirtation.

Even in her turmoil, it occurred to Louisa that they were as brazen as each other. She didn't wish to consider what Charlotte's mother would think of this scene, if she was here to witness it.

'Miss Conrad, do join us for some tea,' Mr Liddell said in the end, gesturing towards one of the seats opposite. 'Is my brother not with you?'

Louisa shook her head as she sat down. 'No... No—he has some business to attend to,' she lied. 'He will be here momentarily.'

Mr Liddell clicked his tongue disapprovingly as he poured her a cup of tea and handed it to her. 'That sounds like my brother—all business and no pleasure.'

That last word made Louisa's heart flutter, and she felt a sudden heat grow in her cheeks. 'I'm sure his tenants appreciate his endeavours,' she replied flatly.

'Are you all right, Louisa?' Charlotte asked. 'You look a little flushed.'

Louisa nodded, then sipped her tea, and was grateful when Charlotte and Mr Liddell's attentions returned to each other. She sat rigid in her seat, listening to the pair of them talk about nothing much, while her mind ran skittishly over everything that had occurred in the library.

Isaac had kissed her, and she had allowed it—more than allowed it, in fact, since she had kissed him in return. Her heart thrummed in her chest as she relived the moment: the soft touch of his lips against hers, the rough hint of stubble brushing her neck, the muscular solidity of his arm beneath her hand. She'd wanted to touch those arms ever since he'd rolled up his sleeves and set about fetching *Don Quixote*. A glimpse of his bare skin, sun-kissed and covered by a layer of fine dark hair, was all it had taken to send her mind to places it ought not to go.

She supposed it was little wonder that she'd surrendered herself so completely to his kiss, when even the mere sight of his flesh seemed to place her on the cusp of ruination.

All the more reason that they must no longer see each other.

At least she'd had the presence of mind to end their embrace. To be firm with him. To tell him that it should not have happened, and to remind him of her grief, of the man she'd loved and lost. That had been as much as she'd been able to say.

There was so much more she could never say to him—so much more he could not know. About her, about her past, about why she was not the sort of woman he should attach himself to. If she allowed a romance to blossom between them, she knew she would not be able to build it on lies. Sooner or later she would have to tell him everything, and she would have to endure the look in his eyes and the inevitable extinguishing of his affection for her. That would be too painful—for him and for her.

He'd already lost his wife and child; he had suffered enough. He needed someone who was worthy of him... someone who did not bear her scars.

It was kinder this way. Kinder to let him go.

And yet she'd made her attraction to him evident, hadn't she? She'd complicated matters with her blushes, and her kisses, and her protest that he was not too old, or too sombre, or indeed in any way disagreeable to her. She hadn't been able to feign dislike or uninterest; she could not have been so cruel. She had pushed him away—but not before indulging herself first. She'd allowed momentary passion to rule her head, to lead to her to go against her better judgement. It seemed she had learned no lessons from the past, after all...

'Are you sure you're all right, Louisa?' Charlotte asked, interrupting her thoughts. 'You look suddenly very pale.'

'I'm fine,' she replied, as smoothly as she could manage. 'However, I do think we ought to begin our walk back to Lowhaven. The afternoon grows late.'

She finished her tea and got to her feet, making her intention to leave clear.

Charlotte rose too, somewhat reluctantly, followed by Mr Liddell, who beamed at them both. Charlotte let out a little laugh at his light-hearted attentions and Louisa bristled, not sure which of them was irritating her more.

'I will have the carriage brought round and my driver will take you back to Lowhaven,' Mr Liddell said. 'Miss Conrad is right—we have detained you here for too long. It is the least we can do.'

'Oh, thank you, Mr Liddell, that is so very kind and thoughtful,' Charlotte gushed.

Louisa watched as her companion took hold of the gentleman's arm, trailing behind them both as they walked out of the warm parlour and back into the cool air of the wide, wood-panelled hall.

'It is a pity we did not have time to show you around Hayton Hall,' Mr Liddell said, glancing at her over his shoulder.

'Another time, I'm sure,' Louisa answered.

'Oh, yes, another time,' Charlotte interjected. 'Perhaps next time Sir Isaac and Louisa won't find themselves detained for quite so long in the library,' she added with a giggle.

Louisa bit her tongue, resolving to say nothing. The enjoyment Charlotte clearly derived from making scandalous remarks was beginning to grate on her nerves. Especially when, in this instance, her insinuations were not so far from the truth.

Finally they reached the front door, and inwardly Louisa breathed a sigh of relief. She had never been so glad to leave a place as she was at that moment.

'Miss Conrad!'

Isaac's deep voice echoed around the hall. Slowly Louisa turned around, felt panic creeping in at the prospect of facing him after all that had happened between them. What they both now had to forget.

Isaac strode up to her, clutching something against his chest. Her mind was so fraught that it took several moments before she realised it was a set of books. He held them up, giving her a broad smile, but she could not fail to see that it did not reach his eyes.

'*Waverley,*' he said, placing three leather-bound volumes in her hands. 'You almost forgot to take it with you. I hope you enjoy it.'

Louisa smiled back at him, conscious of their audience and the need to express a delight she didn't feel. 'Thank you, Sir Isaac,' she replied. 'I am sure that I will.'

# Chapter Seventeen

'Come, my dear, we are going to be late.'

Louisa could hear Aunt Clarissa pacing at the bottom of the stairs as Nan hurried to finish pinning the last curls of her hair into place. She sighed wearily, displeased with the turn her day had taken.

She had been resting quietly in her room, engrossed in the third volume of *Waverley*, when her aunt had knocked on the door and informed her that Mrs Pearson had sent a note requesting the pleasure of their company for tea that afternoon. Louisa, unaccustomed to such last-minute demands on her time, had mildly protested about attending, but her aunt, as usual, had been resolute.

Louisa had known that there was little point in arguing, and Nan had been duly summoned to help her dress for the occasion. Now Louisa emerged from her room in a blue day dress, her hair pulled back into a gentle chignon with a handful of curls framing her face. She just about had time to grab her spencer before Aunt Clarissa hurried her out of the house and across town to the Pearsons' home.

They arrived a few moments after the appointed hour and were shown, somewhat breathlessly, into the parlour.

As Louisa walked through the door she felt suddenly as though she had been thrown into a lion's den. There, sitting on the other side of the small, oval table from Mrs Pearson and Charlotte, were Mr Liddell and Sir Isaac. She felt her breath catch in her throat as Sir Isaac put down his teacup and turned to look at her. Like his brother, he rose to his feet to greet them both, but his face was unsmiling and unreadable.

Beside her, Aunt Clarissa took a step back. 'Forgive me, Mrs Pearson, you have other company. I must have misread the day or perhaps the time on your invitation.'

'Not at all, my dear Miss Howarth,' Mrs Pearson replied with a smile. 'Why...did I not mention in my note that Sir Isaac and Mr Liddell would be joining us? How silly and forgetful of me. Please, do sit down.'

Both ladies did as they were bade, with Clarissa taking the seat nearest to Mrs Pearson, leaving Louisa to sit on the only other available chair, beside Isaac. The prospect of such close proximity to him made her heart beat faster, and she found herself thinking about being with him in the library all over again.

He looked well today, dressed for the occasion in a deep blue tailcoat with contrasting fawn waistcoat and pantaloons, his dark hair tamed into order and his face freshly shaven. Louisa felt his eyes upon her as she eased herself into the seat at his side. She did not look his way, but instead sat back as a maid poured her some tea, trying her best to concentrate on the conversation.

'So Charlotte and I were taken with the notion of a ride in the carriage through Hayton, and who should we see in the village but Mr Liddell? Such a happy co-incidence—and now to have you both here to take tea with us... Such a pleasure,' Mrs Pearson was saying.

Louisa glanced at Charlotte, noting the elated grin on her face, and her eyes darting between her mother and Mr Liddell. A coincidence indeed, thought Louisa.

'It is certainly very good to see you both,' Clarissa agreed. 'Until the ball I had not seen either of you for some time.' She looked apprehensively at Sir Isaac for a moment, then turned her attention back to Mr Liddell. 'I believe you have been travelling in Europe, sir?'

Louisa listened intently as Mr Liddell regaled his audience with tales of his continental travels. Like Mrs Starke, he could no doubt write a book describing his experiences of Paris, Geneva, Rome, Florence and Vienna. He spoke about the places he'd visited so vividly that Louisa could imagine them—although she found herself comparing his accounts with those committed to paper by Mrs Starke, which she had pored over many times.

When he mentioned his visit to Château de Voltaire in Ferney, on the French-Swiss border, she couldn't help but interject.

'Oh, yes, I know of Monsieur Voltaire's house. Mrs Starke wrote of it in her *Letters from Italy*. She says it is unchanged, and that those who have owned it since Voltaire's death have gone to some lengths to preserve it.'

Mr Liddell raised his eyebrows and smiled in delight at their shared enthusiasm for the subject. 'Quite so, Miss Conrad. Although I must tell you that there is one notable thing missing from Monsieur Voltaire's home, and that is his library. It was purchased in its entirety by Catherine, the Empress of Russia, and moved to St Petersburg.'

'Astonishing!' Mrs Pearson exclaimed. 'And you, Sir Isaac, have you travelled, like your brother?'

Isaac gave his hostess a grim smile. 'Unfortunately seeing all that Europe has to offer is not a luxury afforded to a gentleman with an estate to care for—especially when that estate becomes his responsibility at a tender age.'

'Indeed, indeed…' replied Mrs Pearson, apparently somewhat taken aback by Isaac's directness.

'Louisa would like to travel,' Aunt Clarissa said, nodding warmly at her niece. 'I do believe her mother told me that it was one of the reasons she wished to visit me for the summer. Lowhaven isn't quite Lausanne, I grant you, but it has been good for her to see another part of England, I think.'

'I'm not sure I am so keen on the idea of travel,' Charlotte interjected, wrinkling her nose slightly. 'I think I'd much rather remain in a pretty little English village like Hayton and hear all about Europe from Mr Liddell.'

'Of course, my dear,' Mrs Pearson cooed. 'Like Sir Isaac, you know that your responsibilities are here, in Cumberland. Sons and heirs must do their duty, and so must daughters.'

Isaac gave a polite nod. 'Indeed, madam.'

To Louisa's consternation, Charlotte blushed, and she watched as Mrs Pearson eyed her daughter and Isaac keenly. Then she dropped her gaze, occupying herself with drinking her tea and wishing that the ground itself would open up and swallow her whole.

What the devil had he wandered into this afternoon?

Isaac sipped his tea, quietly cursing his brother, who had been responsible for agreeing to this visit in the first place. It was bad enough that since the moment he'd arrived he'd had to endure Mrs Pearson's obvious attempts to place her daughter in front of him, making sure that he knew every detail of her accomplishments. Now the giddy young woman was blushing at nothing, and Louisa had joined them to witness the spectacle.

He wondered if she'd noticed Mrs Pearson's machinations. Certainly, she looked uncomfortable—but then that could be due to his presence more than anything else. For his part, he found it hard to be in the same room as her, drinking tea and knowing what it was like to taste her lips, to feel her pressed against him. He had not expected to see her again so soon; in some ways he had not wished to. Forgetting what had happened between them had been difficult enough, but one glance at her pretty face rendered it impossible.

Isaac fidgeted in his seat. If only he had not come today! He hadn't wished to come, but had felt duty-bound to do so when Samuel had informed him that he'd accepted the invitation on their behalf. He considered himself too honourable a gentleman to deliver such a snub, even to people like the Pearsons, about whom he had to admit to feeling rather wary even before he'd been treated to the mama's scheming.

His brother's growing interest in Miss Pearson had prompted him to make some enquiries about the family, and what he'd discovered was less than encouraging. A trail of bad debt seemed to follow the father, and they lived almost entirely at the whim of his creditors. He'd tried to speak to Samuel about what he'd learned, but he had rebuked him with a speech so well prepared that Isaac suspected his brother of being all too aware of the family's situation.

'If I was to marry Miss Pearson—and I daresay it's too soon to consider that—then the wealth of her family would matter not a jot to me. I have invested my inheritance wisely and I manage my own affairs. When the time comes, I will support my own household. Large dowries and heiresses are no inducement to me.'

Isaac had quickly dropped the subject, in the face of his brother's iron will, and submitted to attending the tea party with resignation. He'd had no idea that Louisa and her aunt would be in attendance also. He still could not decide if that knowledge would have made him more or less likely to attend. All he knew was that between the shock of Louisa's sudden appearance and Mrs Pearson's dreadful efforts to match him with her daughter under his brother's nose, a swift return to the sanctuary of his library felt more tempting than ever.

'Have you managed to read any of *Waverley*, Miss Conrad?' he asked, leaning towards her and speaking quietly in the hope that they might share a conversation.

Fate in the form of Mrs Pearson had forced them together, he reasoned. They might as well make the best of it.

He watched as she hesitated for a moment, as though astonished that he was speaking to her at all. Out of the corner of his eye he could see Miss Pearson observing them, no doubt seeking to include herself in their discussion. He wished then that she would return her attention to his brother, who was engaged in a lively exchange with Mrs Pearson and Miss Howarth.

'Yes,' Louisa replied, 'in fact, I am reading the third volume.' She gave him a reticent smile. 'I must thank you for lending it to me. I have very much enjoyed it.'

'Well, I am glad to hear that. Though I cannot believe

you are almost at the end already. You must have spent a good deal of time reading these past days.'

'I confess that at times I have been unable to tear myself away from the story. The way the author describes the Scottish Highlands is so precise and so vivid that I find myself wishing I could visit.'

Isaac found himself nodding vociferously in agreement. 'I will admit that I entertained the same notion.' He glanced at Miss Pearson, who had mercifully lost interest in their literary discussion and had now been engaged by Samuel on another topic. 'As I think I told you once, I very much lost myself in the pages of that book.'

He watched as Louisa's face coloured slightly at this reference to one of their clifftop conversations.

'I can understand that now that I have read it,' she replied.

She pressed her lips together and he found his eyes lingering on them, his mind wandering to that kiss in his library once again.

'Pray tell, what are the two of you whispering about over there?' Mrs Pearson asked loudly, giving them both a stern look.

'We are just discussing a novel which Sir Isaac has given me to read,' Louisa replied, before Isaac could answer. 'It is called *Waverley*, Mrs Pearson. Perhaps you know of it?'

'No, I don't believe I do.' Mrs Pearson shrank back into her seat. Clearly a conversation about a book was not what she had been expecting to uncover.

'Ah, yes, one of my brother's favourites,' Samuel interjected. 'Its author chooses anonymity, but his identity is a secret not very well kept. I have heard it said on more than one occasion that the poet Walter Scott is the author of *Waverley*.'

Isaac bristled as he observed Louisa's eyes widen in wonder. Trust Samuel to manage to impress with such an assertion, he thought.

To his surprise, Louisa turned to him for confirmation. 'Did you know this, Sir Isaac?'

He shrugged. 'It is mere London tittle-tattle. I would not give it any credence unless the poet acknowledges it to be the truth.'

His answer earned him a nod of agreement from her. 'Indeed,' she replied, 'I would not credit even half of what is said in society.'

He could not mistake the note of displeasure in her voice. He glanced at her, frowning. The impassive expression on her face revealed nothing, but he couldn't help but feel that she was talking about far more than the secret identity of a writer.

'Since we are all gathered here today,' Mrs Pearson interjected, clapping her hands together, 'I would like to extend an invitation to you all. Mr Pearson and I have recently considered how very nice it would be to spend a little of the summer away from Lowhaven. Shortly we intend to travel to our country home, Langdale Hall, and we would be honoured if you would join us there for a few days—perhaps on the Friday after next, if that is suitable?'

Isaac blinked, thoroughly taken aback by the invitation. It was bad enough that Samuel had dragged him here today, but now he faced the prospect of a prolonged social engagement—one which would take him away from his own estate. One which would involve spending several days in Louisa's company.

He stole a glance at her, observing how she stared at Mrs Pearson in apparent astonishment. Clearly she had not expected this either.

'Mrs Pearson, my brother and I would be delighted to accept your invitation—wouldn't we, Isaac?' Samuel said, in his usual flawless way.

'Wonderful,' Mrs Pearson declared, clasping her hands together. 'We will hold a dinner in honour of your visit—won't we, Charlotte?' she added, her keen gaze shifting to her daughter. 'We can invite our neighbours the Suttons and the Coles to join us.'

Miss Pearson gave a vigorous nod, clearly enthused by her mother's obvious machinations. 'With dancing, Mama,' she added. 'Surely we will have dancing?'

'Indeed,' Mrs Pearson replied, clapping her hands together once more. 'Then it is settled.' She turned to her other guests, who still sat, apparently dumbstruck. 'My dear Miss Howarth, Miss Conrad... I hope you will both attend as well?'

Isaac noticed how Louisa's gaze shifted towards her aunt, in the clear expectation that she would answer for them both. The older woman, meanwhile, seemed to take a moment to find her tongue.

'Oh, well...yes, Mrs P-Pearson,' she stammered. 'Indeed we would love to come. But I'm afraid that, as you know, we've... Well, we've no means by which to get ourselves to Langdale Hall.'

The way Clarissa Howarth's face reddened at that final admission made Isaac's heart lurch in sympathy for her, and he felt the heat of indignation rise in his chest at the difficult position Mrs Pearson had put her in. He hoped it was mere thoughtlessness, but he suspected it was not.

'We could take a stagecoach, Aunt,' Louisa interjected, trying to be helpful. 'That will at least get us to the nearest town.'

The thought of Louisa setting foot inside another damnable coach after what had happened to her earlier that summer set Isaac's teeth on edge.

'No,' he said, the word sounding more forceful than he'd intended. He paused momentarily, composing himself. 'It would be our pleasure to escort you. You shall travel with us in our carriage.'

Louisa looked at him then, her dark gaze guarded and unreadable, as somewhere in the background her aunt uttered hurried words of gratitude. In truth, Isaac wanted none of this: no tea parties, no visits to the Pearsons' country home, no long journeys with Louisa sitting in his carriage. But he was a gentleman. He had no choice but to accept invitations and offer his assistance to a fair maiden and her aunt when they needed it.

A fair maiden, he thought to himself. It had been some time since he'd called her that. Much had happened since then—much which could not be undone. Much which, if he was honest with himself, he did not wish to undo.

Isaac glanced at Louisa again as all around them excited chatter about the visit to Langdale Hall grew.

Several days away from Hayton Hall. Several days of seeing Louisa's face each morning. Several days of eating and sleeping under the same roof as her.

Could he bear it? He wasn't sure. One thing he did know, though, was that it would make forgetting that kiss all but impossible...

## Chapter Eighteen

The journey to Langdale Hall took Louisa into the depths of Cumberland's hilly, rugged countryside and away from the sea for the first time in weeks.

For the first couple of hours, as the horses pulled them along at a gentle pace, Louisa gazed out of the window, half listening to her aunt and Mr Liddell make polite conversation, but mostly preoccupied by the increasingly dramatic scenery as it unfolded before her eyes. It was either that, she realised, or risk meeting the eye of the man sitting opposite. A man who sat as quietly as she did, but whose presence nonetheless seemed to fill the entire carriage as they rattled along the uneven country roads.

He had surpassed himself today. The deep blue of his frock coat contrasted sharply with a high white cravat and buff waistcoat, and his attire was completed with a smart pair of fitted grey pantaloons. The only aspect of him which was not agreeable was the expression he wore on his face. His brows were knitted together in a near-permanent frown, his lips pressed together in forbearance. It reminded her of that day, weeks ago, when he and his brother had come to her rescue in the aftermath of the stagecoach accident.

Despite herself, Louisa smiled at the memory. Back then she'd thought him so rude and disagreeable. Now she felt she understood him better. She understood his tendencies to solitude, his aversion to polite society. Indeed, in many ways she shared his feelings.

To her, the invitation to Langdale Hall had been as vexing as it had been unexpected. There was little doubt in her mind that Mrs Pearson had orchestrated this sojourn to further Charlotte's marriage prospects, and increasingly she suspected that Mrs Pearson wished to match Isaac with her daughter.

Charlotte might have spent much of the summer encouraging the attentions of Mr Samuel Liddell but, as Aunt Clarissa had once observed, the Pearsons' circumstances meant that Charlotte needed to marry as well as possible. For her mother, a younger son simply would not do.

The thought of spending several days witnessing Mrs Pearson manoeuvring to secure a baronet for her daughter during endless dinners and dances filled Louisa with dread. The idea of Isaac being betrothed to Charlotte made her stomach churn, as did the prospect of spending so much time in his company after that day in his library. After that kiss.

In truth, she was still reeling from it—from its tenderness, from her unguarded response to it. From the way she'd kissed him back. It brought colour to her cheeks each time she thought about it—which she was alarmed to concede was often. Seeing him every day at Langdale Hall would do nothing to help her forget about it.

The carriage jolted on the road, causing Louisa to start. She caught Isaac's eye, saw the sombre way he regarded her, his gaze holding hers for just a moment too long. It occurred to her then that perhaps the prospect of her presence at Langdale Hall was what vexed him, too.

Around noon they stopped at an inn for luncheon, and to change the horses. Louisa followed her aunt out of the carriage, determined to stay close beside her guardian as they went in search of a parlour and some refreshment. Yet Clarissa, it seemed, had other ideas, and before Louisa could intervene Isaac's brother had joined her aunt and they were striding together across the courtyard, leaving Louisa and Isaac behind.

Louisa couldn't help but wonder if that had been deliberate.

'I'm not sure who is livelier—your aunt or my brother,' Isaac said, moving to stand beside her. 'They barely stopped talking enough to draw breath all the way here.'

Louisa looked up at him, forcing a smile in an effort to seem cheerful and serene. She needed to be at her best, she reminded herself, even if she did not feel it. It was a simple matter of duty.

Isaac moved closer, offering his arm, and she felt herself hesitate—not because she did not want to hold on to him, but because she was frightened of what she would feel if she did.

Something in her demeanour must have betrayed her reluctance, because after a moment Isaac's expression darkened and he withdrew. 'Do you not wish to speak to me, Louisa?' he asked. 'Are we to travel in silence all the way to Langdale?'

His directness perturbed her, and she found herself looking away. 'I doubt that very much since, as you say, my aunt and Mr Liddell are both apt to converse. Besides,' she added, 'I have been enjoying the scenery. I seem to recall you did much the same thing yourself, the first time we travelled in a carriage together.'

Isaac grimaced at the recollection. 'Oh, please don't remind me. I must have seemed like the most disagreeable man on earth that day.'

Louisa nodded, sensing the ice between them breaking. 'You did, but it is all right. I know you much better now.'

Isaac grinned at her, apparently warming to her gentle teasing. 'Should I dare to imagine that I have gone up in Miss Louisa Conrad's estimation?'

She returned his smile. 'Well, you do have excellent taste in books,' she retorted playfully. 'What I mean to say is, I can imagine that a muddy, dishevelled woman and her maid clambering into your carriage was probably the very last thing you needed that day.'

'I was actually most concerned that you were injured,' he replied, his expression growing serious once more. 'Every time we hit a bump in the road you clutched at your side.'

She raised her eyebrows at that. Now she understood why he'd been so insistent about sending his physician to attend her. It seemed that Isaac had not been quite as uninterested as he'd appeared, after all.

'I am sorry if I am not an agreeable travelling companion today,' she said softly, slowly walking in the direction in which her aunt and Mr Liddell had headed. 'I am sorry if my aunt and me are an imposition.'

'I have hardly been talkative and full of cheer, have I?' he answered. 'But you must know that you could never be an imposition, Louisa. Contrary to what my sombre countenance might suggest, it is my pleasure to escort you and your aunt to Langdale Hall.'

'Thank you,' Louisa replied, inclining her head politely. 'And you must know that I understand if our visit to Langdale Hall is the reason you are not feeling so cheerful.'

She drew a sharp breath, poised to change the subject. Their brief conversation had been quite candid enough; she was not keen to know where else it might lead.

'Now, let us go and find my aunt and your brother and something to eat. I am very hungry.'

As his carriage made its way along the drive leading to Langdale Hall, Isaac almost found himself breathing a sigh of relief. The journey had been long enough, taking much of the day and leading them into the very heart of Cumberland with its enticing landscape of lakes and mountains.

Usually the sight of such wilderness would be sufficient to preoccupy him for the hours it took to pass along the web of winding, uneven roads, and he would be content to sit there, watching it unfold and admiring its beauty. Instead, he'd begun the journey in a terrible 'black mood', as Samuel would call it, and had barely noticed the scenery outside.

He was still annoyed with his brother for accepting this invitation and for leaving him no choice but to come. The idea of spending several days with the unsubtle Mrs Pearson and her giddy daughter was bad enough—and that was before he even considered how he felt about Louisa's presence there.

How *did* he feel, exactly? He wasn't sure. The sight

of her sitting across from him in his carriage, silent and steadfastly avoiding his gaze, had provoked him, although he was at a loss to explain why. After all, given the way he'd apparently lost his mind in his library that day, and given the way he'd kissed her, the lady could hardly be blamed for wishing to keep her distance from him. Yet despite knowing this he'd found himself craving a look, a glance, even the smallest interaction.

When they'd stopped for lunch and had that brief conversation he'd felt his bad mood begin to lift. He'd even managed to smile. He'd suggested to her that he was glad to escort her to Langdale Hall—a sentiment which he'd been unaware of until he'd put it into words.

It was all very disconcerting and confusing. Ever since that kiss, it was as though all his thoughts and feelings had been thrown up into the air. They were still falling like autumn leaves, and he was still gathering them up and trying to make sense of them. Trying to understand how he could both long for companionship and yet still feel compelled to remain alone. Trying to understand how to reconcile his grief and his loyalty to Rosalind's memory with his growing attraction to Louisa.

That was what it was, he realised—it was attraction. It was more than mere interest…more than friendship. Those things, he knew, did not lead a man such as him to kiss a woman, or to light up in her company the way that he did.

Louisa understood him—that much was clear. She'd observed his foul mood today and known the reason for it—and, what was more, she'd felt moved to tell him that she knew.

*I understand*, she'd said, *if our visit to Langdale Hall is the reason you are not feeling so cheerful.*

When he'd resumed his seat opposite her, after luncheon, he'd begun to wonder whether the prospect of their stay at Langdale discomfited her too. Feeling suddenly anxious to put her at ease, as well as craving more of her conversation, he'd decided to engage her on a topic he knew she would relish, given her love of the subject matter.

'Did you finish reading *Waverley*?' he'd asked.

'Oh, yes,' she'd enthused, a smile spreading across her lovely face. 'I did, and it was wonderful. I could hardly bear to tear myself away from it! I have brought the books with me. They are packed away in my portmanteau, and I will return them to you later.'

The visible joy those books had given her had stirred something deep within himself, and it had taken all the strength he'd been able to muster for him to acknowledge her intention with a serene nod.

Finally the carriage drew to a halt outside the entrance to Langdale Hall. It was an attractive house—too petite to be called a mansion, but nonetheless impressive, with its red brickwork and elegant embellishments around the windows and doorways.

He wondered how the Pearsons managed to maintain a home such as this, given what he knew about their financial circumstances. Then he reminded himself that it was really none of his business. It was his brother who was nursing a great interest in Charlotte Pearson, not him.

Isaac stepped out of the carriage, swiftly turning and offering his hand to Louisa, who he was heartened to see accepted it without any hesitation. He'd been perturbed when she hadn't taken his arm at the inn, as though she was signalling to him that things between them had changed, that they could never return to the easy familiarity they'd enjoyed before that kiss. That had saddened him—although, to his consternation, he'd realised that it did not lead him to regret embracing her that day in his library.

The Pearsons had come outside to greet them, and a whirlwind of pleasantries were exchanged as all four weary travellers disembarked.

Mr Pearson was briskly introduced to Isaac and Samuel. Isaac was amused to note that the portly, red-haired man looked unenthused, wearing the sort of expression a gentleman wore when he desired nothing more than a newspaper, a stiff brandy and some peace and quiet. Confirmation, if it was needed, that this sojourn had not been his idea.

'I do hope Langdale Hall will feel like a home away from home to you, Miss Conrad.'

Mrs Pearson's shrill voice pierced Isaac's thoughts as she addressed Louisa.

'From what your aunt tells me, you live on a large and very grand estate. Is that where you spend much of your time?'

He watched Louisa hesitate, pressing her lips together momentarily before answering. 'Yes, indeed, I prefer to be in the country,' she replied. 'And, as you say, my home is very lovely. I prefer to spend my time there.'

Mrs Pearson raised her eyebrows. 'But you must spend at least some time in town, surely?'

'I seldom go to town, madam,' Louisa answered her quietly.

'But if an unmarried woman does not go to town, how does she expect to find a husband?' Mrs Pearson continued. 'You must give your mother cause to fret.'

Isaac saw a discomfited look flicker across Louisa's face at such an interrogation, and he felt the temperature of his blood begin to rise in indignance. Clearly Mrs Pearson knew nothing of Louisa's bereavement, or if she did she was being unforgivably callous. He wondered why the older lady felt the need to raise the matter at all. What did she hope to gain, other than to make her guest feel uncomfortable?

'I daresay all ladies are entitled to keep their own counsel on such matters, Mrs Pearson,' he said, giving the woman a stern look.

'Indeed, sir, indeed…' Mrs Pearson stuttered, apparently thoroughly taken aback by his intervention. 'I was merely reflecting upon the concern of all mothers, which is to see their daughters married.'

'Hmm…' he responded, unable to quite trust himself to say anything further on the subject.

Certainly, marriage was foremost in Mrs Pearson's mind. He believed that this was why they'd been invited to Langdale Hall, and he suspected, too, that he was the gentleman Mrs Pearson intended to secure for her daughter, not his brother. Well, Mrs Pearson would have to be gravely disappointed in that regard. Frankly, there was more chance of Louisa kissing him again than there was of him marrying Charlotte Pearson.

Where the hell had that thought come from?

The grateful look Louisa gave him was unmistakable. Emboldened by it, he walked over to her, offering his arm once again. She took it, and as they walked together through the front door of Langdale Hall, he brought his other hand to rest ever so briefly over hers. It was a caring gesture, acknowledging her discomfort at Mrs Pearson's line of questioning. But more than that he hoped to convey how defensive he'd felt of her, and how much solidarity he felt with her.

Earlier today she'd let him know that she understood him. Now, more than ever, he wanted her to know that such understanding was mutual. They were, without doubt, kindred spirits—in grief, and in solitude. In the losses they'd borne, and in the terrible circumstances they'd both had to face.

Still, as he walked by her side he suspected that such an affinity could not begin to explain the way he'd felt when his lips had met hers…or, for that matter, what had possessed him to kiss her at all.

## Chapter Nineteen

Dinner that evening was a trying affair, and to her own surprise Louisa began to look forward to the arrival of the other guests the day after next. At least the presence of some less familiar faces might bring fresh possibilities for mealtime conversation.

Tonight, she was seated at the end of the table, next to Mr Pearson, who had little enough to say to her beyond trivialities about the fine weather and the quality of the soup. Unsurprisingly, that well of superficial talk quickly ran dry, and before long Mr Pearson turned to Isaac, and the two men became engrossed in a discussion about business and investments.

Several times Isaac caught her eye, his expression unreadable, as Mr Pearson wittered on about the price of this or that commodity. If he was bored, he did not show it. Truly, he was every inch a gentleman.

Faced with subjects upon which she could hardly hope to converse, Louisa found herself observing the interactions taking place elsewhere. Directly across from her Charlotte looked flushed, the flirtation between her and Mr Liddell so relentless that Louisa felt almost embarrassed to witness their whispers and smiles. Not that they seemed to notice; they were so preoccupied with each other that they barely looked in her direction.

Still, she thought, at least her peripheral position spared her from participating in Mrs Pearson's topic of choice. Even from here she could hear her engaging Aunt Clarissa at length on the favoured subject of her poor health.

Fortunately, after dinner the evening and the opportunities for good conversation seemed to improve. The ladies retired to the drawing room, where they played several hands of whist, while the gentlemen remained in the dining room, no doubt nursing glasses of port.

For whist, Louisa partnered with Charlotte, who thankfully seemed more composed now she was separated from Mr Liddell, although she was as hopeless at the game as Louisa was. Nonetheless, the card game served to occupy her mind, and for the first time in a while Louisa found herself beginning to relax. Perhaps, she reasoned, this visit to Langdale Hall would not be so bad as she'd feared.

The journey earlier today had served to alleviate much of her discomfort about her forced proximity to Isaac. In fact, at the inn and during the final few miles of the carriage ride, she'd found herself remembering just how much she enjoyed his company and his conversation. Just how open and kind he could be.

Furthermore, she had not been able to help the feeling of admiration which had washed over her when he'd stepped in to defend her against Mrs Pearson's onslaught of questions about marriage. He'd done so with such ease and such tact, but he had known what it had meant to her—the way he'd touched her hand afterwards had told her he had. She could only hope that his intervention had been sufficient to ensure that Mrs Pearson would have no more difficult questions for her, although she suspected that was wishful thinking.

'Oh! We lost again!' Charlotte cried out, startling Louisa from her thoughts.

Louisa smiled bashfully. 'I did say I am no good at this game—whereas I happen to know my aunt is particularly skilled at it. Truly, we did not stand a chance, Charlotte.'

Aunt Clarissa clutched her hand to her chest in faux outrage. 'Me? Whatever do you mean, my dear?'

'I mean my mother told me you and she were an unbeatable partnership as young ladies, Aunt,' she replied with a grin.

'It is all about memory,' Mrs Pearson interjected. 'If you are the sort of person who never forgets a detail, then you can be very successful at whist.'

'Which explains why I am hopeless at it,' Charlotte retorted with a giggle. 'I forget everything.'

'Just as long as you remember to do your duty, Charlotte,' her mother replied, giving her a pointed look. 'We can forgive a lack of skill at cards.'

The sharpness of Mrs Pearson's words cut through the jovial atmosphere like a knife, and Louisa was relieved that at that moment the gentlemen walked in to join them. Instinctively she sought out Isaac among them, catching his eye and offering him a small smile in greeting as he approached their table. He smiled back, then quickly adjusted his cravat and smoothed a hand over his dark hair, which was threatening unruliness again.

She thought of the first time she'd seen him on the

cliffs, his clothing and hair thoroughly windswept. She reflected that, as handsome as he looked in evening attire, dishevelment came very easily to him, and she was alarmed to find herself pondering which version of him she preferred. Clearly she'd had too much wine at dinner.

'Shall we retire to the comfortable chairs?' Mrs Pearson suggested, rising from her seat before anyone could answer. 'I will ring for some tea.'

Louisa did as their hostess bade, sitting down beside her aunt on a well-cushioned sofa. It struck her that the drawing room, like the rest of Langdale Hall, was immaculately furnished and decorated. Nothing about the Pearsons' country home suggested that their circumstances were as dire as Aunt Clarissa believed them to be. In which case, Louisa thought, they had to be living far beyond their means...

'So, who won at whist, Miss Conrad?' Isaac asked her as he took a seat on the sofa opposite.

'My aunt and Mrs Pearson—resoundingly,' she replied, inclining her head towards Aunt Clarissa, who was by now engaged in conversation with Mr Pearson. 'I seldom play the game, so there was little hope for Charlotte and me, I'm afraid.'

Isaac nodded. 'I daresay you prefer to spend the evening reading.'

She let out a small laugh. 'You know me well, sir.'

'Indeed, Miss Conrad,' he replied, lowering his voice. 'I believe I do.'

Although the expression on his face was earnest, Louisa found herself colouring at all the possibilities that remark could contain. Of all that it might suggest. He did, after all, know her mind well. But he also knew the taste of her lips…the feel of her body pressed against his. She knew instinctively that he had not been referring to that, and yet somehow, for some reason, that was where her thoughts had taken her.

'That reminds me—I still have your books in my portmanteau,' she said, grasping at any subject to draw her errant mind back from places it ought not to wander. 'I will fetch them for you shortly.'

He smiled. 'There is no hurry. I know they are safe in your keeping, since you treasure the story as much as I do.'

Louisa inclined her head politely before lowering her gaze, realising to her great mortification that she was still blushing. Truly, what had come over her this evening?

'Miss Conrad,' Mrs Pearson called, interrupting her thoughts. 'I had meant to tell you earlier that it seems we have a mutual friend in Berkshire.'

Louisa looked up at her hostess. 'Oh?'

'Yes—one of the Gossamers. Their estate is not far from Reading. I do believe that you know them?'

Louisa's stomach churned at the mention of that familiar name. 'Indeed, we are acquainted.'

'Mrs Gossamer is an old friend from my youth—our family estates were next to each other in Northumberland. We still write to each other frequently. In fact, I mentioned you to her in my most recent letter…' Mrs Pearson paused, giving Louisa a pointed look. 'I received her reply just a few days ago. She sends you her warmest regards.'

Louisa's heart pounded so hard that she could hear its rhythm in her ears. She'd been blushing before, but now her face burned fiercely, and she was sure she must appear crimson to everyone, even in the dim candle-light. A feeling of utter dread washed over her. Terror at the possible nature of the enquiries Mrs Pearson had made about her, and fear at what might have been contained within the reply.

She glanced at Isaac and saw that he was watching her intently, a small frown betraying his concern. She was sure that he'd read her reaction, that he'd seen her horror. He must be wondering what on earth had provoked it.

She gave Mrs Pearson a polite smile, trying her best to recover. 'Thank you,' she replied, relieved that she sounded more serene than she felt. 'Please convey my best wishes to Mrs Gossamer in return.'

Isaac stood on the terrace and drew in a lungful of the cool night air. He stared out absently, barely noticing the moonlit gardens which sprawled before him. It had been a long day and he was exhausted, his limbs heavy and his senses dulled by tiredness and, he conceded, rather liberal quantities of port. Yet the night was young, by polite society's standards, and as a gentleman he could not retire just yet.

A few moments in the fresh air ought to be sufficient to restore him before he returned to join the party. Although the thought of yet more company and conversation made him inwardly groan. He'd had quite enough of Mr Pearson's talk of wild money-making schemes over dinner—and after dinner, for that matter. It was little wonder he'd indulged in more port than was sensible; it had been all he could do to get through it.

He'd have much preferred to talk to Louisa. He'd sought opportunities to engage her at dinner, but Mr

Pearson's monopoly on his attention had made that all but impossible. That had irked him; he'd felt as though she'd been quite neglected. With a prickle of irritation towards their hostess, he'd had to observe that Louisa's peripheral position at the table was largely responsible for that.

After dinner the ladies had departed for the drawing room, and he'd found himself oddly impatient to join them. When finally he had, he'd been pleased to see that Louisa appeared to be enjoying herself, finding an endearing amount of amusement in being thoroughly beaten at whist. Grace in defeat, he'd thought with a smile. Her face had fallen, though, when Mrs Pearson had mentioned their mutual acquaintance.

That had been odd… It was a fairly innocuous topic, and yet Louisa had reacted like someone awaiting a dreaded punchline at their expense, her eyes widening and her cheeks glowing scarlet. Now that he thought about it, that entire brief interaction had been inexplicably strange…

'Ah! There he is, Miss Conrad.'

Hearing Louisa's name caused Isaac to start. He spun around to see his brother standing in the doorway, grinning, his eyes sparkling after an evening of merriment. Next to him stood Louisa, clutching something in her hands. She looked tired, mustering only a small smile as her eyes met his. He suspected that, like him, she'd had quite enough of being in company today.

'I was just taking the air,' Isaac explained, giving them both a polite nod.

'He's hiding, he means,' Samuel quipped, and let out a hearty chuckle.

Isaac flinched, acknowledging that there was some

truth in his brother's remark. It was all right for Samuel. Social situations always seemed to bring out the best in him, and tonight he was undoubtedly in high spirits. Isaac had not failed to notice that Miss Pearson had been very receptive to Samuel's wit and charm over dinner—a fact which had no doubt contributed to his brother's exuberant mood. Indeed, their flirtation had been so overt that everyone must have noted it... including Mrs Pearson.

Perhaps that would put an end to any ideas the young lady's mother might have about matching her daughter with the older brother.

Isaac could only hope.

'Miss Conrad was looking for you, brother,' Samuel continued. 'She has brought you your books.'

Louisa took a step towards him, holding out the three pristine volumes he'd lent to her that day she'd visited Hayton Hall. That day he'd kissed her.

He forced a smile as he moved to accept the books, pushing that particular memory from his mind.

'I am about to retire for the night, but I wanted to make sure you had these back in your possession first,' she explained.

He nodded. 'Thank you, Lou— Miss Conrad,' he replied, inwardly chastising himself for his accidental familiarity when his brother still stood nearby.

Without doubt Samuel had noticed Isaac's slip, flashing him a mischievous look before clearing his throat. 'Well, I am in very great need of some more tea before I retire. Please excuse me—and goodnight, Miss Conrad,' he added, before bowing and swiftly taking his leave.

'You are retiring?' Isaac asked, turning back to Louisa as Samuel disappeared from view. 'Is everything all right? Are you unwell?'

'I have a slight headache,' she replied, 'but it is nothing to worry about. I am sure I will feel restored in the morning.'

He nodded. 'I daresay sleep will help; you must be fatigued after the journey. Please, let me know if there is anything I can do to assist you.'

'Thank you, Isaac, you are always very kind.'

He watched as she hesitated briefly, before continuing.

'I wanted to thank you for intervening earlier today… when Mrs Pearson asked me about marriage.'

Isaac bristled at the recollection. 'I still cannot understand what possessed her to speak to you in such a way. Does she know about your bereavement?'

'I suspect she does,' Louisa replied quietly. 'Charlotte knows a little of the story. I would be surprised if she had not repeated it to her mother.'

Isaac grimaced. 'Then that is even worse.'

Louisa shrugged. 'I suppose not everyone views these matters in the same way. There is still an expectation in our society that gentlemen and women will go on to marry or remarry after such losses.'

'But not you—or me,' he mused, with a conviction he was discomfited to observe he did not feel quite so strongly as he once had.

'Indeed. Anyway,' she said with a slight shiver, 'it is best forgotten.'

She rubbed her arms, clearly beginning to feel the chill of the night air through the thin muslin of her cream evening dress. Without thinking, Isaac put down the books he was holding and removed his tailcoat, draping it over her shoulders before either of them had time to contemplate the intimacy of the gesture, or how the distance had suddenly closed between them. How, momentarily, his hands had come to rest on her shoulders.

Isaac stepped back, clearing his throat. 'You looked cold,' he explained, as though words were needed.

'Thank you.'

He watched as she ran a careful hand over the sturdy blue fabric.

'If ladies could wear these in the evenings, instead of flimsy gowns, we'd certainly be much warmer.'

'You could try doing that,' he suggested, 'although I daresay you really would provoke comment from Mrs Pearson then.'

She let out a soft laugh, her dark eyes alight with amusement. The sound of it, and the sight of her, did strange things to his heart.

Before he could really understand what he was doing, he stepped towards her again. 'We have never spoken about that day in my library,' he said quietly. 'When I kissed you.'

She looked up at him, her expression unreadable. If she was taken aback by his remark she did not show it.

'You promised you would forget about it,' she said. 'We both should.'

'I did promise to forget,' he replied. 'But I must confess that has proved to be difficult. You know how much I have come to value your company and your friendship, Louisa,' he continued, rubbing his forehead with his hand. 'But I find myself wondering if, perhaps, something more than friendship has started to grow between us.'

Louisa shook her head, just slightly. 'Isaac...' she began.

Behind them, the sound of doors opening and the din of voices intruded.

Louisa glanced nervously over her shoulder. 'We must not discuss this now,' she said, hastily removing his coat from her shoulders and handing it back to him. 'I should go. My aunt will expect that I have retired by now.'

She hurried away, leaving him staring after her, clutching his coat in his hand. What the devil had got into him? He had not meant to say those things—he had not meant to express feelings he was still grappling with himself. Yet in those snatched few moments alone with her he'd done exactly that. He could try to blame fatigue, or port, but he knew it was neither. He knew it was the truth.

Since that kiss he'd felt something shift between them, and within himself. Something he felt less and less able to resist.

As the lively chatter of the rest of the party drew nearer Isaac suppressed the urge to groan. What in damnation was he going to do?

## Chapter Twenty

Isaac sat alone in the breakfast room, clutching a cup of tea in his hands. In front of him his plate sat barely touched as he stared out of the window, his thoughts far from the business of eating.

He'd risen late that morning, after a fitful night's sleep, and had come downstairs to discover that his hosts and the other guests had already breakfasted and gone out to enjoy the morning sunshine in the gardens. Quietly, he had been relieved; he was tired, and out of sorts, and some peace to collect his scattered thoughts was exactly what he needed.

Isaac breathed in deeply and picked up a slice of toast, resolving to eat. The way his conversation with Louisa had ended last night had sent his mind into a maelstrom. He still could not fathom what had possessed him to speak the way he had.

After retiring last night, he'd turned the words over and over in his mind, and somewhere during the small hours he'd confronted his own raw honesty about his deepening affection for a woman who'd wandered quite unexpectedly into his life. He'd never thought he'd feel this way again. His heart had been so broken by grief that he'd genuinely believed himself incapable of such feelings.

Now he realised how wrong he'd been. He had not been incapable, merely unwilling. He'd erected defences around his heart…he'd shrouded himself in solitude. He'd allowed that inner voice to rule him, telling him that to remain alone was to honour his wife's memory, that love was a risk too great and that allowing himself happiness was a betrayal. Over the course of a single summer, though, those defences were being eroded, and if last night was any indication there were not many left to fall.

But how did Louisa feel? That question had plagued him for the remainder of the night.

In the library she'd returned his kiss with an ardour she'd been unable to disguise, yet ultimately she'd ended the kiss, reminding him immediately of the impediment to her heart, of her loyalty to the memory of her dead captain. Last night she'd done little more than remind him of his promise to forget the kiss, said that they should both forget it. Did that mean that, like him, she was unable to quash the memory of it?

How he wished they had not been interrupted—that they had been able to talk for a little longer. How he wished to know what else she might have said, if given the chance.

'Good morning, sleepyhead.' Samuel's cheery voice intruded as he walked in, a merry spring notable in his step.

'Good morning, Samuel,' Isaac muttered, pushing away his plate.

'I regret to inform you that while you were slumbering you missed a truly lovely promenade in Mr and

Mrs Pearson's gardens.' Samuel's grin faded as he sat down opposite his brother. 'Isaac, what's amiss? You look wretched.'

'Nothing. I didn't sleep well that's all,' Isaac replied, getting to his feet and avoiding Samuel's scrutinising gaze. 'I suppose I ought to give my apologies for my tardiness. Is everyone still outside?'

Samuel nodded. 'They are. Come, they'll be pleased to see you. Perhaps you might even manage to rouse a smile from Miss Conrad. She looks about as happy as you this morning.'

Isaac ignored his brother's jibe, following him wordlessly into the fine formal gardens which sprawled at the rear of Langdale Hall. He wondered if Louisa was as tired as he was...if she had also had a restless night. His heart sank into the pit of his stomach as he contemplated that his words might have upset her, and that she might not share similar feelings to his at all.

'Oh, Sir Isaac, a very good morning to you!'

Isaac squinted in the bright light as Mrs Pearson made a beeline for him, her daughter following dutifully at her side. The fabric of their immaculate day dresses swished as they approached, parasols in hand to shade them from the glare of the near-midday sun. He had to admit that Miss Pearson looked very becoming in the soft blue she wore, with loose curls of her red hair framing her youthful face. She gave him a pretty smile, which seemed to illuminate the smattering of freckles on her nose. For all that he had never warmed to her giddy demeanour, he had to admit that it was not difficult to see why his brother was so utterly smitten with her.

He inclined his head politely at the two women. 'Mrs

Pearson, Miss Pearson... I do apologise for my lateness this morning.'

'Oh, do not fret, Sir Isaac,' protested Mrs Pearson. 'I trust you slept well?'

He nodded, offering a smile which he hoped would mask his lie. 'I hope you are well this morning, madam?'

'Oh, yes, very well—very well indeed,' gushed Mrs Pearson. 'I feel considerably restored today. Like you, I rose late. My delicate health requires that I sleep a good deal.'

Isaac looked about him. 'And Mr Pearson is also well?' he asked, noticing that the man was not present.

'Indeed, he has gone wandering in the woods,' Mrs Pearson informed him, waving a dismissive hand in the direction of the trees clustered beyond the gardens. Her eyes shifted briefly to her daughter. 'Charlotte wondered if she might give you a tour of the gardens—perhaps show you some of our prized plants.'

Isaac hesitated, glancing at Samuel. He saw a look of confusion flit across his brother's face before he quickly composed himself once more.

Beyond Samuel, and a short distance away, he spotted Louisa walking alongside her aunt. The two women were sauntering at a snail's pace along the path which led to a walled garden. Their backs were turned to him, but he could see from the gentle shake of her aunt's head and the movement of her hands that they were deep in conversation.

He suppressed a sigh, resigning himself to an invitation which politeness dictated he must accept. He thought about Louisa's observation last night, that society was quite content to see widowed gentlemen like him lining up next to eligible bachelors on the marriage mart. Quite frankly, the thought of spending the rest of his days being sought after by ambitious mamas like Mrs Pearson made his toes curl.

Swallowing his misgivings, he offered Miss Pearson his arm. 'I would like that very much,' he replied, forcing another smile.

The sweet fragrances of the flowerbeds combined with the woody scent of conifer hedges to give Louisa a welcome sense of peace. She'd forgotten how much gardens and greenery could soothe her...how she felt better able to cope with her cares and worries after spending time among plants and trees.

At home they had beautiful gardens, carefully planned and every bit as splendid as those at Langdale Hall. Over the past years she'd walked in them daily, in all seasons and weathers, sometimes with others but often alone. Those daily walks had steadied her, had been her anchor when she'd felt the tides of madness and despair trying to sweep her away.

She realised now that her coastal walks in Lowhaven had been a continuation of that habit, although when it came to the walks she'd taken with Isaac, she suspected they had been less about grounding herself and more about wishing to cast her cares away on a sea breeze. About longing to somehow wipe the slate clean and start anew. About enjoying the solace that friendship could bring.

Only somewhere along the line something more complicated than friendship had begun to flourish, hadn't it?

This morning she was neither losing her mind nor at her wits' end, but she was tired and still reeling from the whirlwind of yesterday. The journey to Langdale, the hours spent so close to Isaac, the way his company and conversation had been her favourite things of the day... The way Mrs Pearson had mentioned her friend in Reading, and how that fleeting piece of conversation had opened old wounds. How she'd worn her pain and her panic on her face.

And then the manner in which Isaac had spoken to her last night—his admission that he still thought of that kiss, that he was thinking about more than friendship. She'd been so lost for words that she'd been almost relieved when they were interrupted by the rest of the party. She was all too aware that, despite herself, her feelings for Isaac had grown too, that she regarded him with an affection and an admiration which went far beyond a friendly acquaintance.

She could not deny that she was attracted to him—that he was capable of provoking desires within her that until this summer she'd believed she'd long since suppressed. However, she also knew that this—whatever it was—could go no further. There could be no future for them; her past had seen to that.

She had to talk to him. She had to find the right words to explain herself. She could not reveal any more about her past—telling him about losing Richard had been as far as she'd been prepared to go. But she could assure him of her friendship. She could appeal to their shared knowledge of grief and loss and ask him to understand that, for her, marriage to any man was out of the question. She could make him see that although she cared for him she could not risk falling for him. Because she could only ever be a spinster, not a wife.

'Are you even listening to a word I say?'

Clarissa had turned to face her niece, raising an inquisitive eyebrow at her. Louisa averted her gaze, staring instead at the handful of sparrows pecking at the ground, hunting for their breakfast. Or was it luncheon? Truly, she'd lost all sense of the time.

After a moment the birds flew away; she listened to the gentle flutter of their wings, wishing she could join them. Right now she wanted to be hundreds of miles from here. She wanted to be in the Neapolitan countryside, or on the shores of Lake Geneva, or indeed anywhere but Cumberland or Berkshire.

Cumberland, she realised, had become as suffocating as her home. She'd absorbed too much of it, let it soak through her skin, allowed it to become familiar with her. She thought again about the pointed way that Mrs Pearson had told her they had a mutual acquaintance in Berkshire. The blessed anonymity she'd enjoyed was ebbing away, and the past had got her firmly in its clutches once more.

'Louisa?' her aunt prompted her. 'What is the matter? Are you unwell?'

Louisa shook her head, taking hold of her aunt's arm once more and leading her through the entrance to a pleasing walled garden bursting with floral displays.

'Last night, after dinner, did you hear Mrs Pearson ask me about the Mrs Gossamer?' she asked quietly, hoping the old stone walls surrounding them did not have ears.

'Yes, your mutual acquaintance—I do recall Mrs Pearson mentioning her. Sometimes it's a small world, is it not?' Clarissa's smile dissolved into a frown as she regarded Louisa once more. 'Why do you ask?'

'Mrs Pearson said she'd mentioned me in a letter to

Mrs Gossamer, and that Mrs Gossamer had replied, acknowledging our acquaintance. The Gossamers are related to…' she paused, struggling to form the words '…to Richard, the man I was to wed. He was their nephew. What if—what if Mrs Gossamer spoke of us in her letter?'

The furrow on Aunt Clarissa's brow deepened. 'I don't quite see the problem. Why would it matter if Mrs Pearson knew about your betrothal?'

Louisa huffed out a breath. 'It wouldn't. In fact, I daresay she's already been informed about it by Charlotte, who I rather foolishly confided in a little while ago. But what if Mrs Gossamer has said more than that?' She shot her aunt a meaningful look. 'They are Richard's relations, after all. We met at a ball they hosted, and he was staying with them at the time. They know far more than most about everything that happened between us.'

She watched as Clarissa chewed her lip thoughtfully. 'Perhaps… But, as his relatives, they will surely wish to guard his memory. Try not to fret, my dear. I doubt Mrs Gossamer has said anything in that letter beyond stating that she knows you.'

'I hope you are right.' Louisa sighed again. 'I wouldn't like to think that I've brought trouble to your door…that my reputation might tarnish yours.'

'I'm an old spinster and the daughter of a long-dead clergyman. No one cares a jot about me—which is exactly how I like it.' Clarissa gave her a knowing look. 'What you're really worried about is Sir Isaac knowing your story. That's what is troubling you.'

Louisa raised her eyebrows at her aunt's perceptiveness. 'Perhaps.'

Aunt Clarissa chuckled. 'There's no "perhaps" about it, my dear. I've observed the two of you often enough by now to see the affinity between you for myself.'

'Isaac knows some of my story,' Louisa admitted. 'He knows I was engaged, and he knows about Richard's death.'

'Ah, so the two of you have discussed more than your favourite books, then?' her aunt teased. She held up a defensive hand. 'Fear not. I don't intend to interrogate you again about the exact nature of your acquaintance with the master of Hayton Hall. You made yourself very clear the last time. I do still wonder about his feelings towards you, however. Certainly he seems to enjoy your company more than that of anyone else here.'

Louisa felt herself begin to crumple. 'He has admitted to me that he feels there could be more than friendship between us,' she blurted, feeling the sudden urge to confide in someone she knew she could trust.

Aunt Clarissa's expression grew serious. 'I see. And what did you say?'

'I did not say anything. I did not get an opportunity as our conversation was interrupted.'

Clarissa frowned. 'Well, you must say something, Louisa. What if he offers marriage?'

'You know I could not marry him, Aunt.'

'Then you must find a gentle way to tell him so—a way of explaining yourself which you can both live with. Do you think you can do that?'

Louisa swallowed hard. 'I hope so,' she replied.

'You don't sound sure.'

'I...'

Louisa's words caught in her throat as over Clarissa's shoulder she spied Isaac, walking up the path with Charlotte on his arm. She felt a strange twinge in the pit of her stomach as she observed the smiles on their faces, and in particular Charlotte's unmistakable giggles and admiring glances as he pointed—presumably to different items of horticultural interest around the vast gardens.

The most powerful heat coursed through her— flames of indignation at the sight of Charlotte walking at his side, clutching his arm and gazing admiringly into his eyes. The strength of the feelings the scene provoked in her were alarming, and not at all reasonable. She could never be anything more than his friend. She could never be his wife. She could not begrudge him if ultimately he sought happiness with another.

Clarissa glanced over her shoulder, following her niece's startled gaze. 'Ah, yes,' she said, taking her by the arm and turning her away as they began to walk once more. 'I hope you are certain of your decision, Louisa, because it seems to me that there might soon be someone else vying for Sir Isaac's affections. And I have the distinct feeling that a certain young woman's flirtatiousness paired with her mother's ambitions will be quite a formidable force.'

'Then let us hope that the end of the summer arrives soon,' Louisa replied, blinking away the sting from the tears which had begun to gather in her eyes. 'Because at least then I will not be here to see it.'

## Chapter Twenty-One

Louisa struggled to eat much at luncheon, her stomach turning somersaults each time she caught Isaac's eye. She forced herself to make polite conversation with the rest of the party, even struggling through a lengthy discussion with Mr Pearson, who seemed keen to tell her all about the undulating fortunes of Lowhaven's port.

She listened as he wittered on, doing her best to look interested, although she'd learned much of what he told her already, from Isaac. She pretended to be thoroughly absorbed in the subject of imports and exports, ignoring the painful hammering of her heart in her chest each time her mind wandered to the conversation she knew that she and Isaac needed to have.

It was for the best, she told herself. She would find a way to be clear with him and then, in a day or two she would return to Lowhaven. Shortly thereafter she would travel home. Isaac would become a distant memory, and in time he would forget about her, too.

'So, you see, Glasgow is the place for tobacco now. It has completely taken that trade over from Lowhaven in every respect,' Mr Pearson continued.

'John, you must be thoroughly boring Miss Conrad with all that talk of trade.'

For once, Louisa was grateful for Mrs Pearson's interjection. She watched as her husband's already rosy cheeks deepened their colour, his head wobbling indignantly on his shoulders.

'I'm not sure what you mean,' he objected. 'These are matters which ought to greatly occupy us all. There can be few in this part of Cumberland who are not heavily invested in the fortunes of the port, and...'

'I wonder...' Isaac began, raising his voice above the ensuing argument.

His interjection caused the assembled party to fall silent, and he smiled appreciatively at them before beginning again.

'I wonder if anyone might wish to walk with me this afternoon? I find the country air is very agreeable on such a fine day.'

Louisa felt her breath hitch as those deep blue eyes of his rested on her, making it clear to whom his invitation was primarily directed. She felt her cheeks colour to match Mr Pearson's, then looked away.

'Charlotte will join you,' Mrs Pearson replied, patting her daughter on the hand.

Charlotte nodded her agreement, although Louisa could not help but note her uncharacteristic lack of enthusiasm for the suggestion. It was not at all like Charlotte Pearson to be so quiet.

Isaac smiled at Mrs Pearson, although Louisa noted that the warmth of it did not reach his eyes. 'Delightful, Mrs Pearson. In that case, I am sure my brother would be happy to accompany us also.'

'Indeed I would,' replied Mr Liddell, inclining his head politely at both ladies.

Charlotte uttered some polite words of acquiescence, fixing a less than convincing smile upon her face. Her mother, meanwhile, appeared thoroughly chastened; her lips pursed, her already pale face turning chalk-white.

Little wonder, really, thought Louisa. No one in the room could have failed to notice how adeptly Isaac had side-stepped her blatant attempt at matchmaking.

'In that case Louisa must go, too,' Clarissa interjected, regarding her niece. 'As a companion for Miss Pearson.'

'Of course,' Louisa replied quietly, accepting her duty to Charlotte as she knew she must.

She bristled as she caught Mrs Pearson glaring at her, clearly still displeased at her machinations being thwarted and apparently now regarding Louisa as an obstacle. That was hardly fair, Louisa thought. Her presence was required for propriety's sake, after all. She could hardly refuse, even if she wanted to.

Did she want to?

She was not sure.

For all that she knew she needed to speak to Isaac, she doubted she would get an opportunity with his brother and Charlotte both present. Perhaps, she reasoned, the walk would be good for her, nonetheless. A little fresh air always helped to restore her and to clarify her thoughts, and Louisa felt keenly the need to do both after last night.

'Excellent,' Clarissa replied, a little too enthusiastically, and Louisa suspected that offering her niece as a companion had been motivated by more than propriety. Indeed, it seemed that Mrs Pearson was not the only woman at the table who was intent upon meddling…

'That's settled then,' Isaac said, clasping his hands together and giving such a genuine smile that Louisa could not help but find it endearing.

Immediately she chastised herself for the thought. She needed to be a good deal more resistant to his charms than that if she was going to speak frankly with him. From now on, she reminded herself, it was her head which had to rule her, not her heart.

Isaac was delighted to discover that Miss Pearson was completely out of sorts. The party of four set out at a steady enough pace, but it was not long before the young woman fell behind, complaining that she had a sore ankle and that she was unable to keep up. Samuel, ever dutiful and attentive, stayed with her.

Isaac had to suppress a chuckle at hearing his genuine concern for her welfare, his pondering aloud if they ought to in fact turn back. Truly, his brother was smitten.

Louisa, on the other hand, seemed determined to march ahead. Together they walked along, side by side, the distance between them and the other two growing by the moment. For some time neither of them spoke, both apparently enjoying the pretty sprawl of the surrounding countryside as they made their way up a gentle incline and into the shadow of the mountains and hills beyond.

Isaac allowed himself to steal the occasional glance in her direction, watching as the wind whipped at her skirts and loosened her blonde curls from under her bonnet. As usual she was immaculately dressed, wearing the same patterned pink day dress she'd worn this morning and at luncheon, and protecting herself from any chill wind with a rose-pink spencer. He tried not to notice how the increasingly rocky, uneven path forced her to lift her skirt away from the ground, revealing a hint of the bare skin above her ankle boots.

With some difficulty he averted his eyes, focussing instead upon the horizon, although his mind remained on improper thoughts of what he had seen—and what he had not.

'I do not think Charlotte finds walking quite so agreeable today,' Louisa said, finally breaking the silence.

'Indeed. Although I believe the fresh air agrees with you very well,' he observed. 'You seem very content.'

She inclined her head politely. 'I'm not sure if I could ever be anything but content in surroundings such as these.' She paused, glancing briefly behind her. 'It seems our companions have turned back. Should we join them, do you think?'

Isaac shook his head, not turning around. 'My brother is more than equal to the task of assisting Miss Pearson.'

'It was clear that Mrs Pearson wished for you to accompany Charlotte. She seemed quite put out when you insisted that Mr Liddell would join you.'

'I was hardly going to promenade with Miss Pearson alone, whatever her mother may or may not wish,' Isaac countered with an amused laugh. 'Besides, it is my brother's duty to assist Miss Pearson, since it is he who wishes to court her.'

'I think Mrs Pearson wishes it to be you who is courting her daughter.'

Her directness took him aback. He looked at her, observing the obstinate way she set her jaw, half intent upon the path in front of her, half intent upon—what? Provoking him?

He thought again about their conversation last night…

the way he'd spoken of his feelings. The way that she'd remained silent about hers. Was she trying to tell him something about them now?

'Do you think that I should?' he asked, choosing to answer fire with more fire.

'I think that would hurt your brother, given his obvious attachment to her,' she replied.

'And what about how *you* feel, Louisa?'

Again, she clenched her jaw. She did not look at him. 'We are friends, are we not? I wish for you to be happy, Isaac. Just perhaps… Well, perhaps not with Charlotte Pearson.'

He raised his eyebrows in amusement at her assertion. 'Do you not regard Miss Pearson as being a suitable match for me?'

She glanced at him, a smile pulling at the corners of her mouth. 'With all due respect to Charlotte, I think her excitable nature would drive you to distraction.'

He gave a brisk nod. 'Very perceptive. Fear not, Louisa, my interest does not lie with Miss Pearson, but elsewhere. Indeed, I think I said as much to you last night.'

Isaac watched as she drew a deep breath, realising that his heart was thudding in anticipation of what she might say. He did not wish to vex her, but he had to speak with her honestly, had to understand how she felt. To understand if she might feel the same way as he did. And it had to be now—just the two of them, alone in the countryside, with Miss Pearson and his brother well and truly out of sight. It was possible that they might not get the opportunity to speak like this again.

'I do care for you, Isaac,' she said at length. 'But I cannot be anything more to you than a friend. I decided long ago that I would remain unwed. Surely you must understand why, given all that you have also lost?'

'I do understand,' he agreed, his heart at once sinking at the plain tone of her refusal whilst also being buoyed by her admission that she cared for him. 'I have spent much of the past two years convincing myself that I should remain alone, that love is something to be altogether avoided—feared, even. But nursing such convictions, I have discovered, brings much unhappiness.' He gave her a hopeful glance. 'If we both care for each other, then perhaps that is something we ought to embrace.'

She gave a slight shake of her head. 'It is not possible, Isaac. I came to Cumberland to visit my aunt for the summer, and I will be going home to Berkshire soon. We will be hundreds of miles apart. Indeed, we are unlikely to ever see each other again.'

'You do not have to go,' he ventured, his throat suddenly dry at the prospect of her departure. 'That day on the cliffs when you told me about Richard, you said how much you liked it that hardly anyone here knows your story. Perhaps that anonymity has afforded you the fresh start you needed. Perhaps the distance between you and Berkshire has liberated you. Perhaps it has helped you to move on.'

'But the past is always there, Isaac,' she replied. 'You know that as well as I do. Surely that was why you were content with my friendship? Because, like me, you could not truly countenance anything else?'

'Even asking for your friendship was a considerable step forward for me,' he admitted. 'After Rosalind died, for the longest time it was as though I had died, too. I wallowed in my library. I drank too much and ate too little. And I saw no one but my servants. But over time I began to remember that I am in fact alive, and moreover I began to want to live. This summer, for the first time in two years, I have lived a full and happy life. I have been dancing, I have visited my tenants, I have enjoyed tea and conversation in parlours and I have walked arm in arm on the clifftops with a captivating woman.'

He smiled bashfully at his own frankness.

'The past is always there,' he said. 'But so is the future. It seems to me that what has grown between us this summer represents another chance of happiness, if only we will take it.'

They halted as a stream crossed their path, its fast waters flowing noisily over the stones it had carried down from the nearby peaks. Isaac glanced up, noticing how heavy grey clouds had started to gather on the hilltops, and he wondered how much time they had left. He leapt over the stream before turning back and extending his hand towards Louisa, indicating that he would help her. He bristled to see her hesitate, glancing down first at the stream and then at her skirts, as if to assess the situation for herself.

After a moment, and apparently accepting that she had no viable alternative, she hitched up her skirt slightly with one hand and grasped his hand with the other, before leaping towards him. She reached the other side, narrowly missing the water's edge and losing her footing, causing her to stumble.

Instinctively Isaac caught her, and found duty dissolving quickly into pleasure as he grew conscious of his own hands upon her slim waist. Despite his better judgement he did not release her once he felt her feet become steady on the ground. Instead, he allowed his arms to encircle her, pulling her closer to him. To his surprise she did not resist. At first her hands pressed against his chest, before moving up on to his shoulders. Her dark eyes gazed into his, the tips of their noses touched, their lips were barely an inch apart…

'Isaac…' she began.

He pressed his mouth against hers, stemming the flow of her words. The kiss was as fierce as it was urgent, and the strength of his ardour surprised even himself. Even more disarming was the way Louisa responded in kind, looping her arms around his neck, her body clinging tightly to his.

Even through his frock coat he was aware of every detail of her petite, alluring form, from the legs he'd glimpsed earlier brushing his to the soft curve of her breasts pressed against his chest. His heart pounded as desirous thoughts ran unbidden through his mind, warming the blood in every part of him.

Around them the wind continued its frenzied dance, and behind them the stream continued its ceaseless babbling. Time marched on even as he willed it to stop, willed it to suspend them both in this perfect, delicious union. Alas, he knew it would not. He knew that words must be spoken…that questions must be answered.

'Please stay in Cumberland, if only for a while longer,' he breathed. 'Being with you this summer has made me see my life clearly—made me see that I've allowed my grief to cast its shadow over everything for too long. Being with you has made me confront what it is that I truly want, and it is not to be miserable and alone. I want laughter and conversation, companionship and affection. I do not want to forget the past. I want to live with it rather than allowing it to rule me. My brother once said to me that Rosalind would have wanted me to be happy. At the time he made me angry, but he was right—she would. And I believe Richard would have wanted only happiness for you, too.'

'It is not as simple as that…'

She pulled away from him, stepping back towards the water as though she might turn and flee at any moment. The look of horror on her face in response to his honesty made his heart lurch.

'I do not understand,' he began, shaking his head. 'You have said that you care for me. I did not realise that the admission of my feelings would be quite so unwelcome.'

'I do not mean to offend you…' She paused, her lip trembling as tears welled in her eyes. 'I do care for you, Isaac. Please believe that.'

He stepped towards her again. 'Then do not deny yourself happiness, Louisa. You deserve so much more than to do that.'

'I do not deserve anything,' she replied, tears running unabated down her cheeks. 'I care for you, but this…this affection between us—it must cease. I cannot allow myself to love you, Isaac, and for your own sake you cannot love me. I am not the sort of woman you should have in your life.'

He frowned. 'I do not understand. What does that mean? Are you trying to tell me that your objection to me is about more than your lost sea captain?'

She shook her head. 'I am sorry, Isaac. I cannot explain…'

'The devil you can't!' he replied, his frustration growing. 'Surely you must know by now that you can trust me, Louisa,' he continued, doing his best to soften his tone. 'If there is more to your story than I know, then please tell me. Tell me whatever it is, so that I can assure you that it makes no difference to how I feel.'

Those brown eyes stared into his, and he watched as she bit her trembling lip, trying to regain some modicum of control. 'I am sorry, Isaac, but I will never be able to bring myself to say those words to you.'

'I see,' he said, his voice grave. 'Then you are a coward, Louisa. Plain and simple.'

Overhead the sky had darkened further, and the thick clouds seemed to beckon the low but persistent rumbles which could be heard in the distance. Isaac let out a sigh of resignation, his mood blackening like the weather as he realised there was nothing more he could say to her. He cared for her, and she cared for him, and yet it seemed he was doomed to lose her without even understanding why.

'Come,' he said grimly. 'Let's make haste and return to Langdale. There is a storm brewing.'

## *Chapter Twenty-Two*

Just as Isaac had predicted, a storm did indeed arrive, bringing heavy rain which battered Langdale Hall's windows, and thunderclaps loud enough to set everyone's nerves on edge during dinner. Not that the inclement weather was the only reason that tension hung in the air—as Louisa knew only too well.

Dinner was a torturous affair. The sight of Isaac seated across the table from her, immaculately dressed in his deep blue tailcoat, made Louisa's breath catch in her throat and her heart race.

She was far beyond the point of being able to deny her feelings for him, even to herself. She cared deeply for him and was hopelessly attracted to him. Her eyes sought him every time she entered a room. She craved his attention, his conversation. His embrace. Worse still, she now knew the depth of the regard he had for her. She'd heard it in his every word today, felt it in that kiss. And yet those feelings were all for nought. There could not be any future in what they felt for each other.

As she sat at that table, sipping her wine and wishing she could muster an appetite for the food in front of her, it occurred to Louisa how different this was from her attachment to Richard. Back then she'd been so youthful, so simplistic about love. She'd also been naïve, trusting in that affection as it carried her along, never thinking it would bring her such heartache. Now she knew better. Indeed, it was that awareness, that experience, which made her involvement with Isaac so complicated.

Standing by that stream, with the sky looming thunderously above them, she had so desperately wished she could tell him everything—that she could trust her feelings just as she had all those years ago. Knowing she could not…knowing how the truth would only serve to condemn her in his eyes and confirm that they were lost to each other…was as painful as refusing his affection had been.

There had been no good choices today—but then, Louisa reflected, that had been the case for her for a very long time.

After dinner, Louisa retired to the drawing room, occupying a window seat away from her aunt and the Pearson ladies and nursing a cup of tea. She watched absently as bolts of lightning lit up the black night sky, making a pretence of being fascinated by the spectacle so that she might remain undisturbed. She was not in the mood for light conversation tonight.

The gentlemen hadn't joined them yet, clearly preferring to remain around the table with their glasses of port—a fact which Charlotte had remarked upon several times in as many minutes, her head bobbing up and down to look at the door.

She'd seemed uncharacteristically on edge ever since returning from her walk, and Louisa had caught enough of the whispers exchanged between her and her mother to surmise that the outing had not proceeded according to either of their plans. If she'd been in a better state of mind Louisa might have tried to speak to Charlotte herself, to discover what was amiss. As it was, she found herself still consumed by the events of her own afternoon, replaying them over and over, tormenting herself with every last detail.

The way Isaac had spoken of his feelings for her. The way he'd kissed her. The way he'd insisted that whatever had happened in her past did not matter.

That final declaration had torn the ground from beneath her feet. How could he say that when he did not know the nature of what he so readily dismissed?

A gentleman like Sir Isaac Liddell could not love a woman like her; it was out of the question. Even if he could care for her in spite of her past, his association with her would taint him and his good name. The whiff of scandal would plague them for ever. It would destroy her. It would destroy them both.

No, she reminded herself. Of course she could not tell him. She could not risk ruining herself further, or seeing the light go out in his eyes when he regarded her. It was better this way, even if it meant Isaac thinking that she was a coward. Better that than him thinking she was a scandalous woman.

'Are you all right, my dear?'

The kindly face of Aunt Clarissa looking down at her startled Louisa from her thoughts. She nodded, forcing a smile for good measure as her aunt sat down beside her.

'Mrs Pearson and Miss Pearson are going to retire for the evening,' she said, as both ladies departed from the room with the briefest and, it seemed to Louisa, the most curt of farewells.

'Charlotte has not seemed happy this evening,' Louisa observed, once the door had closed behind them.

'Nor have you,' Clarissa countered.

Louisa inclined her head, deciding not to deny it. 'I daresay Charlotte's reasons are different from my own.'

'Or perhaps not, since I suspect both of you have reasons that are rooted in your feelings for a certain pair of brothers.' She patted her niece on the hand. 'Come, we are alone, and I think the gentlemen are unlikely to join us now. Tell me what happened.'

'I spoke to Sir Isaac earlier today. I made it clear that we could not be more than friends.'

Clarissa's eyes widened. 'Oh, I see. And what did he say?'

'He left me in no doubt about the depth of his feelings for me.' Louisa felt her lip begin to tremble, her fraught feelings bubbling to the surface once more. She tried to quash them, but to no avail. 'He spoke so honestly, Aunt, and I am afraid I said more than I wished to when I refused him.'

'Did you tell him about your…about all that happened?' Clarissa asked, lowering her voice to a whisper as she chose her words carefully.

Louisa shook her head. 'I could not bring myself to. He knows there is more to my past than losing Richard, but that is all. He told me that whatever happened doesn't matter to him, but surely that cannot be true?'

Clarissa frowned. 'Sir Isaac is no starry-eyed youth, Louisa. He is a respectable gentleman. If he has given his word to you, then what reason do you have to disbelieve him?'

'His respectability and status are the very reasons

why I would be entirely unsuitable for him, Aunt—you must see that.'

'Oh, my dear, perhaps it would have been better if you'd just told him and let him judge the situation for himself,' Clarissa replied.

'Please do not be angry with me, Aunt,' Louisa replied, sobbing. 'I could not do it. I could not bring myself to tell him. What possible good could come from him knowing? All it would do is serve to ruin me all over again—this time in his eyes.'

Clarissa placed a comforting hand on Louisa's shoulder. 'You have a lot of regard for the opinion of a gentleman you once claimed barely to know,' she observed, giving her niece a knowing look. 'I'm not angry with you, my dear. I am saddened, though. Your summer in Lowhaven has not turned out as I'd hoped. I wanted you to leave here with a lighter spirit and a spring in your step, not weighed down by more difficulties.'

'Oh, but I have enjoyed my time here with you,' Louisa said, sniffing as she finally brought her tears under control.

'Yes, but it has not been the respite that I wished for. I wanted Lowhaven to be an escape for you...to be somewhere you could feel free from the past, even if only for a month or two. And, rather selfishly, I had hoped you'd grow to love it so much that you might wish to stay.' Clarissa paused, a watery smile spreading across her thin face. 'Your company has brought me great comfort these past weeks. It is not an easy thing, to be on your own. That is something you will learn, Louisa,' she added pointedly.

'I admit I have much to learn when it comes to being independent. But if I have learned anything in Lowhaven it's that I cannot run from the past, no matter how much I might wish to, or how hard I might try. I will live with its consequences for the rest of my life. And the only way I can do that is on my own.'

'And in doing so you are prepared to deny yourself love?'

Louisa wiped her eyes with a firm and steady hand. She had shed enough tears today. 'Fate has denied me love, Aunt,' she replied. 'God has denied me love. Napoleon himself denied me love when he took Richard from me. I lost all hope of love a long time ago.'

'I'm the wrong brother, Isaac. That's the problem. I'm the wrong brother…'

Isaac sat at the dining table with Samuel, the pair of them finishing off what had once been a healthy decanter of brandy. Mr Pearson had departed a few moments earlier, summoned to bed by his wife, and, rescued from the need to sustain an interminable conversation about investments, or gambling, or some other gentlemanly pursuit, the brothers had seized the chance to speak frankly for the first time in days.

Samuel had started first, his tongue loosened by drink and his heart apparently sore after today's ill-fated promenade with Miss Pearson.

'She has as good as told me that I must end my pursuit of her,' Samuel said miserably. 'She's made it clear that her father will not permit any such courtship, and has declared she is not ready to marry. She said that her mother plans to take her to London soon, so that she might experience "proper society", and that it will be a long time before she will return.'

'This is the mother's doing,' Isaac replied, before

gulping down another generous measure of the strong drink. 'A typical ambitious mama, if ever I've seen one.'

'Indeed… Why have the younger brother when you could have the baronet?' Samuel replied, and the bitterness was unmistakable in his voice.

Isaac raised his eyebrows at that. 'Mrs Pearson's efforts to foist her daughter on me have not gone unnoticed, brother, but I can assure you I am completely indifferent to that young woman. Let them try their luck in London, for they shall have none here. I am bone-weary of the female heart,' he added sourly.

'Oh? Pray tell, brother, which female heart has so grievously wounded you? Dare I suppose that it is the heart of a certain Miss Conrad to which you are referring?'

Isaac groaned, rubbing his temples with his fingers. 'I have told Miss Conrad that I care for her,' he admitted.

Samuel sat bolt upright. 'Good heavens, why on earth did you do that?' A mischievous grin spread across his face. 'I knew there was something between the two of you—although I did not imagine for one moment that you'd reached the stage of professing your undying love.'

'I most certainly did not do that—and besides, there isn't anything between us,' Isaac replied, shaking his head. 'She told me that anything more than friendship is impossible.'

Samuel's face fell. 'Really? Why?'

Isaac hesitated. As miserable as Louisa had made him, he could not stop himself from feeling protective towards her. 'It transpires that a number of years ago she had a fiancé—a naval captain who was killed fighting

Napoleon. It seems that her grief still troubles her,' he explained, settling on telling half the story.

The half he knew, he reminded himself, since the rest remained mere conjecture. Mere imagination, since she had given nothing away.

Samuel frowned. 'But you are a widower, and you are clearly prepared to remarry.'

'Perhaps there is more to the story than Lou—than Miss Conrad is willing to say,' Isaac replied, feigning a nonchalant shrug. 'Or perhaps she really is quite content to be alone, whereas I am not. I quite despise it, if the truth be told.'

'Then let that be the lesson here, brother,' Samuel said, refilling both their glasses. 'If meeting Miss Conrad has made you realise that you want a wife, then a wife is what you must find.'

He paused, holding his glass up in front of him as though considering its contents.

'I have seen a change in you this summer, Isaac. And if some of that is because of Miss Conrad then, frankly, we ought to thank her. You must keep moving forward now. If you do not want to be alone, then do not remain alone. If Miss Conrad will not have you, then you must find a woman who will.'

He took an enormous gulp of brandy, almost draining the glass in one swift movement.

'But not Miss Pearson, because I would never forgive you.'

Isaac laughed. Despite the trials of the day, the brandy-fuelled conversation with his brother had somewhat lightened his spirit.

'You've clearly drunk too much of this, Samuel,' he said, waving his glass, 'if it is giving you wild ideas about Miss Pearson and me.' He drew a deep breath, not quite able to believe what he was about to say. 'You are right, though, about me finding a wife. I think it is time I made a concerted effort to remarry—for companionship, yes, but also to fulfil my duty to this family. I am not getting any younger, and we Liddells need sons and daughters if we are to survive.'

Samuel rested his chin on his hands, giving Isaac a considered look. 'And what about love?' he asked.

Love. Indeed, Isaac thought, what about it? Love had been the sight of Rosalind, dressed in white, walking down the aisle towards him. It had been the smile on her face as she'd patted her swollen belly. It had been the cold clamminess of her hands as she'd gripped the bedsheets and clung to the hope of living.

This summer he'd come to hope for love once more—only to have those hopes dashed in the midst of the Cumberland countryside by a woman who'd wept as she'd rejected him. A woman who cared for him but could not bring herself to tell him the truth about her past.

All love seemed to have done, Isaac thought, was break his heart.

He gulped down the last of his brandy. 'Perhaps, brother, I've had quite enough of love,' he replied.

## Chapter Twenty-Three

Louisa sat beside her aunt in the drawing room, running her finger absentmindedly over the rim of her wine glass and paying little attention to the surrounding conversation. The party had assembled for dinner, dressed in their finest clothes as they awaited the arrival of the handful of further guests who would be attending for the evening. Two had just joined them—a Mr and Mrs Sutton of Ashwell Park—and a further three were apparently expected at any moment.

Louisa suppressed a shiver, feeling cold in the pale blue muslin gown Nan had packed for her. She leaned towards the fire, grateful for its heat. She'd declined to have much involvement in the selection of her dresses—a decision she now regretted. Sometimes, she reflected, she could be her own worst enemy.

The day had passed quickly, with most of the household preoccupied with preparations for the evening's festivities. Keen to keep out of the way, Louisa had embraced the excuse to keep to her room as much as possible, busying herself with her books until the appointed hour, at which time a maid had arrived to help her dress for dinner.

She had not spoken to Isaac since they'd returned from their walk yesterday, their interactions having been restricted to polite nods of acknowledgement at mealtimes. She had noticed his sombre countenance whenever their eyes met over the dining table, and she didn't doubt that she looked just as unhappy. Being in the same room with him had become such torture that she longed to return to Lowhaven. Except, she reminded herself, it was Isaac's carriage which would take her back tomorrow.

The very thought of spending so many hours sitting close to him, after all that had passed between them, made her chest tighten and her stomach churn. She had no idea how she was going to bear it.

'Miss Howarth, Miss Conrad...may I present Mr and Mrs Edmund Cole and their daughter, Miss Carolyn Cole?' Mr Pearson said, interrupting her thoughts.

Louisa got to her feet, inclining her head politely at the final guests to arrive. Mr and Mrs Cole acknowledged her stiffly, before turning back to be introduced to Isaac, who had now joined the party in the drawing room. Their daughter, however, gave her a warm and hopeful smile. She seemed young, perhaps even younger than Charlotte, her green eyes filled with the anxious wonder of a woman not long out in society.

Louisa smiled in return, musing on the composition of the assembled party. The small size of it struck her, as did the obvious omission of eligible young gentlemen. It was a clear indication that Mrs Pearson's schemes had indeed been focussed upon securing one of the Liddell brothers for her daughter, and Louisa had well-founded suspicions as to which one she preferred.

Her smile dissolved as she spotted Charlotte sitting

quietly beside her mother, looking unmistakably glum. She wondered again what might have happened to provoke such a change in her, and felt a stab of guilt that she had not tried to find out.

'Are you quite well, Miss Conrad?' Miss Cole asked her. 'You look a little uncomfortable.'

'Oh, yes I am well…just a little cold in this dress,' Louisa replied as smoothly as she could manage. 'It seems I am not yet acclimatised to summer in Cumberland. I am visiting from Berkshire, you see.'

The young woman's eyes widened. 'Indeed! I daresay it is warmer in the south, though I have never been. I should be so happy to go—especially to London. I suppose you will have been to London many times?'

Louisa laughed, finding it hard not to be encouraged by Miss Cole's enthusiasm. It was hard to remember how exciting a prospect London had seemed to her at one time. 'Yes, although these days I prefer life in the country. It is possible to tire of town, after a while.'

'Oh, I don't believe that! Cumberland is so dull that I hardly think I could be anything but merry in London,' Miss Cole gushed.

Louisa smiled, and without even thinking found herself gazing over the young woman's shoulder towards Isaac. She drank in the details of him, from his immaculate deep blue tailcoat and crisp white cravat to the curl of his dark hair, which had been tamed into order.

As though sensing her looking, he turned his head, and for a moment their eyes met. She watched as feigned indifference melted into curiosity, and felt a familiar heat rise in her belly as the hue of those blue eyes deepened with desire. She looked away, unable to bear the intensity in them a moment longer. Unable to bear the longing his stare had conveyed. Unable to bear knowing just how much he cared for her when his affection was futile.

'I find that Cumberland could be described in many ways,' she replied, recovering herself, 'but in my experience "dull" is most certainly not one of them.'

Dinner was announced, and the party made their way into the dining room to find their seats. Louisa found herself hoping that she might be seated near to Miss Cole. The young woman had a pleasant and easy manner about her, and the sort of light conversation she would doubtless offer would make this difficult final evening at Langdale Hall more bearable.

Alas she was not, and furthermore Louisa's bad luck was Charlotte's good fortune, since the young ladies had been placed opposite each other at one end of the table. Suppressing a sigh, she continued to peruse the name plates, hoping that at the very least she'd been placed near to her aunt. Heaven forbid that she should have to endure another meal beside Mr Pearson...

'You are at the other end, Miss Conrad, beside my brother,' Mr Liddell called over to her, with an unmistakably mischievous smile.

Louisa nodded, trying to conceal her alarm at the placement. She watched as Samuel Liddell rested a hand upon his own seat, beside Charlotte, arching her eyebrows as Charlotte immediately turned away from him with a look of haughty indifference. It was quite a change from the ceaseless flirtation of recent days, and Louisa could not mistake the look of hurt as it flickered across Mr Liddell's face.

Something indeed was terribly amiss.

'Forgive me, Miss Conrad, I do believe my brother

has swapped the name plates.' Isaac spoke discreetly, his low voice behind her making her stomach flip. 'I am sure we can change it if you like.'

'It is fine,' Louisa replied, in an equally hushed tone. 'I daresay your brother has his reasons for the change, although I fear his suit does not fare well.'

'Indeed,' replied Isaac, his eyes momentarily shifting towards Mr Liddell. 'It seems that neither of us has had much recent success when it comes to matters of the heart.'

Louisa stared at him open-mouthed, unsure how to retort. It seemed that tonight she did not have the monopoly on forthright remarks.

She watched, dumbstruck, as Isaac turned his attention to Mrs Pearson, giving her the most magnanimous smile.

'I must compliment you on your table settings, madam,' he said.

Mrs Pearson beamed at him, although her smile quickly faded as she observed Louisa taking her seat at Isaac's side. A seat Louisa had not even wanted. And now, thanks to Mr Liddell's meddling, she had provoked Mrs Pearson's ire once more.

Louisa sipped her wine, trying to ignore how her senses were heightened with awareness at Isaac sitting so close to her. Trying not to remember the warm feeling of him as he'd wrapped her in his arms and kissed her beside that stream. Trying not to think about just how much she wished she could reach out now, touch his hand and tell him that she would be his.

Truly, she thought miserably, tomorrow could not come soon enough.

\* \* \*

The sight of her in that sky-blue dress was positively arresting. From the moment he had spotted her coming down the stairs he had been unable to tear his eyes away from her. All the resolutions he'd made during his conversation with Samuel the previous night had immediately fled from his mind, his thoughts fixed instead upon the glow of her fair skin, bared by a plunging neckline and short sleeves, and the neat curve of her waist as the floaty fabric skimmed over it.

Unable to entirely trust himself, he'd not followed her into the drawing room, but lingered instead in the hall, feigning interest in the portraits on the wall. Now she sat beside him at dinner, her familiar lavender scent wafting beguilingly towards him, haunting his senses, provoking his memories. How foolish he'd been to think that he could simply set aside his feelings for her and seek someone else. How awful he'd been to consider a union without love.

If he could not have Louisa he would have no one else.

'The game is very good, is it not, Sir Isaac?' Louisa asked, nodding approvingly at her fork.

He agreed, then continued with his own meal. Conversation between them was stilted, at best, and he wondered if she too was trying to maintain her composure in the presence of so many listening ears. Certainly, Louisa's aunt seemed to be paying close attention whenever they spoke to each other. He wondered how much her guardian knew about their involvement this summer.

'I daresay that here in Cumberland we have the finest fare—wouldn't you agree, Miss Conrad?' Mrs Pearson asked, having clearly caught Louisa's remark.

'I would certainly agree, Mrs Pearson,' Louisa replied. 'There are many things I will miss about Cumberland when I return to Berkshire.'

'Chief among them are my cook's cakes, I should think,' her aunt interjected, provoking a few murmurs of amusement around the table.

'I imagine you will miss the beautiful scenery as well, Miss Conrad,' Mrs Pearson continued. 'Indeed, you must have spent a long while enjoying it yesterday, since I hear that neither you nor Sir Isaac returned to Langdale for some time after Mr Liddell escorted Charlotte home with her injured ankle.'

The woman paused, staring at Louisa, her expression impassive as she let the damning insinuation her words contained sink in around the table.

'Charlotte feared you had both become lost, after you continued walking. She said you were completely out of sight,' she added, apparently for good measure.

Isaac felt the heat of indignation rise in his chest. He could not believe what he had just heard—could not believe that Mrs Pearson had the audacity to sit at the dining table and make such thinly veiled scandalous accusations for all her guests to hear.

It was bad enough to hear such suggestions being made about *him*, to have *his* honour called into question, but as a gentleman he knew he would survive it. For a lady like Louisa reputation was everything—once ruined, it could never be recovered. Such was the cruelty and such was the difference in standards applied to men and women by so-called polite society.

Isaac glanced at Louisa, saw how her cheeks had reddened and her eyes had widened in horror. It was true that they had been alone together yesterday. They had talked of their feelings. They had embraced. But Mrs Pearson could not and would not know anything of that. He would make sure of it.

'I'm afraid you are mistaken, madam,' he replied, meeting her eye with a cool and steady gaze. 'Miss Conrad and I turned back immediately. However, Miss Conrad had twisted her ankle on the rocky path, and had to rest, which meant we returned to Langdale a few moments after my brother and Miss Pearson did.'

He watched as the older woman's nostrils flared. 'That is not what I was given to understand...' she began.

'Perhaps Miss Pearson's recollection is not complete, given she was in such discomfort. But I can assure you we never lost sight of either Miss Pearson or my brother.' Isaac turned to Samuel, who was regarding him carefully, his fork poised in his hand. 'Indeed, did I not wave to you several times, brother, to assure you we were just a little way behind?'

'Yes,' Samuel replied seamlessly. 'That is correct.'

Isaac gave Mrs Pearson a satisfied smile. 'I hope this eases your mind, madam. I'm sure that, as her guardian, Miss Howarth appreciates your concern for her niece.' He glanced at Louisa's aunt, who looked thoroughly dismayed at what was unfolding before her. 'It is regrettable that sometimes accidents happen...especially in the countryside. However, I can assure you both that Miss Conrad was appropriately attended throughout the entire short promenade. You have my word as a gentleman.'

Briefly he regarded Louisa. She acknowledged his explanation, inclining her head gracefully, and he felt another wave of protectiveness grip him as he noted the look of sheer relief in her eyes. How he wished he could reach out and place his hand over hers, reassure her that all was well, that he would always be there for her. That he would not allow the likes of Mrs Pearson and her spiteful tongue to harm her. That he wanted to care for her always, if only she would let him.

Around the table his final remarks were being met with murmurs of agreement about how dangerous the paths could be, and how regrettably commonplace such injuries were. Mrs Pearson, however, looked rather as if she had just swallowed a lemon. He watched as the woman exchanged a glance with her daughter. Whatever the look communicated, it seemed sufficient to wipe the small smile from the younger lady's face.

He suppressed a wave of irritation at their behaviour. How glad he would be to be away from these Pearsons and their scheming ways.

Hopefully Samuel's heartache concerning the daughter would be short-lived.

Hopefully, his own would be, too, although somehow he doubted it.

After their meal was finished, the party retired swiftly to the drawing room for drinks and dancing. It seemed that during dinner Louisa's aunt had been persuaded to do the honours on the pianoforte, and despite her mild protestations of being out of practice, before long she was delighting them all with a merry tune from her repertoire.

Isaac watched with some amusement as Samuel keenly assembled the dancers, persuading first the Suttons and then the Coles to participate in a dance. To his surprise, his brother then approached Miss Cole and requested a dance, and he watched as she accepted his hand with a shy smile. On the other side of the room the Pearsons had gathered, watching the festivities unfold, clutching glasses of wine as red as their faces.

It would have been an uncomfortable scene if it had not been so thoroughly deserved.

'Won't you dance, brother?' Samuel asked him.

'I hardly think Miss Pearson looks in the mood to take a turn,' he replied, making the observation quietly enough so as not to be overheard.

'What about Miss Conrad?' Samuel persisted.

'I believe she is turning the pages for her aunt,' he replied, inclining his head to where Louisa stood by the piano.

'I daresay someone else could do that,' Samuel said, raising his voice. 'What do you say, Miss Howarth? Could you spare your niece so that she may dance with my brother?'

'Gladly, sir,' Louisa's aunt replied. 'It is surely the duty of all young people to be dancing on such an occasion, is it not?'

Isaac did not miss the wily look the woman gave her niece, and nor did he miss the look of consternation Louisa gave her aunt in return. He strode towards her, holding out his hand and giving her the broadest smile.

Perhaps it was the wine, or perhaps it was the breath-taking sight of Louisa in that pale blue dress, but something emboldened him—made him determined to charm her once more. It was as though this summer, each clifftop walk, each conversation, each kiss, had led them to this dance. To spending a few final, fleeting moments in each other's arms, quietly acknowledging all that had passed between them and all that could never be.

'Pray tell us, brother, what dance would you have us perform?' Isaac asked, as Louisa accepted his hand.

Her touch seemed to set his fingers alight, and he found himself swallowing hard, grappling with the sudden tide of emotion which threatened to overwhelm him.

Samuel grinned at him, clearly enjoying himself. 'I had thought a country dance, but in truth I am now minded towards a waltz.'

Miss Cole's eyes widened, and Samuel smiled at her with what could only be described as rakish charm. For a moment Isaac almost pitied her. She was young, and only just entering society, and he hoped that his brother was not simply suggesting the performance of such an intimate dance in order to make Miss Pearson jealous.

Although if that was his intention it seemed to be working. Miss Pearson still hovered on the periphery of the room, looking completely put out, whilst her mother's pinched face had turned white with anger. Still, he thought, conscious again of Louisa's hand resting in his, he could not concern himself with his brother's romantic entanglements—not when he had such an insurmountable one of his own. How his heart would survive waltzing with her, he did not know.

Miss Howarth began to play, and the couples took their positions in the centre of the room. He smiled warmly at Louisa, trying his best to compose himself, to calm his racing heart. Louisa, however, looked worried, casting her eyes down and chewing intently upon her bottom lip.

Isaac felt his resolve begin to waver. 'What is the matter, Louisa?' he whispered.

'I don't believe I know the steps,' she admitted with a heavy sigh. 'It has been a long time since…'

Her voice faltered, but he knew her meaning well enough.

Isaac smiled again, taking his position at her side and holding her hands in his. The last time he had danced a waltz it had been with Rosalind. How many lifetimes ago that felt now.

'Please do not worry,' he said. 'Just follow my lead and all will be well.'

Tentatively he led her through the first few marching steps before turning to face her, their eyes meeting as he took one of her hands in his, above her head, and placed his other hand upon her waist. The feeling of her form curving below his fingers took his mind back to their country walk, and his blood heated with thoughts of the embrace they'd shared the previous day.

Louisa's hand came to rest on his shoulder, and if he'd been warm before, now his flesh was searing at the temptation offered by her touch. She looked up, those brown eyes bewitching him, daring him to hold her gaze, to be this close and yet not kiss her.

They turned and turned again, melded together, fixed on each other, not caring if the room around them was empty or full, not concerned about whether everyone or no one was watching. It had been a long time since Isaac had felt so light, so uncontrolled.

'Thank you for what you said earlier,' Louisa said quietly. 'To Mrs Pearson…about our walk. What she was suggesting…it was…'

'Let us not speak of her now,' Isaac murmured.

He felt her draw closer to him. 'I just want you to know what it meant to me. You defended my honour.'

'You must know by now that I would do anything for you, Louisa,' he replied. 'You can trust me.'

She nodded, her expression heavy with thoughts he could not read. 'I know.'

'You are the most beautiful lady in this room,' he whispered. 'I wish you knew how happy being with you makes me feel.'

Her dark eyes widened a little more, and her lips parted as she searched his face in earnest. 'I think about you all the time…' she breathed. 'I confess, I do not know what to do…'

The music stopped, ending the dance, breaking the spell. Louisa stepped back, taking her hand from his and smoothing it over her skirts as she cast her eyes about—first at the other dancers, then towards her aunt. He saw at once the rapidity of her breath, the flush of colour in her cheeks. She had felt it, too. Undeniably, she had felt it.

'Louisa, I…' he began, reaching towards her.

He had to say something, and yet at that very moment words seemed to fail him.

She took another step back, wrapping her arms around herself. 'Forgive me, Sir Isaac,' she said. 'I am a little cold. I need to fetch my shawl.'

Isaac blinked at her, as though startled, his arm still suspended awkwardly in the air. She had cut him adrift once more, and there was nothing he could do but watch as she turned away from him and hurried out of the drawing room.

# Chapter Twenty-Four

The rules of etiquette forced Isaac to remain with the other guests, to keep a smile fixed upon his face and pretend that nothing was amiss.

The dancing continued, and mathematics conspired with politeness to ensure that he participated. With more ladies than gentlemen present, he could hardly decline—much as he wished to. Much as he wanted to run from that room and seek out Louisa. Much as he wanted to kiss her fiercely upon the lips and ask her all over again to stay in Cumberland, to stay with him.

At length he took two turns with Miss Pearson, after the sullen young woman's mother all but shoved her daughter towards him in the aftermath of Louisa's sudden departure. Fortunately that single waltz seemed to have sated Samuel's appetite for the borderline scandalous, and the party occupied themselves with a cotillion, followed by a lively country dance.

Still Louisa did not return, and Isaac found his gaze repeatedly drifting towards the door, wondering how it could take so long to retrieve a simple shawl.

'I am sure Louisa is quite well, Sir Isaac,' Miss Pearson insisted in the end, clearly trying to recapture his attention. 'She has always struck me as very…robust.'

Isaac forced a smile, not wishing to indulge her on this subject. 'An astute observation, Miss Pearson,' he replied, immediately regretting the note of sarcasm which had crept into his voice.

Thankfully, Miss Pearson did not seem to notice. 'Still,' she continued, 'if she does not return then you will have to dance with me for a third time! But I should not wish to hear us *talked* about,' she said, with laughably feigned concern. 'I should not wish anyone to think that we have formed an *attachment*.'

Isaac suppressed the urge to roll his eyes. The young woman was as ridiculous as her mother. What his brother saw in her, he could not fathom.

'Miss Pearson,' he replied, giving her a steely look, 'I do not think that anyone could look at the two of us and believe we are attached.'

Her nostrils flared, and to his eternal shame he felt no small measure of satisfaction at having provoked her.

'I daresay it is impossible to tell who has become attached to whom from mere observation,' she said smoothly. 'My mama says people will always surprise you—that those you dismiss are often the ones who remain constant, whilst those you pursue are most likely to trifle with your heart.'

He scoffed at that. 'You mean just as you did with my brother's?'

Miss Pearson's face flushed scarlet. 'I do not know what you mean, sir.'

Mercifully, at that moment Louisa's aunt stopped playing, signalling the end of the dance. Conscious of the sudden quiet in the room, Isaac checked himself, painting an insincere grin on his face as he bowed politely at his dancing partner, who gave him a furious curtsey in return.

'I am sure you do not, Miss Pearson,' he replied. 'Now, please, excuse me.'

With a reassuring nod in Samuel's direction, Isaac walked out of the drawing room as casually and confidently as he could manage. Once out in the hall he paused, taking a lungful of cool air. It was chilly tonight, he realised, and those light, fashionable gowns women wore were no match for the northern climate, even in summer. Little wonder Louisa had felt the need of her shawl.

But that did not explain why she had stayed away for so long. The reason for that, he expected, lay in what had passed between them during that waltz. It had enraptured him, and he was still in thrall to his feelings. Goodness knew what effect that dance must have had on a woman determined to deny herself love if she'd felt even half of what he had.

He made it across the hall and up the first half-dozen steps of the staircase before his thoughts forced him to pause again. What was his intention now, exactly? He could hardly burst into her bedroom, even to ask her if she was all right.

He took a deep breath, felt his heart rattling inside his ribcage. As improper as it was, he would knock on her bedroom door and ask to speak to her. He would not go in; he could say what he wished to say in the doorway. But he had to say it. This was likely the last chance he would get.

When he reached her door he knocked tentatively, his sense of honour rendering him uncertain about his chosen course. He was Sir Isaac Liddell, a baronet and a gentleman—not the sort of rapscallion who went about summoning women from their bedchambers. His means might be questionable, but his intentions were noble, he reminded himself. Noble and tender.

'Louisa?' he said softly. 'Louisa, it's Isaac. Are you all right?'

His words were met with silence. He stood still for a moment, his ear hovering close to the door, listening for any sound coming from within. But there was nothing—no answer, no footsteps…nothing.

'Louisa?' He tried again. 'I only wish to make sure you are well. I…' He faltered, trying to decide what to do. 'I will go,' he continued after a moment, 'but I will ask Mrs Pearson to send a maid to attend you.'

With a sigh he walked away, his footsteps heavy on the floor as he headed back along the corridor and down the stairs. He felt his mood shift from concern towards frustration. If she was not in her room, then where the devil was she? And if she *was* in her room, why had she ignored him? Why would she not simply speak to him? Tonight they'd found themselves in each other's arms once again, forced to confront all that had blossomed between them this summer, and she'd chosen to run from it.

She'd run from him.

Outside the drawing room he paused, feeling suddenly unable to face the party, to disguise his misery with a smile and bury his lovelorn heart beneath layers of obligatory merrymaking. Instead he turned away, making his way down towards the Pearsons' library. He would re-join the party in a little while, but right now he needed a few moments of sanctuary in the sort of place where he could always find solace.

He wandered in and shut the door, glad to be greeted by the same scent of leather-bound books that gave him such comfort at home.

Except that wasn't all that was there to greet him.

She was sitting in a wingback chair, a shawl wrapped around her shoulders, her legs curled up beneath her. She looked up at him, her dark eyes wide, surprised and unsmiling. As though he was intruding. As though he was the last person she'd expected to see.

*That makes two of us*, he thought to himself.

He had not expected this at all.

'Louisa,' he said, finally finding his voice. 'What are you doing in here?'

'I could ask you the same question.'

Louisa stared at him in something of a daze. She hadn't answered his question because she did not have an answer. She still wasn't sure what had possessed her to wander in here after fetching her shawl. Despair, perhaps. Desperation. The realisation that she could not return to the party and face everyone as if nothing had happened.

As if she hadn't just danced a waltz with a man whose gaze, whose touch, whose mere presence made the earth shift beneath her feet.

'I needed a few moments of peace,' he replied, both his expression and his tone remaining sombre. 'Do you mind if I join you?'

'It's not my library, Isaac,' she replied. 'Strictly speaking, we ought to ask Mr Pearson's permission to be in here.'

Strictly speaking, she thought, they ought not to be in here together and unchaperoned at all. She did not wish to imagine what Mrs Pearson would make of it if she caught them.

She watched as Isaac removed his tailcoat and sat down opposite her with a sigh. For several moments she continued to stare at him, drinking in the sheer deliciousness of those dark features against the sharp white linen he wore. His hair, threatening disobedience as always, had begun to curl on top, and she found herself dwelling on what it would feel like to run her fingers through it.

'I don't think I could live without the peace and quiet of a library to retreat to,' he said softly, casting his eye over the Pearsons' immaculate room.

'I could not live without books,' Louisa replied. 'Without being able to escape into the worlds they contain.'

He nodded. 'Hiding away in libraries and stories is a reliable way to avoid life's difficulties,' he said, looking at her pointedly.

He knew—of course he knew. He always did. He knew her. He understood her. He deserved to know everything, whatever the consequences.

'Isaac, I…'

She got to her feet, and so did he. They moved towards each other, drawing close. Through his shirt and waistcoat she could see the rapid rise and fall of his chest and instinctively she reached out, laying a hand over his heart, feeling its furious rhythm playing against her skin. She dropped her gaze, staring at the broad, solid frame hidden so tantalisingly beneath the fine fabric of his attire. He hooked a finger under her chin, lifting her eyes to meet his. Blue—so blue. Just like the ocean.

'Isaac…' she began again, searching his gaze, struggling to find the right words.

'Stay…' he breathed. 'Do not leave Cumberland. Stay here with me.'

Even as she began to shake her head she found herself pulling him towards her, running her hands over his shoulders and around to the back of his neck, her fingers finding those curls of dark hair. She pressed her mouth against his, revelling in the firm, muscular warmth of him, feeling the heat of passion rise in her as he wrapped both his arms around her waist and pulled her closer to him.

She knew she should not kiss him—that what she was about to tell him would likely break their bond for ever. That he would never look at her in the same way again. Perhaps that was why she kissed him—to feel his closeness, to feel his affection one final time before the truth parted them for good.

'Isaac.' She tried yet again. 'I have to tell you what happened—with Richard. I have to tell you everything…'

He shook his head. 'I do not need to know,' he replied, caressing her cheek. 'It is in the past. It can make no difference to this—to us.'

'You do not know that,' she replied, stepping back from him. 'When Richard and I were together, before he returned to sea, we…' She faltered again, the words sticking in her throat. Words she could hardly bear to speak. Words she'd have to live with from the moment they fell from her lips to the end of her days.

'I am sorry that I called you a coward yesterday,'

Isaac said quietly. 'I should not have said that. And I should not have asked you to tell me everything. I understand how much pain it causes you to speak of this; I can see it. Please, do not tell me.'

He placed a tender kiss on her forehead, and despite herself, despite all her better judgement and reason, Louisa pulled herself close to him once more.

He brushed the curls back from her face as his lips found hers, softly and gently, and the earlier passion she'd felt dissolved into an overwhelming need for comfort and solace. For reassurance. For a kiss to say everything that she had not been able to put into words. For it to tell him her secrets so that she might never have to speak them...

'Well, I daresay *this* will cause a scandal.'

A shrill voice intruded, causing them both to fly apart.

Louisa felt her cheeks begin to burn, the intimacy of a moment suddenly overcome by the sting of shame. She heard Isaac cough, saw him press his fist to his mouth, as though he too was struggling to compose himself. Her eyes flew towards the door, although she already knew from the voice she'd heard who had entered and caught them together.

Her heart sank as she met that familiar cold gaze and observed the self-satisfied curl of those thin lips. There was no doubt in her mind that this discovery would be her downfall.

'I am quite shocked,' Mrs Pearson continued, in a voice which did not sound very shocked at all. 'Although, given what I know about Miss Conrad, I cannot say I am altogether surprised that she has seduced you, Sir Isaac.'

Isaac took several steps towards her. 'She has not…
What on earth can you mean, madam?'

Louisa bowed her head, feeling her heart and her
stomach descend into her feet.

Mrs Pearson knew. She knew it all.

Mrs Pearson, meanwhile, was smiling. Louisa could
not see it, but she could hear it, along with the note of
something like triumph that was ringing in her voice.

'Oh, Sir Isaac, she hasn't told you, has she?' she
continued, her tone honeyed even as her words bit like
vipers. 'Then it is fortunate that I arrived when I did.
I think there is something about Miss Conrad that you
should know.'

## Chapter Twenty-Five

Isaac glared at the spiteful older woman, challenging her to do her worst. He watched as she dallied towards them both, running a carefree hand over the back of a nearby armchair, her expression haughty and disapproving. Beside him, he sensed Louisa's frozen form. He glanced at her, beholding her ashen face and staring brown eyes. It was as if all of her was suspended in dread. Mrs Pearson, meanwhile, seemed to be relishing the moment, a smile twitching at the corners of her mouth as she turned to look at him once more.

'Well?' he demanded. 'You should know, Mrs Pearson, that I care little for idle gossip.'

'Oh, this is not gossip, Sir Isaac,' she replied, her tone irritatingly silken. 'You see, I have learned the truth about Miss Conrad from a very good authority on the matter.' She looked at Louisa, clicking her tongue disapprovingly. 'And to think, when she first arrived in Lowhaven I thought she would be an improving influence upon my dear Charlotte...'

He saw how Louisa visibly shuddered, and instinctively he reached for her hand. His heart sank as she drew herself away from him, retrieving her shawl, which had earlier fallen from her shoulders, and replacing it around her even tighter than before.

'I presume Mrs Gossamer did not spare any detail in her letter?' Louisa spoke quietly, her voice suddenly hoarse.

Mrs Pearson chuckled at that, which only served to rankle Isaac further. He frowned, his thoughts racing as he tried to make sense of what was unfolding.

He recalled Mrs Pearson's talk of an acquaintance she shared with Louisa, to whom she wrote. Her name was Gossamer, wasn't it? He thought about that dinner, and how perturbed Louisa had seemed when Mrs Pearson had raised the subject. At the time he found it strange. Now he was beginning to realise there had been an undertone to her words, a threat contained within them which he had not understood.

'Who is this Mrs Gossamer and why should I give a single damn what she says?' he asked, anger flashing through him now. Anger at Mrs Pearson—at her intrusion, her taunts.

At length, it was Louisa who answered him. 'Mrs Gossamer is…was Richard's aunt,' she whispered, venturing to look at him. 'You might recall that when I talked of him I told you that we'd met while he was staying with his relatives? Their family name is Gossamer.'

He nodded, holding her gaze, pained to observe how broken she looked. She had said that. He searched her dark eyes, as though he might be able to find answers in their depths. Mrs Pearson knew Richard's aunt—why was that significant? What on earth could the correspondence of two women contain that would leave Louisa looking so defeated?

Mrs Pearson, meanwhile, was not to be discouraged. 'Ah, but it seems to me, Miss Conrad, that you have not told Sir Isaac all that you ought to have told him about your dalliance with that young captain.'

'It was no dalliance, Mrs Pearson,' Louisa bit back. 'Had life dealt us a kinder hand he would still be here and we would be wed.'

'Life is cruel, to be sure,' Mrs Pearson answered her, just as sharply. 'Although a young woman can do much to protect herself against its evils if she is of good moral character. If she is not prone to wanton behaviour.'

Incensed, Isaac stepped forward. 'Mrs Pearson, I hope you are not suggesting…'

'Indeed, I am, Sir Isaac,' the woman spat. 'Imagine my horror to learn from a dear old friend that her poor dead nephew's memory has been sullied by his association with this strumpet! To this day, she remains so appalled by what was said that she could barely bring herself to write the details to me. Were it not for the duty she felt, to warn me against any association with such company, I doubt she would ever have mentioned any of it. To lose such a dearly beloved young man to war is bad enough, but then to hear society whispering about him leaving a woman behind, unwed and with child, is simply unthinkable.'

'A woman?' Isaac repeated. 'You cannot mean…?'

He turned to Louisa, searching her expression for something—he did not know what. A denial, perhaps? An explanation? Had he any right to ask for either? The colour had returned to her face now, and a hot fury was gathering in her cheeks to match the indignant look with which her eyes beheld Mrs Pearson.

The older woman, meanwhile, continued her dramatic remonstrations.

'Have you no shame, Miss Conrad?' she asked, her arms wildly outstretched. 'Have you no sympathy for the pain already borne by his grieving family?'

'I understand their pain well enough, Mrs Pearson,' she replied, her voice low but steady. 'Their loss was also mine. As for shame—I cannot own the portion you would give me, since I am not guilty of all that you have accused me of.'

'So, you were *not* with child?' Mrs Pearson rounded on her. 'You did *not* accuse that young man of going to war and leaving you in such a condition?'

For the longest moment Louisa just stood there, not answering, not even looking at her accuser but staring beyond her, her brown eyes eerily vacant and unmoved.

Isaac watched her intently, awaiting and dreading her answer in turn. So much made sense now—so much of what she had said to him over these past weeks and so much of what she'd left unspoken. Yet at the same time there was much still to be untangled—a good deal of rumour and insinuation which needed to be separated from the truth. Louisa's truth. The only truth, frankly, that he cared to hear.

'Louisa…' he prompted her gently.

Her eyes snapped back to Mrs Pearson then, but where that affronted expression had previously been, Isaac now saw only sadness.

'I was with child,' she replied, her voice trembling as her tears began to fall. 'Richard's child. The child did not live.'

Instinctively Isaac moved towards her, overwhelmed by the desire to comfort her, to wrap her in his arms and to never let her go. To make her understand just how profoundly he understood her sense of loss. To tell her just how little the opinions of society and its preoccupation with so-called scandal mattered to him.

But Louisa simply shook her head and stepped away. 'Now you see why I can never marry,' she sobbed, rushing past Mrs Pearson towards the door. 'Please forgive me. I should not be here.'

Then she left the library, leaving unanswered questions hanging in the air and, he realised, her dancing shoes abandoned on the rug.

She never allowed herself to think of the child. For these past years she'd made Richard the sole focus of her grief—a grief she'd worn like a shroud, owning it as a justification for her melancholy, her insistence upon solitude and her complete withdrawal from society.

She'd loved and lost, it was true, but she had not permitted herself to count those losses or to acknowledge the depth of them.

As she ran up the stairs and into her bedchamber it struck her that tonight was the first time she'd spoken of the child since he'd slipped from her body, limp and small, his tiny lungs not yet ready for breath.

Her child.

Her son.

Pressing herself against the door, she wept as she thought of the words that had been placed alongside him. Dalliance…wanton behaviour…strumpet. Shame. She had felt shame—shame for being swept away by passion, for her secret being discovered despite her efforts to conceal it. For all the things Berkshire society had said about her—some true, but most not. For not having the good sense to marry the man she had loved before taking him to her bed.

But she had not felt ashamed of the child. As she'd brought him into the world and watched him pass straight on to the next she'd felt overwhelming guilt and the deepest sorrow, but never shame. Perhaps that was why she could never bring herself to think of him. Because confronting that pain was hard enough without being reminded of what she was expected to feel but could not.

Feeling suddenly weak, she let her weight drop to the ground, slumping down on the cold, hard wooden floor. Isaac had known how she felt; she had seen it in his face—seen his own pain breaking through as he'd placed it next to hers. They'd long since realised that they shared an understanding; now they both knew just how deep it ran.

Except Isaac's was an acceptable sort of loss. Hers was not.

Not that any of it mattered now, of course. Isaac knew the truth about her, and whatever his feelings were for her he knew, just as she did, that any association between them was at an end. Cumberland, it seemed, had not been far enough away for her to outrun the past. It had got her in its grip once again. She could feel its pull, dragging her back to Berkshire, to loneliness and isolation, to daily reminders of all that had been and all that was gone.

It was time to go home.

Taking a deep, shuddery breath, Louisa forced herself off the floor and hauled herself to her feet. She glanced down at her flimsy gown in irritation, suppressing the memories it provoked—memories of tonight, of dancing, of Isaac holding her in his arms as they twirled.

Such dresses were no good to her now. She would have to change into some warmer clothes and put on some boots, since she realised now that she had nothing on her feet. Furiously, she pulled off her evening clothes and dressed herself in the plainest day dress she could find, along with the largest bonnet, the thickest shawl and the single pair of boots she'd brought.

Thank goodness Nan had had the good sense to include some items suitable for long country walks in her portmanteau. Her heart lurched as she thought of her loyal maid back in Lowhaven, blissfully unaware of her mistress's imminent departure as she retired for the night. How worried she would be when she learned of it. How worried Aunt Clarissa would be, too.

She hurried over to the little desk in the corner of the room, scribbling a brief note to her aunt. She would leave it on the hall table, just before she departed.

Louisa adjusted her bonnet and wiped her watering eyes, steeling herself. She retrieved her reticule, tucking the note she'd written into it and hoping that the money she'd brought with her to Langdale would be sufficient for her journey home. Not that there would be any coaches going south at this time of the night; she would have to wait until morning for that.

In the meantime she would have to find somewhere to hide—somewhere that no one would find her. Somewhere that Isaac would not find her. Quietly, she slipped out of the bedchamber, every step accompanied by a silent prayer that the solid floors of Langdale Hall would not betray her as she made her bid to find sanctuary and thereafter to get away unseen.

\* \* \*

Isaac didn't know how long he'd been staring at those dancing slippers. Long after Mrs Pearson had departed, with a brisk nod and a muttered goodnight, he found himself still fixated upon them, as though a simple pair of shoes might hold the answer to what on earth had happened that evening.

Merely an hour or two ago he'd held that beautiful, beloved woman in his arms, losing himself in her gaze as they waltzed together. In the library he'd asked her to stay, he'd embraced her and told her that the past did not matter. But then Mrs Pearson had intruded, and she'd brought it all crashing down with her stories and her gossip.

How that dreadful woman had crowed over Louisa… how determined she had been to bring her low. Well, he told himself now, he was just as determined that she would not succeed. He cared nothing for scandals, for reputations. The only part of that sorry tale to affect him had been learning about all that Louisa had lost. He did not wish to condemn her, only to console her.

Only to love her.

That thought made his breath catch in his throat, but it was true. What he felt for her had ventured far beyond the friendship they'd begun earlier that summer. He loved her. He understood that now.

He picked the slippers up, holding them tightly in his hands as he hurried out of the library and up the stairs towards the bedrooms. He would go to Louisa and he would declare himself to her.

It had been a little while since she had left the library. He could only hope that sufficient time had passed for her to calm herself, that they might talk candidly now that they'd been freed from Mrs Pearson's poisonous presence.

He needed her to know that what he'd said was true—there was nothing in her past that could change his feelings towards her. If anything, knowing about her past had only served to deepen his affections. She had borne terrible losses and had been greeted not with the sympathy she deserved but with callousness and censure from those in society.

He understood now that she'd been all but forced into a life of solitude, robbed of the right to properly grieve as a widow and a bereft mother otherwise might. Her past was not a scandal; it was a tragedy.

'Louisa?' he said, knocking loudly on the door. 'Louisa, please—I need to speak to you.'

He waited for several moments but received no reply. Tentatively he placed his hand on the doorknob, in a quandary about what to do next. He ached to be with her, to speak to her, but bursting into her bedchamber was hardly the right or proper thing to do.

He listened at the door, trying to detect the smallest movement, the subtlest sound. He felt sure she must be in there. After all that had unfolded in the library, he could not imagine she had returned to the party. Perhaps, he reasoned, she'd been so exhausted and overwrought that she'd simply fallen asleep. Or perhaps she just could not bring herself to face him right now.

Either way, he decided he ought not to intrude. He let go of the doorknob, resolving to leave her in peace. He would speak to her in the morning. He would hope that in the light of a new day she would be able to see that all would be well. That his intentions and his affections remained steady and unchanged.

'Goodnight, Louisa,' he said softly. 'I will see you tomorrow. I want you to know that this changes nothing when it comes to how I feel about you.'

Isaac withdrew and walked towards his own bedchamber, his head swimming with the evening's events and his heart still yearning for her to change her mind and open her door to him. To see her face, to feel her embrace. To hear, at the very least, a 'goodnight' in reply.

## Chapter Twenty-Six

Louisa slumped down against the wall of an old stone hut, listening to the wood pigeons as they cooed on the roof. She groaned, clutching her ankle as it throbbed painfully in her boot and chastising herself for not being more careful. She'd been sore enough already as it was, her legs aching after hours on her feet, and her back and neck stiff from spending the night in the cramped linen cupboard she'd found at Langdale Hall.

Not that she'd slept, she reminded herself. Indeed, each time she'd closed her eyes she'd revisited that scene in the Pearsons' library, from the condemnation in Mrs Pearson's words as she'd revealed Louisa's scandalous past to the sympathy and sadness Louisa had seen in Isaac's eyes.

In the early morning she'd crept out of the cupboard and then out of the house, leaving the note addressed to Aunt Clarissa on the hall table, before making her way to the stables. There she'd asked a bleary-eyed young groom for directions to the nearest coaching inn from which she might begin her long journey south. A look of confusion had flashed momentarily across his face, but he had imparted the necessary instructions, which had seemed straightforward enough.

In practice, however, she'd quickly lost her way, the seemingly endless woodland and lack of discernible landmarks leaving her disorientated. The burning heat of panic had begun to rise in her chest, clouding her thoughts, and moments ago she'd stumbled over a tree root, painfully twisting her ankle and falling to the ground with a thud.

Now she was filthy, and she was injured. She needed rest, but there was no time for that. She knew she had to carry on. It was either that, she realised, or return to Langdale Hall.

Going back, she knew, was not an option.

Wearily she hauled herself upright, gritting her teeth as she forced the injured leg to bear her weight. Tears pricked in the corners of her eyes as the overwhelming desire to escape which had driven her all morning began to give way to the harsh reality of the situation she faced. She had no idea where she was, or how far it was to the nearest inn, or indeed if she was heading in the right direction at all. She had some money, but no food or drink to sustain her. She had to find her way, and soon, otherwise she really would be in peril.

'Stop it,' she muttered to herself. 'Fretting will do no good at all.'

She swiped a hand across her watering eyes and forced her mind to focus. She had to get out of the woodland and on to a road—preferably one with inns and coaches, with other travellers and people who could tell her where she was. There was nothing else she could do; there were no other options. She had to keep going.

With renewed determination she began to limp along,

biting her lip at the pain which pulsed through her ankle. At least the day was fine and bright, with the sun streaming through the gaps in the trees. She inhaled deeply, filling her lungs with the crisp air as she forced herself to keep moving forward. Around her the pigeons sang their farewell, and although she was tired and sore she gave them a watery smile.

She would find the road, she told herself. She had to. Her life, as bleak and lonely as it was condemned to be, likely depended upon it.

'I've asked the groom to ready the horses. She cannot have got very far.'

Samuel's insistent words cut across the silent room. Isaac dragged his hands down his face, the shock of her sudden disappearance giving way to his sheer horror at the thought of her out in the countryside alone.

A myriad of thoughts raced through his mind. If only he had gone to her last night... If only he'd decided to walk into her bedchamber and offered his reassurance and his heart... If only he had not waited until morning to speak to her... If only he had not risen later than usual, after a fitful night's sleep...

Then he might have discovered her disappearance sooner. If only he'd been more impulsive and less gentlemanly, he might have been able to prevent her from fleeing at all.

'The young groom said that Miss Conrad approached him early this morning and asked where she could find the nearest coaching inn,' Samuel continued. 'However, she did not give him any indication as to where she might wish to travel from there.'

'And this groom did not think it odd? A lady like Miss

Conrad leaving Langdale alone shortly after dawn?' Isaac snapped.

'He's a boy, Isaac,' Samuel replied. 'He was hardly going to be disobliging.'

'You're right…forgive me,' Isaac said, rubbing his forehead.

In truth, he did not know what to do with himself. He could do nothing until he knew Louisa was safe and well. Until he had her back here, with him.

'At least we know which coaching inn she is heading for,' Samuel continued. 'We also know that she is on foot. On horseback, we should be able to catch up with her.'

'Unless she reaches the inn before that and catches a coach,' Isaac replied. 'If that is the case we will have no idea where she is going.'

'I think I know.'

Louisa's aunt walked into the parlour, her lined face drawn, her eyes red and swollen with tears. She had been the one to discover Louisa's disappearance, having gone into Louisa's bedchamber after knocking and receiving no reply. She had not stopped weeping since.

Miss Howarth held up a letter. 'One of the servants just found this in the hall. It is from Louisa, and addressed to me. She thanks me for welcoming her into my home, but says that she must return to Berkshire now, and that…' The older woman paused, pressing her handkerchief against her mouth as she fought to suppress her sobs. 'She says that now everything about her is known, regrettably her time in Cumberland is at an end.'

'Please try not to fret, Miss Howarth,' Samuel said, doing his utmost to comfort her. 'We will find her safe and well, I'm sure of it.'

'She seemed troubled last night,' Louisa's aunt continued between sobs. 'I should have gone after her when she left the dancing. I should have spoken to her last night instead of waiting until this morning. I should have known, after all she's endured these past years...' She looked up at Isaac. 'This is my fault, sir. I suggested that it might be better if you knew all about her. I never imagined—' Her voice broke, her words faltering once again.

Isaac regarded her grimly. Such a remark, so laden with meaning, left him in little doubt that Miss Howarth knew the whole story of her niece's past. He drew a deep breath, knowing he had to say something. That he had to try to explain.

'Samuel, perhaps you could check on the horses,' he suggested, knowing that speaking with Miss Howarth about something so delicate could only conceivably be undertaken in private.

His brother gave him a look of surprise, but quickly caught on. 'Ah—yes, of course,' he acquiesced.

Isaac gave his brother a grateful nod as he left and closed the door behind him, before he turned back to Miss Howarth, who dabbed her eyes with her handkerchief.

'I know how profoundly your niece has suffered, Miss Howarth,' he began, speaking quietly. 'I know all of it. But I can assure you...'

'So that is why she has run away, then,' she sobbed, interrupting him. 'Oh, my poor Louisa! She never speaks of the baby, you know. Never. Telling you would have taken a deal of strength, and clearly she cannot bear it. Oh, my dear girl...'

Isaac's heart lurched at her assumption that Louisa

had confided in him. How he wished that she had. How he wished that he'd let her. How he wished that he'd heard the story in her own words, rather than from Mrs Pearson's venomous tongue.

He decided that he wouldn't tell Miss Howarth about Mrs Pearson's involvement in its revelation—at least not yet. Knowing about that right now would only cause her more grief.

'What a frightful journey for her to attempt…on the stagecoach alone!' Miss Howarth continued. 'Think of it—a young woman, unchaperoned, wandering about the inns…'

Isaac could not decipher the rest, since Miss Howarth had buried her face in her handkerchief, her words muffled then eventually overtaken entirely by a set of deep, racking sobs.

'I promise you, Miss Howarth, I will do all that I can to find your niece.' He spoke gently, in an effort to calm her. 'Please do not blame yourself. You must know that I care for her a great deal, and what I know now does not alter that. I will ride all the way to Berkshire for her, if necessary.'

The older woman nodded, composing herself as she attempted a watery smile. 'I believe you will, sir.'

A knock at the door startled them both, and before Isaac could answer it Samuel burst in. 'Sorry to disturb you, but I thought you'd want to know that the horses are ready.'

Isaac gave his brother a brisk nod, walking closer to where he stood in the doorway. 'We should leave immediately and go directly to the inn,' he said.

'Assuming she has found her way to the inn,' Samuel added. 'She cannot know this country well, given that she has been here for such a short time. She might just as easily be lost.'

'And if that is the case I will search every inch of Cumberland,' Isaac replied, rubbing his face with his hands.

He needed to wash, having had time only to change for riding. Alas, that was something else which would have to wait.

'I have to try everything, Samuel. I will not rest until I find her.'

His brother rested a sympathetic hand on his shoulder. 'I know,' he said.

Isaac sighed, glancing over his shoulder at Louisa's aunt. 'Before we leave, perhaps you could ask someone to come and sit with Miss Howarth.'

He sighed heavily, considering the options. The Coles and Suttons lived nearby and had left late last night in their carriages, before Louisa had disappeared. The Pearsons, meanwhile, had apparently not risen yet. Not that Isaac wanted to see any of them right now.

'Fetch a maid, perhaps,' he suggested, 'and ask her to bring some tea.'

Samuel nodded. 'I'm surprised Mrs Pearson has not been down to console Miss Howarth,' he mused. 'Where *are* the Pearsons, anyway? I have not seen any of them since last night.'

Isaac suppressed a growl at the mention of that family. He could not wait to be many miles from them—but he had to find Louisa first.

'Making themselves scarce, I hope,' Isaac replied. 'Mrs Pearson in particular.'

'Oh?' Samuel stared expectantly at his brother, frowning.

Isaac's gaze shifted briefly to Miss Howarth, who had begun to weep all over again. 'I will explain all while we ride,' he replied, his tone hushed. 'But believe me when I say that I wish never to lay my eyes upon that woman again.'

'I'm not sure which part of this I find most shocking,' Samuel remarked as they rode on to the turnpike road, having been apprised of all that had been revealed last night. 'That the sensible and serious Miss Conrad has a scandalous past, or that Mrs Pearson has the capacity for such ill behaviour. And to think I'd been considering pressing my suit with her daughter just days ago.'

'Indeed,' Isaac grunted, cantering alongside him. 'I'd say you had a lucky escape, brother.'

'I could say the same for you, Isaac, if all that Mrs Pearson has said is true. Miss Conrad has done you a good turn by refusing your affections.'

Isaac looked at his brother sharply. 'My feelings are unchanged, Samuel, and I intend to tell her so once we find her,' he said. 'Indeed, I wish to marry her if she will have me.'

Samuel looked aghast. 'But there will surely be a scandal. It does not sound as though Mrs Pearson can be relied upon to keep her own counsel on the subject. The news of Miss Conrad's disgrace will be the talk of Lowhaven soon enough.'

'What disgrace, Samuel? I should think it a terrible misfortune, not a disgrace, to lose the one you love to war.'

'But she was with child and unwed. You are no fool, Isaac. You understand how society views these things.'

'I knew Rosalind before we were wed,' Isaac said,

shooting him a meaningful look. 'If Rosalind had ended up with child, and I had died before the wedding could take place, she would have been left in the same situation. It is rank hypocrisy from so many among our society to condemn others for falling foul of risks that they themselves have often taken. And I would wager that you, brother, are no innocent, but are as yet unwed. Which means that…'

'Yes, all right, your point has been well made,' Samuel interrupted, screwing up his face in discomfort. Then he shook his head, smiling at Isaac in disbelief. 'You really have fallen for Miss Conrad, haven't you?'

Isaac looked straight ahead, not meeting his eye. 'I believe that I love her, Samuel. And I believe that she loves me, too.'

'Then you have my blessing. Not that you need it, of course.'

Isaac glanced at him then, offering a small smile. 'Thank you. I might not need it, but I do value it, brother.'

'Now, let's find this woman you wish to wed,' Samuel declared. 'We are not so far from the inn now, and look—there is a mail coach stopped ahead. We will ask the driver and guard if they've seen a woman walking along here.'

Before Isaac could say anything Samuel galloped ahead. Inwardly Isaac groaned. Its requirement for speed and efficiency meant that the postal service never took kindly to any imposition on its time. And if they were stopped here, and not at an inn, that meant they were already delayed. He was not keen to provoke an irritable guard, armed with pistols and a blunderbuss.

By the time he caught up with Samuel he saw that

his brother was already in conversation with the driver, an older man with a keen stare and a roughly shaven face. The red-coated guard, meanwhile, watched warily from his perch at the back.

'Thank you for your offer of assistance, sir,' the driver was saying. 'But we are about to be on our way. We hit some tree branches on the road a little further back; they got caught in the wheels and one of the horses seemed spooked. You can't be too careful.'

'Quite right,' Samuel agreed enthusiastically, effortlessly deploying that easy manner of his. 'Before you go, I wonder if you might have seen a young woman walking along this road? She has a very handsome face, brown eyes and fair hair. She might have seemed a little…distressed.'

The driver raised an eyebrow. 'I see, sir. Well, I daresay the course of true love never did run smooth for any of us.'

'It is not like that,' Isaac interjected, feeling suddenly defensive, although he wasn't sure why. 'The woman has had some bad news regarding a relative who lives some distance away,' he explained, the lie falling easily from his tongue. 'We fear she may try to catch a coach going south, and are gravely concerned about her making such a journey alone.'

'I see, sir,' the driver said again, although he looked far from convinced. 'Well, I'm afraid we haven't seen such a woman on the road.'

He inclined his head politely and began to ready his reins.

'There was that young lady at the last inn, John,' the guard reminded the driver. 'She looked much like the woman the gentleman has described.'

The driver nodded. 'Oh, aye—in a bit of a state, she was. Her dress looked all muddy and she was walking with a limp. She approached me just as we were leaving; she must have seen we'd nought but the mail on board and thought she'd try her luck. This last leg of our route can be quiet, as a lot of passengers leave us at Penrith. Anyway, she seemed tearful when I told her we were bound for Lowhaven.'

Isaac and Samuel exchanged a look, half hopeful, half fretful. If this woman was indeed Louisa, then she had already reached the inn. It also sounded as though she was injured.

Isaac felt his stomach lurch, a potent mix of anxiety and desperation gnawing at him. The need to find her was more pressing than ever.

'Thank you both,' Samuel said with an obliging nod. 'I think we will ride to the inn and make some enquiries.'

The driver began to ready his horses once more. 'You'd best make haste if you wish to find her there, sir. Many coaches pass through in the morning. She's bound to find a seat on one of them.'

Isaac did not need urging twice. With a brisk word of thanks he was off at a gallop, his brother speeding to catch him. Coaches be damned, he thought to himself. Let them all be filled. Let her be still stranded at the inn.

Quietly he appealed to his maker, casting out something like a prayer as his horse's hooves frantically churned dust on the road beneath. He hadn't prayed in a long time, but he would do so now. He prayed for Louisa, and for her safe return to Langdale Hall.

For her safe return to him.

## Chapter Twenty-Seven

Louisa sat alone in the lowly kitchen, picking at an unappetising meal of stale bread and cheese, accompanied by a sour-tasting watery beer. Moments ago the room had been a flurry of activity, with half a dozen travellers hurriedly helping themselves to the refreshments on offer while their stagecoaches changed horses outside.

All scruffily dressed and smelling ripe, they'd eyed her suspiciously as they'd shovelled bread and beer into their mouths before departing to take their seats once more—no doubt the cheapest ones, outside and atop the coach, exposed to all the elements.

Seats Louisa would have never contemplated occupying, until today.

Now she would take any seat, any means, to get where she wanted to go.

Upon arriving at the inn she'd received a hostile reception; travellers on foot, it seemed, were not particularly welcome. The portly, rosy-cheeked landlord had glared at her before pointing her wordlessly in the direction of a woman whom Louisa presumed to be his wife, a short and no less rotund individual, whose manner had been equally inhospitable. She'd pursed her lips as she'd looked Louisa up and down, no doubt noting the filthy fabric of her skirt.

Louisa had tried to enquire about coaches travelling south, but the woman had brushed her questions away with a brisk shake of her mob-capped head.

'You'll need to get to Penrith for that,' she'd said, her voice thick with the local accent. 'Penrith coaches do come through here, but you'll be lucky to get a seat on one.'

The woman had been right about that. After an hour or more of trying, Louisa had not managed to find a seat on any of the coaches travelling in the right direction. In the end, feeling faint with hunger and exhaustion, she had tearfully admitted defeat and approached the woman again, this time to ask if there was any possibility of a drink and a warm meal.

'There's the parlour,' she'd said, raising her eyebrows as she regarded her dirty clothing once again. 'Or there's bread and beer in the small kitchen, which you might prefer.'

Not wishing to make a spectacle of herself in the parlour, and conscious that she needed to keep most of her money for coach fares, Louisa had settled upon the cheaper option. The woman had directed her to this cramped, untidy room at the rear of the inn, and it was here that Louisa had sat ever since, forcing herself to eat the unappealing fare and trying to gather her strength for the long walk ahead. If she could not get a coach to Penrith, then she would have to get there on foot.

She shuddered, pulling her shawl tighter around her shoulders as she considered what lay ahead of her. Getting herself this far had been a trial. Her ankle had worsened, growing more painful and swollen with each mile, and conspiring with her growing fatigue to hinder her progress as she limped along. She wasn't sure how she was going to face more hours on her feet, enduring pain and lacking both sleep and proper sustenance. She did not even know if she would reach her destination before dark, or where she would rest if she did not.

'What is the alternative, Louisa?' she muttered to herself, shredding the dried bread with her fingers. 'You can hardly go back—not now.'

A tear slipped down her cheek as for a moment—the briefest moment—she allowed herself to despair. Last night, her life had seemed to unravel at such an overwhelming pace that she'd felt she had no other option but to flee. Yet her flight had not lightened her load; instead, it had only added further difficulties, which seemed to multiply and mount up by the hour. Running away, it turned out, had been no answer. It was self-destruction, plain and simple.

She wiped her eyes as a young maid flew in through the door, her small hands laden with dirty bowls which she dumped unceremoniously on the table in front of her. Servants had been to-ing and fro-ing like this ever since she'd been there, using this small area to abandon the used crockery that they had presumably collected from the parlour.

This maid, however, did not leave immediately; she lingered, her pretty emerald eyes regarding Louisa curiously for a moment. Normally Louisa would have found this impertinent, but she had no energy for such feelings today. Instead, she offered the maid a small smile, then filled the silence with another sip of the flavourless beer.

'Is your name Louisa?' the maid asked after a moment.

'Y-yes,' Louisa stammered, taken aback at being so bluntly addressed. 'Why?'

'There's a fine-looking gentleman in the parlour asking about a young woman called Louisa something-or-other. The description he gave sounded like it might be you.'

Louisa felt her heart descend to the pit of her stomach. It was Isaac—it had to be. She ought to have realised he would come looking for her. Ought to have considered that, whatever he thought of her now, her sudden disappearance would grieve him.

'Oh,' she replied. 'And what did you say?'

'Nothing,' the maid scoffed. 'He didn't ask me—he asked Mrs Sym. She's keeping tight-lipped, of course. Doesn't like to get involved with runaways. We get a lot of that here, what with being close to the border. Mind you, if he offers her a few coins that'll likely loosen her tongue,' she added. 'Anyway, miss, you might want to slip out of here now—if you don't wish to see him, that is.'

Louisa nodded her thanks, but didn't move from the hard wooden stool upon which she was perched. She sipped her beer again, her heart still racing but her mind strangely blank. She was tired, and she was injured, and at that moment she realised that she had neither the will nor the energy to carry on.

The young maid regarded her carefully, her freckled face screwed up in confusion. 'Or perhaps you do wish to see him, after all?' she asked.

Louisa felt the heat of tears prickling in her eyes as she considered the question. 'Yes,' she whispered finally. 'But I cannot. It is better this way.'

The maid's brow furrowed deeper. 'With all due respect, miss, I don't see how moping in here is better than going out there to talk to him. If it makes any difference, the gentleman looks as miserable as you. Worried, too. I'll bet he's travelled miles, trying to find you. If I had a gentleman like that looking for me, I wouldn't be staying put in Mrs Sym's kitchen for a moment longer, that's for certain.'

Her spirited tone made Louisa smile. 'So, if you were me you'd go and see him?' she ventured to ask.

The maid grinned. 'I'd do more than see him. I would marry him and go to live in whatever grand house he's come from. Then I wouldn't have to work all hours in this place and give most of my pay over to my father just so he can spend it on ale. That's what I would do.'

Louisa sighed. 'I ought to have spoken to him last night, instead of running away from him. I was just so overwhelmed, and I got it into my mind that it would be best if I left.' She tugged at her skirt. 'Now look at me—all I've managed to do so far is injure myself, be a nuisance to every coach driver I've encountered today, and no doubt upset everyone who has ever loved me.'

'The gentleman must care very much about you,' said the maid thoughtfully. 'Whatever has happened, is it really so terrible that you must run away?'

Louisa grimaced, thoughts of last night's revelations flooding unbidden into her mind. 'Yes, it was terrible,' she replied, slowly getting up from her seat. 'However, I don't think I am running any more.'

'Are you going to see him, then?' the maid asked, raising an eyebrow. 'If you are, you'd best hurry.'

Louisa nodded, suppressing a groan at the pain that shot through her ankle as she began to walk. 'Thank you,' she said. 'If it wasn't for you I'd have never known that he was here.'

The maid shrugged. 'I just thought you had a right to know. That way, you could decide what you wanted to do about it.'

'I'm still not sure I have decided,' Louisa replied. 'I just know that I need to talk to him.'

'Then you *have* decided, in a way,' the maid answered her. 'Now, go on, miss—go and find him. But take care with that leg; you've turned very pale all of a sudden.'

Louisa smiled at her, her head feeling suddenly light as pain, nerves and anticipation potently mingled. Mustering the very last vestiges of her strength, she limped out of the room, trying to ignore the way the ground swayed beneath her feet and the world swam before her eyes.

Isaac made his way back across the courtyard to where Samuel was patiently waiting with the horses. Frustrated, he kicked at the dusty ground, cursing aloud and causing a couple of young grooms lingering nearby to cast him wary looks. The innkeeper's wife had been rude and evasive, and had all but refused to answer his questions.

'It's a busy place,' she'd kept telling him. There was no way to account for who passed through or when they might have been there.

Her unwillingness to look him in the eye had told him that she was lying, but there was precious little he could do in the face of such obfuscation.

'Did you not offer her a few coins for her trouble?' Samuel asked, when Isaac informed him that he'd failed to discover anything. 'Everything has a price in these establishments—even information. She might have been a bit more forthcoming with a shilling or two in her pocket.'

'No. I hadn't thought of that,' Isaac replied, putting his head in his hands. 'Perhaps I should have sent you in there instead, brother, for it seems I am truly hopeless. Louisa could be anywhere by now. What am I going to say to her aunt? To her family?'

To his surprise, a slow smile spread across Samuel's face as he looked over Isaac's shoulder. 'You can tell them that you've found her. Look.'

Isaac spun round, his heart leaping into his throat as he laid his eyes upon the slight young woman limping towards him. For a moment he did not believe it could be the same lady he'd waltzed with just a day earlier, such was the extent of her transformation. Her bonnet looked to be damaged, and some of her fair curls had escaped from it and come to rest on her shoulders, which were adorned with a filthy shawl. Her dress was in an equally ill condition, and as she drew closer he saw that her pale face seemed almost grey, with pronounced dark circles beneath her brown eyes. She looked up at him, attempting a smile, but managing only a grimace.

'Good God, Louisa,' he said, darting towards her. 'What has happened to you?'

Without thinking he wrapped a supportive arm around her. She looked fragile enough that one gust of wind might blow her away.

'Please don't fret. I am quite well,' she said, but her voice contained an odd, strained note which told him that she was anything but fine. 'When I heard you were here I realised I must see you. I needed to tell you I am sorry…'

Isaac gathered her into his arms. 'No, *I* am sorry. Sorry for what happened last night. Sorry for everything that has happened to you. Sorry that you felt you had no choice but to leave Langdale. To leave me.'

Her lip trembled. 'I should not have run away. I should have spoken to you and…' She paused, a pained look flickering across her face as she leaned against him, grabbing hold of his coat and clinging on for dear life. 'I am sorry. My ankle…it's…'

She did not have to say another word. Without a moment's hesitation Isaac lifted her up, taking her into his arms and striding towards the inn. He carried her through the door and into the parlour, where a dozen or so gawping genteel faces awaited, with their wine glasses and their steaming bowls of soup.

He cared nothing for their whispers, nor their judgement. Propriety be damned, he thought. Society be damned. Society had brought Louisa nothing but condemnation and misery. It had left her feeling as though she deserved no happiness…as though she had no good choices left to make. If this was what society and its rules would do to a woman, then he wanted no part in it.

'Your best room, man—now!' Isaac bellowed to the ruby-faced innkeeper. 'With fresh sheets and a fire lit. And send for a physician immediately. Tell him that Sir Isaac Liddell of Hayton Hall requires his assistance. This lady is injured.'

'You're making a scene,' Louisa said quietly. 'You'll be the talk of Cumberland.'

He gave her a tender smile. 'Then so be it. Let them gossip. I care nothing for it as long as you are by my side.'

She searched his gaze, her brown eyes seeming to

darken further. 'You cannot mean that. Not now. Not after learning the truth about me.'

'I mean it more than ever,' he replied, as the inn-keeper beckoned them into a large and comfortable room. 'Indeed, Louisa Conrad,' he added, smiling at her once more, 'I mean to marry you, if you will have me.'

## Chapter Twenty-Eight

He wanted to marry her.

As the young maid she'd met in the kitchen had fussed around her, and a physician had arrived to tend to her, Louisa had turned Isaac's words over and over in her mind. He cared nothing for gossip. He wanted her by his side.

He wanted to marry her.

She'd been unable to answer him at the time, such had been her shock at his declaration, and as propriety had required him to leave the room once the maid had come to help her remove her filthy dress and get into bed, he'd not had the opportunity to say anything further. Now, as the physician finished bandaging her ankle, she found herself wondering where he was. Wondering when she would be able to speak to him again and say all the things she knew needed to be said.

'It will heal,' the physician said brusquely, inclining his head towards her foot. 'With a few days of rest and a good deal of care there should be no lasting damage.'

Louisa offered him a meek smile and a nod of thanks before the maid escorted him to the door. The room she'd been given was comfortable and warm, with a low fire burning in the grate and the curtains drawn against the world outside. She sank back against the crisp bedlinen, trying to rest as she'd been instructed, but finding she could not relax.

Her mind raced, her thoughts scattering like leaves in the wind. He knew every detail of her scandalous past, and yet he wished to marry her. She'd run away from him like a reckless coward, and yet he wished to marry her. How was this possible?

A knock at the door startled her, and the maid flashed her a knowing smile. 'That'll be your gentleman, I expect.'

'He's not my gentleman,' Louisa said, sitting herself upright.

'He most certainly is,' the maid insisted. 'I'll let him in, shall I?'

Louisa nodded her agreement.

Inexplicably, she held her breath as the door creaked open and she caught sight of those familiar blue eyes, that dark, dishevelled hair with a will of its own. He was, without doubt, the most handsome man she knew. He was kind, and loving, and decent. And he wanted to marry her.

'Come in, sir,' the maid said. She gave Louisa another knowing look. 'I do believe Mrs Sym is looking for me, so I shall leave you both in peace.'

Hurriedly the maid departed, pulling the door shut behind her. For several moments neither of them spoke. Isaac busied himself by fetching a chair from the corner of the room and bringing it to her bedside. Louisa, meanwhile, found herself watching him, her eyes lazily wandering over his tall frame, over his broad shoulders.

He had removed his coat and wore only a shirt which had been rendered off-white, no doubt by his exertions. The sting of guilt rose in her stomach then, as she was reminded of all the grief her actions would have caused him.

'I have sent Samuel back to Langdale,' Isaac said, sitting down next to her. 'He will return in my carriage with your aunt and your portmanteau. The physician has advised that you would be best to rest here for a day or two, so you will need some provisions for that.'

Louisa nodded, lowering her gaze and feeling suddenly very conscious that she wore only her chemise beneath the bedsheets. 'Thank you, Isaac,' she replied. 'For everything. You must think me very foolish and reckless.'

'I do not think you are either of those things,' he countered. 'The way Mrs Pearson behaved towards you was unconscionable. It is little wonder that you felt you had to leave.'

She bit her lip, still not looking at him. 'I do not just mean that. What I did in the past…'

Isaac shifted in his seat, clearing his throat. 'What happened to you in the past is not your fault, Louisa. You were dealt a cruel hand, but neither you nor your fiancé did anything different from what scores of men and women have done since the beginning of time.'

She smiled. 'You sound like my aunt.'

'Well, your aunt is right.' He paused, as though searching for the right words. 'I just— I wish I had allowed you to tell me what happened. I wish I had not had to hear it from that dreadful Mrs Pearson.'

She felt her smile fade as her thoughts were overtaken by recollections of that scene.

'I think the satisfied look on her face will haunt me. Her version of events…the insinuations she made…' Louisa bit her lip, shaking her head in disbelief. 'I am not a strumpet. And I never accused Richard of anything. And I never—I never lay with anyone but him. By the time I discovered I was with child he was at sea. I told no one—not even my mother. Instead I waited, hoping beyond hope that he would return soon, that we could marry quickly and no one would be any the wiser. Then the news of his death reached me. It all… it all unravelled after that. I told my parents—I had to. But I told no one else. To this day I do not know how the rumours began—the careless talk of a maid, perhaps, or the prying eyes of a visitor who spotted my swollen belly. Being with child and unwed was scandalous enough, but some of the things which were said were appalling—that I had taken many lovers, that I was no better than a harlot. I've often wondered if it was Richard's family who said those things—to discredit me and to protect his memory, I suppose. It seems that the vitriol spouted by Mrs Pearson is some confirmation of that.'

Louisa sniffed, wiping crossly at the tears which had begun to form in the corners of her eyes. Isaac, meanwhile, got up, and to her surprise he perched on the bed next to her, taking her hand in his.

'You said yesterday that you lost the child,' he said. 'My son did not live for many hours after his birth… nor did Rosalind. She succumbed to fever a day later.' He paused, a pained expression briefly flashing across his face. 'I understand all too well the grief you feel. But I'm not sure I can put into words my anger at the way Mrs Pearson tried to shame you, or my sorrow for your loss. I am so sorry, Louisa.'

She gave him a watery smile. 'Thank you. You are the first person to say that to me. Even my parents, as kind as they were in the circumstances, never could bring themselves to say they were sorry.' She felt her face crumple as more tears began to fall. 'I wish I had confided in you, Isaac. I wish I'd trusted that you would understand.'

He squeezed her hand. 'Perhaps you would do me the honour of putting your trust in me now,' he said quietly, searching her gaze. 'Will you marry me, Louisa?'

She hesitated. Ever since he'd first uttered his intention as he'd carried her into this room, she'd been grappling with her answer. With what her heart desired and what her head still told her she could not have.

'You are a gentleman of impeccable repute, Isaac,' she said. 'Please consider what connecting yourself to me would mean for your name, for your family.'

'Reputations be damned,' he replied. 'I will not live my life for society's approval. I will be forty years of age soon, and I have endured quite enough pain in my life. I love you, Louisa. I wish to be happy, and I wish to make you happy. More than anything. Please, trust me. Trust that this is all that matters to me—not society, nor scandal. Just you. Just us.'

She nodded. 'I do trust you,' she replied, feeling the depth of truth in those words.

She could trust him—he had more than proved that to her. Over these past days he'd defended her, protected her, cared for her and sought to rescue her, even after learning her terrible truth. Now, when he said her past was no impediment to his heart, she trusted him. She believed him.

'Then the only question that remains is, what do you want, Louisa?'

His eyes continued to search hers and she knew he was glimpsing her answer, even if she had not yet put it into words.

She had spent so long fixed upon the past that she had never allowed herself to consider the future. Never permitted herself to contemplate being happy. Never dared to imagine loving and being loved in return. Yet the desire for those things had always been there, she realised now, lying dormant beneath layers of grief, sorrow and shame. This summer Isaac had awoken that desire—perhaps in the candlelight of the Assembly Rooms or on the breezy clifftops, or perhaps in his old library, when she'd first enjoyed his warm embrace.

She could not truly say. What she did know, however, was that this was a desire she must finally admit to.

She swallowed hard, holding his gaze. 'I want you,' she said. 'I will marry you, Isaac.'

By the time Louisa's aunt arrived with Samuel, Isaac felt as though he was ready to burst with joy. He wanted to rush downstairs and announce his news to his brother in the middle of the inn. He wanted to tell all of Cumberland that Louisa Conrad had accepted him. As it was, he tried his best to maintain his composure, reminding himself that there was a proper way to handle these matters. And as Louisa's guardian, Miss Howarth needed to be informed first.

After showing her to Louisa's room he tried to excuse himself, believing it was best to give the two ladies some time alone to reconcile, and for Louisa to deliver her news in her own way. However, Louisa would not permit it, insisting that he should remain. She seemed anxious about seeing her aunt again, and he suspected she was worried that the older woman would be angry with her for leaving the way she had. As it was, she need not have feared. More than anything, Miss Howarth seemed relieved to find her niece safe and well, except for an injured ankle.

Now that they were all happily far away from Langdale Hall, Isaac took the opportunity to inform Miss Howarth about Mrs Pearson's regrettable involvement in the revelation of Louisa's past. It was a task he did not relish, but he knew he had to do his duty.

Miss Howarth's mouth fell open in horror as the full extent of the woman's unpleasantness became apparent to her, and she turned back to her niece, regarding her tearfully.

'Oh, my dear, I am so sorry,' she said, shaking her head. 'I must admit that I was perturbed when I heard the suggestions Mrs Pearson made at dinner, about you and Sir Isaac promenading alone, but now I am truly horrified. I cannot believe she did that to you. It is no wonder that you ran away from Langdale.'

'Even so, I am sorry I caused you such distress, Aunt,' Louisa replied. 'I hope you can forgive me.'

'There is nothing to forgive,' Miss Howarth insisted. 'On the contrary, it is me who should be asking you for forgiveness. I regret the day that I ever introduced you to Mary and Charlotte Pearson. Please know that I will never welcome either of them into my home again. Our acquaintance is at an end.'

With that, Miss Howarth seemed to consider the matter of her callous former acquaintance closed, and their conversation turned to the future—specifically, the next few days.

In his elated state, Isaac had given little thought to

the practicalities of what lay beyond today, and he found himself rather taken aback to witness Louisa's aunt take charge of the situation. Neither he nor Louisa seemed to be able to get a word in edgeways as the older woman launched into listing all that needed to happen, and all that needed to be done.

'And Mr Liddell has been very attentive, and has secured me a very nice room here,' she continued, singing the praises of Isaac's younger brother. 'So I will stay while you convalesce, as is right and proper. Oh, and I will need to write to your mother. I know she is expecting you back in Berkshire by summer's end, but I will write to explain that there may be a delay on account of your injured ankle.'

'Aunt…' Louisa began, clearly trying her best to interject.

'Oh, but how shall we travel back to Lowhaven once you are well enough?' Miss Howarth began to fret. 'Sir Isaac and Mr Liddell will surely have departed by then.'

Louisa tried again. 'I doubt Sir Isaac will have gone, Aunt, since…'

'Oh! Well, then, sir, would you be so kind enough to take us back to Lowhaven in a day or two?'

Isaac glanced at Louisa, an amused smile twitching at the corners of his mouth to mirror the one she already wore. 'It would be my pleasure, Miss Howarth,' he said, beginning to chuckle.

Louisa's aunt furrowed her brow, regarding them both seriously as Louisa began to laugh, too. 'Pray tell, what is so funny?'

'I have been trying to tell you, Aunt,' Louisa replied, obviously composing herself. 'Sir Isaac has asked me to marry him, and I have accepted.'

The older woman clasped her hands together in delight. 'Oh! How wonderful!' she exclaimed. 'Why on earth did you not say anything before? I feel rather foolish now, talking of writing to your mother about your return to Berkshire. I shall have to write and tell her there is to be a wedding. Oh—and in your grandfather's old church, too. She will be delighted.'

He watched as Louisa sat bolt upright. 'The church in Hayton?' she repeated.

Miss Howarth nodded. 'Well, of course—the master of Hayton Hall can hardly get wed anywhere else, can he? I'm sure the whole village will turn out for it—and probably a good number of families from Lowhaven, too.'

Isaac saw Louisa's smile fade. She closed her eyes, a small frown gathering between them, as though she was trying to steady herself. His heart lurched as he realised something troubled her. Something that he sensed she was not prepared to reveal in front of her aunt.

'Miss Howarth, perhaps you would be so kind as to give me a moment or two alone with your niece?' he asked.

Perhaps noticing the sudden tension in the room, Louisa's aunt assented and swiftly departed, closing the door behind her.

Isaac sat down at Louisa's side, his heart thudding in his chest, his emotions swelling up into a lump in his throat. Dread. Anticipation. Agony. Hope.

'Is something the matter, Louisa?' he said softly. 'Do you not wish to marry me, after all?'

'Of course I wish to marry you,' she replied without a moment's hesitation. 'It is not that. It is…it is the thought of the banns, of church. Of the whole village watching us wed. Of what they will say.'

'You know I care nothing for any of that.'

'It is easy to say that you do not care when you have never been marred in scandal,' she countered. 'Besides, you are a gentleman, and a baronet—you will always command respect, even if tainted by your association with me. I, on the other hand, will always be considered a disgrace. I am not sure I can face the scrutiny… if I can manage to stand up in church in front of society and endure their whispers while making my vows.'

An idea dawned on him then, and he could not repress his smile. 'Then don't,' he said. 'Let's not marry in front of them at all. We don't have to marry in Hayton, and we don't have to wait until the banns are read. Indeed, I do not care for any of it as long as we are wed.'

She frowned. 'What do you mean?'

He took hold of her hands, clasping them in his. 'I mean, let's go to Scotland. Let's elope, Louisa, to Gretna Green. We can travel as soon as you are strong enough.'

Her eyes widened at the suggestion. 'An elopement? That will cause another scandal!'

He drew her fingers to his lips and kissed them. 'It might, but it will be our scandal. Together.'

She smiled. 'Sir Isaac Liddell, I do believe that you've lost your mind.'

'Oh, I have,' he answered her, laughing. 'Earlier this summer a beautiful woman climbed into my carriage after a stagecoach accident, and days later my horse almost collided with her on the clifftops near Lowhaven. My life has not been quite the same since.'

'Nor has mine,' she replied, stroking his rough, unshaven cheek. 'I'm not sure what I expected from my summer in Lowhaven, but I certainly did not expect this.'

'Well, you did once tell me that you wished to travel,' he said. 'And, since we both adored *Waverley*, Scotland seems as good a place as any to start.'

'To start?'

'Indeed,' Isaac answered with another smile. 'I think you and I have had our fill of hiding away. There's a world out there, and I'd like us to see it together.'

The look of utter joy on her face was a sight to behold. Isaac leaned over once more, enveloping her in his embrace and saying a quiet prayer that he would always manage to make her as happy as this.

## Chapter Twenty-Nine

They were married not before an altar but an anvil, in a short ceremony conducted by the village blacksmith. Louisa did not take her eyes off Isaac throughout, and the words of the would-be priest washed over her as she assuredly made her vows.

The past few days had been strange and exciting, taking them across wild open countryside and into a succession of comfortable but often raucous inns as they made their way north.

Isaac had insisted that they take their time, travelling only as far as the horses could manage each day. She was still recovering, he'd pointed out, so a more leisurely pace would be better for her health. Louisa, in turn, had expressed her desire to be wed as soon as possible.

'I may have to reconsider my opinion that you are neither foolish nor reckless,' Isaac had teased.

She'd laughed and conceded the point, agreeing to be sensible just this once.

Their church on that fine summer's day was the blacksmith's shop, a humble building with whitewashed walls and a ceiling supported by exposed wooden beams. Their congregation comprised two witnesses tempted out of the nearby inn with a few coins for their trouble. For wedding clothes they'd made do with their country attire, although Louisa did not believe Isaac had ever looked a finer gentleman than he did now, in his dark frock coat, fawn pantaloons and black Hessian boots.

It was all very irregular, and far from sensible, and yet Louisa could not have been happier. Standing there in that little room, observed by no one who knew them as she committed herself to the man she loved, she realised that for the first time in a long time she felt truly free.

Isaac took hold of her hands as the blacksmith brought his hammer down on his anvil, sealing their union with the tools of his trade. Then he pulled her close, confirming it himself with a lingering kiss on her lips. She kissed him back ardently. Their first kiss as husband and wife.

'A very handsome couple,' one of the witnesses remarked. 'I wonder why they had to run away to get wed.'

'Let them wonder,' Isaac whispered in Louisa's ear. 'Although they are right,' he added, kissing her on the cheek. 'The bride in particular is a great beauty.'

Louisa blushed, glancing down at her plain cream day dress, conscious of the curls she'd struggled to tease into order that morning bouncing around her face. For all her delight at the way in which she'd been wed, she had missed the help of her maid.

Aunt Clarissa had assured her that Nan would remain at her home in Lowhaven until she could be reunited with Louisa when the new mistress of Hayton Hall returned. The thought of it caused Louisa to pause. That was what she was now: the new mistress of Hayton Hall. Isaac's wife. It was hard to believe the changes to her life which had been wrought by one summer sojourn to visit her aunt.

Aunt Clarissa, for her part, had been somewhat taken aback by their decision to elope. Ultimately, though, she had been supportive, understanding their reasons for doing so, albeit with some reservations about exactly what Louisa's parents would make of it.

Sharing her aunt's concern, Louisa had written to her mother directly before they departed for Gretna, explaining her decision and expressing her hope that her parents would be happy for her.

'We will invite them to visit once we return to Hayton,' Isaac had said when she'd broached the subject of how her parents might greet her news. 'I have no doubt that will allay any concerns they may have.'

'Are you telling me that the brooding Isaac Liddell plans to charm my parents?' Louisa had teased him.

'No, I thought I'd let Samuel do that,' he'd replied, grinning. 'For my part, I intend to impress them with my large estate and title.'

Smiling now at the memory, Louisa leaned against Isaac, steadying herself. Her ankle was slowly healing, but it still ached after any length of time spent on her feet.

'This has been quite an adventure, hasn't it?' she remarked, gazing up at him. 'Once we return to Hayton, I think it will feel like a dream.'

Isaac grinned at her. 'Alas, I have no plans for us to return to Hayton just yet.'

'You don't? But what about the estate?'

'I have written to Samuel, and I'm sure he will manage my affairs for a little while longer,' he said, wrapping his arm around her waist as together they walked outside to where their carriage was waiting.

'Poor Mr Liddell… I fear he has been rather put upon of late,' she remarked, referring to all the to-ing and fro-

ing the poor man had done across Cumberland, seeing
Aunt Clarissa home safely and bringing the eloping
couple provisions before returning to Hayton himself.

Isaac chuckled. 'He has enjoyed it. As a very beautiful and perceptive lady once told me, my brother likes
to arrange things. And, please, call him Samuel. You're
my wife now; hearing you call my brother "Mr Liddell"
sets my teeth on edge.'

'In that case, shall I expect to hear you calling my
aunt "Clarissa" when we next visit her for tea?' Louisa
asked, unable to suppress her smirk.

'Oh, heavens, no! She will be Miss Howarth until the
end of my days.'

They paused next to the carriage, and he pulled her
closer to him.

'Anyway,' he continued, his thumb caressing her
cheek, 'do you not wish to know where we are going,
if not back to Hayton?'

She gazed up at him. 'Indeed. Enlighten me.'

'It occurred to me on our journey to Gretna that I'd
like to see something of Scotland with my wife. How
does Edinburgh sound?'

'Edinburgh sounds wonderful,' she gushed, resting
her head against his chest. 'I love you, Sir Isaac.'

Isaac placed a tender kiss on top of her head as the
driver opened the carriage door, signalling the start of
their next journey together. Beyond the charming little border village were more miles of roads, more open
country, and eventually a city beckoned.

'I love you too, Lady Liddell,' he replied.

\* \* \* \* \*

Spinster with a Scandalous Past
*is Sadie King's debut.*
*Look out for her next book,*
*coming soon!*

# Get 3 FREE REWARDS!

**We'll send you 2 FREE Books plus a FREE Mystery Gift.**

FREE Value Over $20

Both the **Harlequin® Historical** and **Harlequin® Romance** series feature compelling novels filled with emotion and simmering romance.

---

**YES!** Please send me 2 FREE novels from the Harlequin Historical or Harlequin Romance series and my FREE Mystery Gift (gift is worth about $10 retail). After receiving them, if I don't wish to receive any more books, I can return the shipping statement marked "cancel." If I don't cancel, I will receive 6 brand-new Harlequin Historical books every month and be billed just $6.19 each in the U.S. or $6.74 each in Canada, a savings of at least 11% off the cover price, or 4 brand-new Harlequin Romance Larger-Print books every month and be billed just $6.09 each in the U.S. or $6.24 each in Canada, a savings of at least 13% off the cover price. It's quite a bargain! Shipping and handling is just 50¢ per book in the U.S. and $1.25 per book in Canada.* I understand that accepting the 2 free books and gift places me under no obligation to buy anything. I can always return a shipment and cancel at any time by calling the number below. The free books and gift are mine to keep no matter what I decide.

Choose one:
☐ **Harlequin Historical**
(246/349 BPA GRNX)

☐ **Harlequin Romance Larger-Print**
(119/319 BPA GRNX)

☐ **Or Try Both!**
(246/349 & 119/319 BPA GRRD)

Name (please print)

Address     Apt. #

City     State/Province     Zip/Postal Code

**Email:** Please check this box ☐ if you would like to receive newsletters and promotional emails from Harlequin Enterprises ULC and its affiliates. You can unsubscribe anytime.

### Mail to the **Harlequin Reader Service:**
**IN U.S.A.:** P.O. Box 1341, Buffalo, NY 14240-8531
**IN CANADA:** P.O. Box 603, Fort Erie, Ontario L2A 5X3

**Want to try 2 free books from another series?** Call 1-800-873-8635 or visit www.ReaderService.com.

*Terms and prices subject to change without notice. Prices do not include sales taxes, which will be charged (if applicable) based on your state or country of residence. Canadian residents will be charged applicable taxes. Offer not valid in Quebec. This offer is limited to one order per household. Books received may not be as shown. Not valid for current subscribers to the Harlequin Historical or Harlequin Romance series. All orders subject to approval. Credit or debit balances in a customer's account(s) may be offset by any other outstanding balance owed by or to the customer. Please allow 4 to 6 weeks for delivery. Offer available while quantities last.

**Your Privacy**—Your information is being collected by Harlequin Enterprises ULC, operating as Harlequin Reader Service. For a complete summary of the information we collect, how we use this information and to whom it is disclosed, please visit our privacy notice located at corporate.harlequin.com/privacy-notice. From time to time we may also exchange your personal information with reputable third parties. If you wish to opt out of this sharing of your personal information, please visit readerservice.com/consumerchoice or call 1-800-873-8635. **Notice to California Residents**—Under California law, you have specific rights to control and access your data. For more information on these rights and how to exercise them, visit corporate.harlequin.com/california-privacy.

HHHRLP23